SYNADOR

A Dystopian Fantasy Anthology

SYMADOR

A DYSTOPIAN FANTASY ANTHOLOGY

KRISTEN DOVNIK   LIV EVANS   G. R. THOMAS

JUDY LIU   DANIELLE HUGHES   EMMIE HAMILTON

EA ROBINS   KATIE CIVITELLI   VICTORIA JADE MOSS

KATE SCHUMACHER   JP MCDONALD

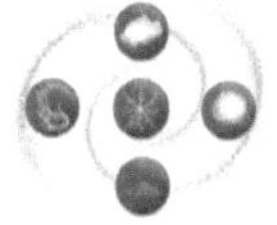

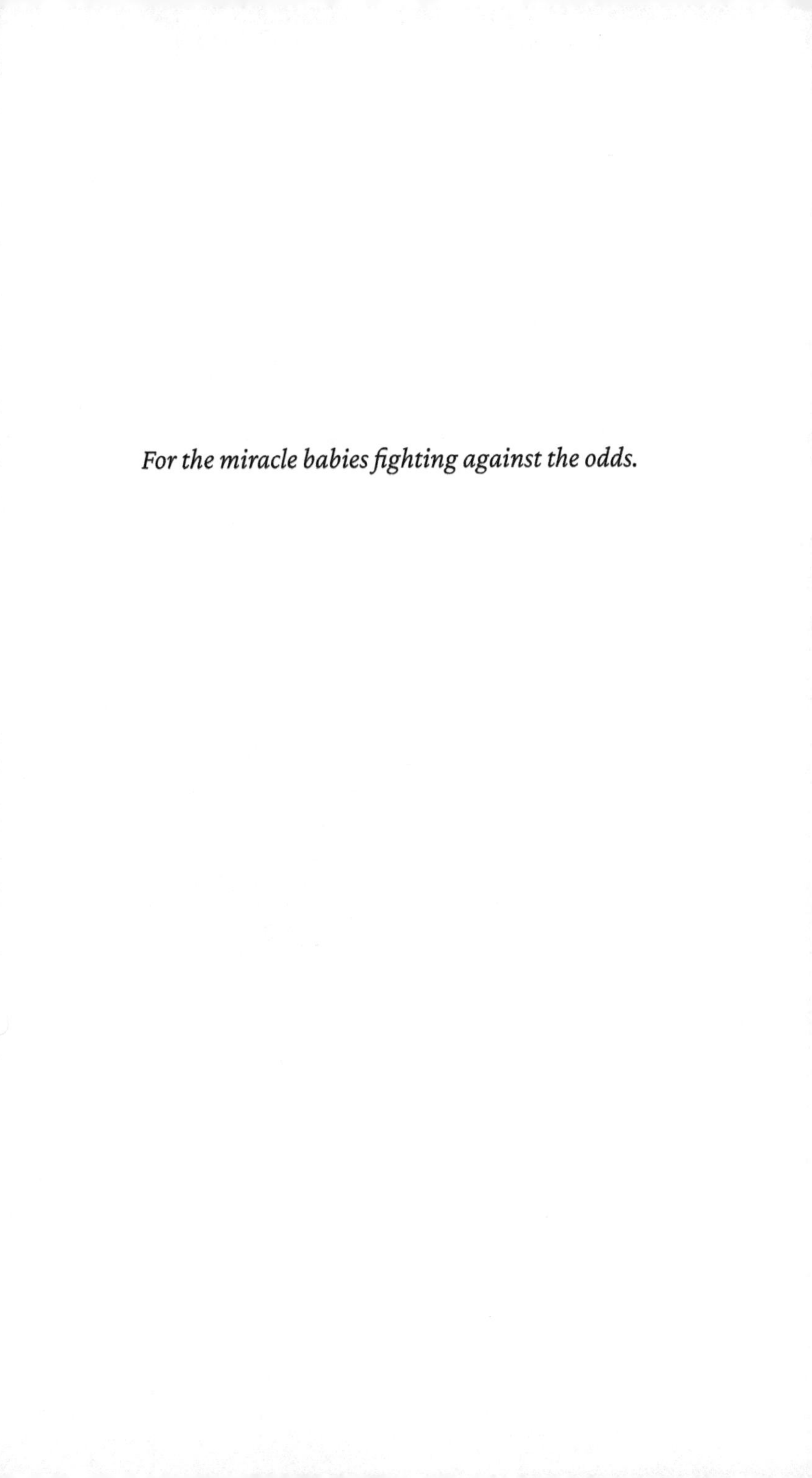

For the miracle babies fighting against the odds.

FOREWORD

KRISTEN DOVNIK

Eleven authors have collaborated to create a collection of stories set in a world that requires faith to persevere, mirroring the charity we have chosen to support. Families with infants in the SCN or NICU need to believe that their children will be okay. As a parent who has been through this experience, I understand how difficult it is to witness your child being hooked up to machines and surrounded by bright lights. However, I had to remind myself regularly that my son was receiving the best possible care.

Miracle Babies Foundation is Australia's leading organisation supporting premature and sick newborns, their families and the hospitals that care for them.

Every year in Australia around 48,000 newborn babies require the help of a Neonatal Intensive Care Unit (NICU) or Special Care Nursery (SCN). 27,000 of these babies are born premature and up to 1,000 babies lose their fight for life.

For families, the experience of having a baby come into the world not as expected or planned is life-changing.

Without support, this overwhelming and traumatic experience can have lifelong effects on the emotional well-being of these miracle families. It affects the entire family unit.

That is why we have decided to donate proceeds from all ebook, Amazon, and Ingram Spart to The Miracle Babies Foundation.

Miracle Babies provide support to families of premature and sick newborns through our NurtureProgram, including NurtureLine (24 Hours Family Support Line **1300 622 243**) NurtureTime (in-hospital emotional support) and NurtureGroups (community play and support groups, for after discharge). Your support will also help continued distribution of our family NurtureProgram Resources, via hospitals.

SYMADOR
PLEASE NOTE: This map was constructed from Chronicler archives. There may be
geographical discrepancies due to variation in reports.

OBSERVATIONS OF THE HEAD CHRONICLER

LIV EVANS

"History is written by the victors."
- Winston Churchill

HISTORY IS ALL ABOUT PERSPECTIVE.

It doesn't matter how many accounts you read, from all different sources, there will never be a single cohesive truth.

Everyone experiences the world in their own way, through their own lens. Two people could have the exact same conversation and walk away with entirely different impressions of what it was about.

The real, telling factor is that the history that gets saved and pushed into the common consciousness is the history written by the victors.

At least, it used to be.

That was a long time ago, though. Well before the soil turned rancid and the air toxic. The stories that survived about humanity's triumphs and crimes were recorded by those in power, by *only* those in power. The stories of real people, the minute decisions and small acts that triggered a flurry of future actions, those were left out. Records that survived any great era were the ones held by those in charge. Countless small but crucial voices were caught in the swell of the past and washed away by the tide of time.

The unbalanced recording of events meant that people only had a sanitised, convenient version of the past. One that allowed them to pretend they learned from the mistakes of those before them. This provided justification for why the happenings of the now were acceptable. It seems there have been critics of this over time, but very few people tried to change it.

There was hope, though, a little bit of light back in the twenty-first century, when people mobilised and refused to take the tall tales of their leaders for granted. They learned that what they heard in the news and read on their electronic books was biased. It was a promising time, but their awakening came too late. Too late to save them. Too late to save the world they lived in.

Thankfully, a small group of people who survived the horror of the initial radiation kept the fire of resistance burning. A band of like-minded scholars who realised that real accounts of the unfolding of time and humanity were essential. They wanted to ensure that the truth existed out there. That the stories of people, no matter who they were or where they came from, were recorded.

As a result of these stories being matters of perspective, they do not always match up. There are conflicting accounts, tales without resolutions, and outright delu-sions. However, it isn't the job of humanity to determine what *is* and what *is not* worth knowing. Every word of every story has value, and when the current world is built off too many lies, the Chroniclers see it as our solemn duty to record reality for those in the future.

For when the liars in power fall, people need to know the truth.

"History is written by the people."
— The Chroniclers

THE RUNNER

KATE SCHUMACHER

THE RUNNER

KATE SCHUMACHER

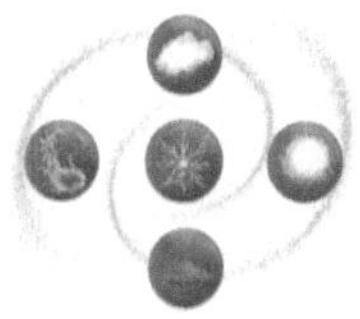

Dust crept over the city. It wasn't a storm, not today, but it was dust all the same. Dirty, choking, radioactive red dust that coated everything in its path.

Sia shut the window. It didn't close properly, like most windows in the Lower Sector of Symador, so she slipped off her threadbare jumper and jammed it against the base of the frame. Her mother was sleeping on the cot in the corner, skin stretched tightly over her bones, a thin blanket resting over her body. The sickness had taken hold a month ago, and it moved quickly – the poison sucking all the vitality from her body as it raced through her system.

There was no cure for the radioactive wasting disease, just like there had been no cure for the others; the ones Sia remembered only when it was dark, when the past gnawed at the corners of her mind like a rabid animal, chewing and feasting on the blackness that lay inside her like a sickness of its own.

She remembered the children – tiny, mewling things with scrunched faces and claw-like hands. They had been born broken and ridden with poison. There had been Burnings, and she remembered the tiny bodies slowly disappearing into ash and fed to the dust-covered ground.

Sia re-checked the window and the front door. There was nothing she could use to cover the thin strip of light beneath the door and, as she watched, it slowly turned red. She pulled her scarf up to cover her mouth and nose, glancing at her mother's exposed face. Habit wanted her to try; rational thought told her not to bother, and riding close behind that was the guilt.

Her father would wait for the dust to settle before coming home and, even then, he would need to be careful. Sia tried to remember if he had taken his mask with him that morning, but she hadn't been home. He would have, she told herself.

Would he? A little voice whispered. Since her mother had fallen to the sickness, her father had changed. A once vital presence in their home, he moved like a man defeated, shoulders curled in on themselves, eyes turned to the floor. Sia wanted to shake him, to remind him that she was still here, that she needed him.

With a final look at the bloodied light easing in beneath the door, Sia returned to the window and watched the dust pile up against the glass, wanting to come in.

THE BOY WAS SO CLEAN HE ALMOST SHONE IN THE DREARY WORLD. Sia narrowed her eyes, instantly suspicious. She watched him from the shadows that stretched across the street, her scarf pulled tight around her mouth and nose – the dust storms came without warning, and to wander about without protection was the quickest way to die. They used to be given proper masks, designed to filter the air. Sia remembered lining up for them when she was small, but now, no one came down here handing out protection. No one up there cared if those in the bowels of the city lived or died. So, people used whatever they could find.

The scarf she used was thin and she had discovered a hole in it, close to one of the ends. One hole would become another, and then eventually another, until the scarf was useless and she would have to find something else. Again.

Not far from her, a stunted tree clung to life between the cracks in the footpath. The boy looked left and right before crossing the road and Sia snorted. No one did that anymore, not down here. They hadn't seen a car in years – she could barely remember them. The last skeletal truck had been long scavenged for scraps. Sia had found it both alluring and horrifying, a symbol of what had been, a civilisation and a people that were long gone, leaving the residents of Symador scrabbling through the dust in their wake.

The boy approached the tree. He didn't bother to check if anyone was watching him as he reached out and touched it, running smooth fingers over rough bark. He seemed sad, like he was personally affected by what he saw.

Sia narrowed her eyes more. This boy, whoever he was, was a stranger to this part of the city. She was surprised no one else had noticed him. People moved past him, not shifting their eyes, not moving from their path. Sia chewed her lip beneath her scarf, feeling the dry skin crack a little before she tasted blood, the salty tang of it.

The boy was about her age, dressed in smart grey trousers and a black shirt. He was tall and slim, his limbs long – it didn't look like he had an ounce of muscle on him anywhere. His face was free of the dust that she was never able to get rid of, no matter how hard she scrubbed. If she had hot water and soap, maybe she would look like he did.

She examined her hands, noticing the ring of red around the cuticles and how the cracks in her skin were also tinged with red. Even the boy's hands were pale – she could see that even from a distance. He stuck them in his pockets, pulled them out again. Nervous, perhaps. She couldn't tell.

Sia glanced up, noticing the sky had darkened. She tugged down her scarf and sniffed the air – dust, maybe twenty minutes away – and quickly pulled the scarf back over her mouth. The boy on the street could smell it too. She knew it from the way he looked up, his eyes suddenly frantic.

She sighed. She should just go home. Sybil's voice was in her head. *'You're always collecting junk, Sia. Just leave it. The underground market is full of scammers and rip-off merchants – you're wasting your time.'* No one had seen Sybil for a month and Sia had already resigned herself to never seeing her friend again. Sybil was always poking her nose into things that didn't concern her.

The sky darkened a little more. Sia picked up her bag and slipped it over her shoulder. Losing her bag would be a sure fire way to lose her job; and the scant amount of rations her job earned was needed, especially now. The boy was coming down the footpath, eyes darting side to side.

He looked more worried now than he did before. If he hadn't spent all that time stroking a tree …

He'd obviously not seen Sia hiding in her shadows and he jumped when she stepped in front of him. He was older than she'd thought – a boy on the edge of being a man. He was clean-shaven, but she could see the shadow that graced his jaw. His dark hair gleamed in the muted light.

'What are you doing here?' she asked him bluntly.

He started. 'I'm …'

'Because we don't want your sort around here,' Sia continued, keeping her distance. 'Nothing but trouble comes when you people step outside your walls. You need to leave.'

She couldn't tell if he was armed, but he probably was. It was no secret the Select had access to weapons, relics of a world that no longer existed.

'I can't,' he said. His voice was soft but clear, as if he'd never pulled the dust into his lungs.He regarded Sia warily with deep brown eyes, pushing the hair from his forehead. It was long. Most people down here kept their hair short. It was easier that way. 'I'm lost.'

'Lost?'

'Yes,' he sighed. 'I've … got a food token and I don't know where I'm going and my sister … she's hungry,' he added defensively.

'We're all hungry,' Sia snapped, wondering about this strange boy's sister. How old was she? Did she breathe okay? Somewhere nearby, a siren wailed and a cracked voice spoke static over the magical loudspeaker attached to the wall of the building opposite them.

Sia turned to go. It had gotten darker and she had ten

minutes, tops, before the dust came creeping over the outer walls, slinking through the streets like mist.

'Can you show me? Where to go?' the boy pleaded.

I'll show you where to go, Sia thought. 'I can't be seen queuing for food, can't be anywhere near the depot. I've already been this week.'

He hesitated, then reached into his pocket. Sia tensed, ready to run, to fight, to die. It was always this way. She bit the inside of her cheek; blood mingled with adrenalin on her tongue. That taste was a well-known friend. He pulled a food coupon free and waved it at her.

'Are you stupid?' Sia eyed him like he was crazy, and maybe he was. His eyes had taken on a wild, twitching sense. 'Put that away before someone sees. People have died for less.'

He crammed the coupon back in his pocket, glancing around nervously. The loudspeaker crackled again.

'Look,' Sia said quickly. 'Forget the food. You, *we*, need to get home before the storm comes.' She glanced at the sky again. 'Five minutes. Where do you live?' She didn't like him, but she didn't want to come back tomorrow and find him dead on the footpath, buried in red dust. His body would lie where it fell until someone claimed it. Sometimes, no one did. She had seen that once before, a body bloated with the heat, the skin stretched tight, ready to pop. Sybil had made her move away, but Sia had wanted to crouch there all day and study the way death operated.

'I live back that way,' he answered, gesturing across the street.

'You might make it,' Sia said. She didn't wait for his reply before she pulled the scarf over her mouth and ran.

IN THE YEARS AFTER THE DISASTER, IT USED TO RAIN. SIA WASN'T born then, of course, but her grandmother had told stories before she died of the water that fell from the sky, and the great rivers and creeks that used to run like giant serpents through the landscape. Sia had listened, wide-eyed, at the stories of floods. All that water! Clean water.

It had still rained occasionally when Sia's mother was born but then, when her mother was a girl, the radiation that seeped through the ground from the contaminated water table could not be contained anymore. The grass became dust and the trees lost their leaves and, eventually, the rain stopped falling altogether. Great storms still wracked the earth, teased to life by the radiation that coated the planet, but all that fell was ash and dust. In an atmosphere devoid of water, the temperature climbed and, soon, the ice caps melted and the seas rose, grey-tipped waves rolling towards the shore, sinking their teeth into the earth before they were pulled back out again, and the coastlines were soon devoured by the angry sea.

All that water, but it was useless.

And without water, without food, without the comforts people were used to, a world that had gorged itself on capitalism, on wealth, found itself living in darkness as the radiation spread. The great cities of mankind quickly tumbled into ruin, swallowed in the earth's revenge.

The riots began, and what followed were what Sia's grandmother's generation called the Dry Dark. Water was currency, economy, and power, and those that had it guarded it with fierce hands and brutal hearts. The dams that fed water to billions of people dried up, becoming nothing more than great pans of cracked and shrivelled earth. The great basins that lay beneath the ground, that artesian water that had been stored for thousands of years, once regularly replenished by the rain, were drained.

No one could say where the radiation came from to begin with – that knowledge was lost, forgotten by time and hunger and thirst. All the world knew now was that, outside the walled cities, was death.

DUSTY FOOTPRINTS FOLLOWED SIA AS SHE DARTED THROUGH THE winding streets of Symador. She ran with one hand clutching the empty bag slung over her shoulder.

The Trials were due to start soon and, like last year, there would be dozens of messages to ferry across the city from one district to the next. Without the old world technology, running messages was an important job, given mostly to children from Sia's sector. There were two reasons for this – runners were not expected to live long lives, with all the dust and radioactive particles that coated the air; and it was assumed the children used as runners could not read, so the information they carried was safe.

Only, assumptions were not always correct.

As she ran, Sia let her hand slide towards her hip, fingers caressing the hard shape of the knife she carried. She had found it on the street while scavenging for anything useful, anything she might be able to sell on the underground market that she was certain the Select knew about but ignored. The knife was blunt, but it was all Sia had. Information was worth more than fresh water – the life of a runner was not.

If it came to it, she was expected to die protecting the secrets she carried. If what they carried couldn't be protected, every runner had instructions to destroy the information in their charge. The ink on the paper was magical, a system devised using a combination of fire and earth magic. If a runner was under threat, they had to simply scrunch the scrolls they carried – as the paper crinkled, the ink would turn to dust and fall free of the page. Then, they were allowed to die.

The Trials used to happen once every three years, but now it had become an annual event. The radiation had taken so much from the world, but it had also given a strange gift – the power to control the elements. Magic, some called it, like from the stories Sia's mother used to tell her. Fairy tales, that was what they were called. Stories of princesses and princes, of curses and terrible magic that could make or break a world. Stories of girls trapped in towers, waiting to be rescued by men on white horses who slayed dragons and battled giants to reach the woman they were destined to love.

Sia knew nothing of white horses and dragons, but she did know about being trapped. And she had not decided yet if magic was a blessing, or a curse.

Pausing to rest before she began the ascent into the Upper Sector, Sia chewed on her lip. She was seventeen. One more year until her Tests, and then, if she was lucky, the Trials.

Last year, two kids from her district were uncovered at

the Tests. One could manipulate fire, something that would be useful in the Lower Sectors of Symador. Fires were common when people lived like rats, buildings smashed together and cobbled out of whatever was lying around. A magic user who could control fire could prevent catastrophe.

There had been a rumour, long-ago whispered but not quite forgotten, that the fires were not accidents at all, but were unleashed on purpose. What better way to rid a city of the vermin that took up food, water and space? No one knew this for certain. The Chroniclers would know, but Sia had never met one. No one she knew had. Sia wasn't even sure they existed, and if they did, what was the point of them? To watch and not help, when the world around them was falling to pieces?

The other kid had energy, a rare and sought-after talent, used to fuel the lights of the upper reaches of the city. Sia had seen them at night, a series of glowing beacons set high above her, like an invitation to something she would never be able to attend. Were there princesses in glorious silk up there? White horses and men who would fight dragons for the women they loved? Sia spoke about it with Sybil once. Her friend had laughed, calling Sia a romantic fool.

'There is nothing but corruption and greed up there,' Sybil had said, gesturing to the inner walls of Symador. 'We are better down here, Sia.'

'How so?' Sia had argued, and Sybil had given her a long, knowing look.

'We're free,' she'd said eventually.

Sia adjusted her scarf and set off again. She had never

felt the presence of any sort of magic within her. When she was a child, she had wished for it, knowing even then, as everyone did, those magical talents were important, and that Symador's leader, Imperator Vaarem, would reward them. A child's longing for a different life for her family was quickly squashed when she learnt, talent or not, it would only be her leaving the dust-choked world of Lower Symador for the fresh air and sunshine. The kid with electricity in his fingertips was taken to the upper district, beyond the grey stone wall, and no one had ever seen him again. With his disappearance, Sia's romantic fantasies were squashed.

Now, with the Trials looming, Sia wondered how many others with magic would be taken away, sent to serve those who spent their existence looking down on others. She wiped her forehead free of sweat and glanced up. High above her, set on top of the hill Symador was built around, was the castle. The building was smooth grey stone and could be seen from every part of Symador, and those within could keep watch on the rest of the city, as well as what lay beyond the walls.

Sia no longer believed in princesses and men on white horses riding to their rescue, but she was consumed with a fierce yearning to *know* what went on up there. As a Runner, she had come closer to the Upper Sector than anyone else she knew. She had peered through the great gate as it opened just enough for her to stick in her hand and wait while someone whose face she had never seen placed letters in her palm and gave her terse instructions, spoken slowly, like she was feeble minded.

As the streets crept higher and she passed through the

first checkpoint, pausing only to have her nano tattoo scanned, the buildings around lost their grime; sunlight bounced off smooth walls and there was no litter choking the footpaths, no queues for food rations or water, no one waving coupons around, no shouting or the wailing of hungry children. The ground beneath Sia's feet lost its permanent tinge of red as she left the dust behind.

This was the Middle Sector, home to those more fortunate than Sia's people, but not so fortunate as to be allowed entry into the world of the Upper Sector and the Select. Sybil had spoken once about a girl she knew from the Middle Sector. She'd been gifted to a man in the Upper, in the hope that her marriage would be the ticket out for her family. It wasn't, though, Sybil had said. A prize brood mare doesn't mean the whole stable gets to eat better. It didn't stop other families from hoping for the same thing, and Sia often wondered how many girls had been sent to the Upper Sector against their wishes.

Princesses and silk gowns. Maybe they did want that life.

In the Middle, people could attend school. That was what Sia wished for more. Not silk gowns and white horses or a husband with privilege. She wanted to learn. Her mother had broken the rules and taught her how to read. No one needed to tell Sia how important it was that no one found out. The information she carried in her satchel everyday was power and, although she had wanted to, she had never looked. The scrolls were sealed with wax. If she so much as peeked at the words that lay inside that roll of paper, she would Burn for it.

Sia's steps slowed as she reached the markets. Fruit in

bright colours winked at her. Ruby-red apples and bright oranges rested in crates alongside things she could not name. Whatever was left over from the day would slowly make its way to the food depot, and by the time anyone from the Lower Sector got their hands on it, it would be shrivelled and bitter. The stall owner eyed Sia suspiciously. She patted her satchel, resisted the urge to give him the finger, and hurried on, her stomach grumbling.

The next checkpoint came into view. The gates to the Upper Sector were heavy steel, well fortified. It would take ten men to open them, if it wasn't for the electrical magic that operated them. Sia would not be allowed through. Someone would meet her and the other runners at the gate. As Sia drew closer, she realised with dismay she was the only one there. She was late. The Symguard, red uniform like a beacon in the Upper Sector sun, swept his eyes over her and a grin pulled at the corners of his mouth.

'Perhaps you're getting too old for this job, Sia.'

'Piss off, Robert,' she mumbled. Robert had been a guard for as long as she'd been a runner. While not friends in any way, they were friendly enough with one another to be able to share a joke like this. Symguards were always from the Middle Sector. Robert was not much older than Sia was, with a boyish face that made him seem younger. He wore his hair long, like some of the Select. 'Get a haircut,' she said bossily.

'Like yours?'

Sia ran her hand over her head. Her hair was freshly shaven.

'You look like a boy,' Robert told her.

'That's the point, dickhead,' she said with a roll of her

eyes. Boys didn't get hassled. They didn't get leered at. They didn't get snatched off the streets and sold to brothels by Raptor addicts looking for their next fix. 'Better do my job, then.' She peered around him; the gate was open a crack, just wide enough for a hand to slip through and pass out a scroll or two. Sia never usually saw the faces of those who handled the scrolls. The fresh and clean boy from yesterday flashed into her mind. She hadn't found him dead in the street, so figured he'd managed to get back to where he belonged.

Robert glanced over his shoulder, then waved Sia up to the gate. She kept her eyes on it as Robert scanned her nano tattoo. A slim hand appeared, a scroll held gently so as to not disrupt the ink. Handling scrolls with magical ink was a skill – it was so easy to mess with the magic and if that happened, Sia was certain she would be blamed for it.

Shoot the messenger indeed.

She was not supposed to touch the scroll at this end. She opened her satchel wide, but the hand holding the scroll did not let it fall. Sia frowned. There was something oddly familiar about that hand.

'Shiny boy,' she whispered, lifting her eyes and meeting his dark gaze. 'So, this is what you do for a crust? Never mind. Where am I going first?'

'The City Office on Fourth Street, Middle Sector,' he said, voice all business-like, dropping the scroll in her satchel. The City Office was the grandest building in the Middle Sector. The people who worked there were tasked with planning – mainly how to feed and water a walled city caught like a rat in a trap on the edge of a radioactive wasteland. There were great greenhouses and hydro farms manned by water wielders on the far side of the Middle Sector. Probably where those shining apples came from, Sia thought.

She went to move away, but the boy shook his head. A second scroll appeared in those slim fingers. Sia raised her eyebrows. She never carried more than one message at a time. It was too dangerous in case she was found with two. Raptor junkies had been known to steal scrolls and pass them to the highest bidder, usually one of the Rebels. A runner would collect a message, deliver and return to the Upper Sector gates for another. The more messages you ran in a day determined your worth. Sia hated when she was sent to the furthest places because it meant she would have to forfeit a job to someone else. There was no love amongst runners and competition was fierce. Everyone had families to help feed.

Sia locked eyes with the boy beyond the gate. 'Do I get paid for it?'

He nodded.

'Where to then?' she asked.

The boy hesitated, then, voice low, 'Langhorne Bridge. You're to leave it—'

'What's taking so long?' A new voice cut in. Deep and harsh. Sia gulped, willing the boy to hurry. He dropped the scroll into her satchel and she snapped it closed and stepped back. She caught the flash of fear in the boy's eyes as he darted away. Before the gate was closed, Sia saw a dark-skinned face and sharp eyes.

She was slow to get moving, and Robert noticed.

'Hey, you okay?'

'Fine.' She did not need a Symguard, even one who was

half a friend, remembering what had just happened. She forced a smile and gave him a mock salute. He gave her the finger. She turned and ran.

LANGHORNE BRIDGE WAS A CRUMBLING MONSTER THAT SPANNED what used to be a river. Nothing but cracked earth and metal skeletons flowed along its bed now. Sia did not look at them. She kept her eyes on the bridge and her fingers on her satchel. The dark-eyed Shiny Boy had not had time to tell her where to leave the message. Sia had delivered the scroll to the City Office and kept running, pushing her way through the Middle Sector before dropping back through the checkpoint and into the Lower, the Symguard on the gate barely looking at her and not bothering to scan her tattoo. No one came to the Lower Sector unless they had to.

'Fuck,' Sia growled. She should just leave the scroll, but something told her that would not be wise. She glanced around; she couldn't see anyone, but she could feel eyes on her. The Bridge was a known haunt of Raptor addicts. She remembered the day her and Sybil had encountered a pair of them, reaching up to touch her shaved head. The lack of hair and the permanent smudge of dirt on their faces had saved them. Raptor addicts weren't looking for dirty boys.

Sia kicked at a miserable tin can; it bounced away, echoing dully as it turned over and over against the crumbling cement bridge, before it sailed over the edge through a gap in the railing.

'Fuck,' she said again. She couldn't return to the Upper

Sector with a scroll she was certain she was not supposed to have, nor could she just leave it here. She glowered at the bridge, then slunk away. She wouldn't go far. She'd wait and see if someone showed up to collect the mysterious scroll.

She settled into the shadows of an abandoned cart, wondering what had happened to the horse that pulled it, and the Carter who drove it. Her scowl deepened. She could be on other runs right now, but the boy had said she'd be paid, and if this was illegal underground stuff, maybe that payment might be something worth waiting for.

An hour. She'd give it an hour. Sia was fast. She still had time to return to Robert's gate and collect another message for the day.

Footsteps crunched across the dirt; Sia pulled her rusty knife free, shifting into a crouch. A pair of black boots was approaching; she watched them moving closer and then, when the owner of the boots came around the edge of the cart, she leapt out, her arm swinging, the blade of the knife glinting in the sunlight.

It was the boy. He yelped in fright and jumped back.

'Shit, Sia!'

Her eyes narrowed. 'How do you know my name?'

'I heard Robert—'

'Bullshit you did,' she snarled. A thought struck her. 'If you think I'm letting you touch me, you're very mistaken.'

He blinked at her, bewildered. 'What are you talking about?'

'I know what boys like you are looking for. Didn't daddy give you enough for a visit to the brothel?' Girls, and some boys, traded their flesh for food coupons or freshwater. Sia had done it once, years ago, and straight after decided she'd rather go thirsty. The man's bristly beard had scratched her face and he'd hurt her in his desire to taste a different sort of flesh.

'You've got the wrong idea.'

'Do I?' She gripped the knife tight; the handle was starting to fall apart and soon all she'd be left with was a blade, but a naked blade was better than nothing. 'Are boys more your thing?'

'No one is more my thing.' He swallowed. 'If you kill me, they'll come looking for me, then they'll come looking for you.'

'Is that a threat?' Sia hissed, but hesitated, her thoughts shifting quickly to her parents.

'Sybil would care,' the boy said quietly.

The hand gripping the knife trembled. 'What?'

'She asked me to find you.'

'Bullshit, Shiny Boy,' Sia shot back.

'She trusted no one else with her message,' he said, his eyes flickering to Sia's satchel, then to the crumbling edges of the bridge. 'Come on. I'll show you where to leave it.'

'Fine,' Sia snapped. She did not put the knife away, following at a distance as he led her onto the bridge. No one used it anymore and the further they went, Sia could see why. The concrete base of the bridge was collapsing in places, and everything was cloaked in dust. With a curse, Sia pulled her ratty scarf over her mouth and nose, but the boy didn't attempt to cover his face.

He stopped suddenly, and dropped to his haunches, lifting something from the ground. Intrigued, Sia moved closer, her knife held at the ready. She had never stabbed anyone, but now was as a good a day as any.

'Here,' the boy said. He had removed a small slab of concrete from the surface of the bridge; beneath it was a metal box, which he pulled out and flipped the lid. Sia peered over his shoulder. The box was empty. She made an unimpressed noise. He glanced at her, a small smile on his mouth. 'What were you expecting?'

'Something exciting,' she said, opening her satchel and retrieving the scroll. Quickly she placed it in the box, and he returned it to the hole, sliding the slab of concrete back into place. When he stood, he rubbed his boot over it, smearing the hiding place with red dirt.

Maybe he wasn't so dumb after all.

'You said you'd pay me,' Sia reminded him as he walked away from her. 'Hey!' She ran to catch up to him, grabbing him by the shoulder and spinning him around, adjusting her grip on the blunt dagger. He shoved her away. She opened her mouth, then froze. Dust. A great plume of it was rising from the wastes beyond the city. She reached out and wrapped her fingers in the smooth fabric of the boy's shirt. 'A storm is coming. Move.'

She should just leave him. He wasn't her problem. She wondered how long it would be before the rats started to chew on his pretty face when he died? But he said he knew Sybil, and that was enough, for the moment. Sia glanced over her shoulder, pulling her scarf up higher as she did so. The boy didn't have a scarf. He covered his mouth and nose with his fingers, scurrying along awkwardly behind her as they left the ruined Langhorne Bridge and headed towards the city.

Shining, pale, stupid, to come down here without something to protect himself.

If he was lying to her, she'd open his flesh and leave him in the sewers. See who found him first. The smell of dust became stronger. Sia quickened her pace, until she was running. She didn't look to see if he was following her – she could hear his feet slapping against the cracked concrete, could hear his ragged breathing. As she led the way between two buildings, she sensed him falter, then hurry to catch up when she didn't slow.

Sia glanced up; the slice of sky between the crumbling building was beginning to turn red with dust. She swore, sidestepping a pile of rubbish as the alley narrowed and the sky disappeared where the buildings leant to embrace one another. This part of the city had been declared too dangerous, the buildings too unstable, and no one was to live here, a law made by the Guard, who had never bothered coming down to enforce it. Sia could feel eyes watching from behind broken windows, but she didn't stop, scuttling over the skeleton of a car.

The boy followed, saying nothing, not stopping until she led them to the sewers.

They were in the very bowels of the city now.

Sia lowered her scarf, smelling the air as she turned to face the boy. 'You got a name?'

'Cas,' he said, his voice muffled from behind his fingers.

She gestured to the gaping black mouth of the first sewer tunnel. 'After you.'

He baulked. 'The sewers?'

'Yes.'

'But—'

'Look, you can either face the dark,' she said, gesturing again at the yawning concrete mouth, 'or that.' She nodded at the plume of red dust rising over Symador's walls. The sun was covered now, the sky a deep red. Dust had begun to float down to coat the lower city. It was strangely beautiful, the way those tiny red particles embraced everything they touched.

Cas rubbed at his chin. 'The sewers it is, then,' he murmured.

Sia stepped aside. 'After you,' she repeated.

His eyes narrowed. He didn't trust her. Good. Trusting the wrong person was another way to die. Cas sighed in resignation and disappeared into the darkness; Sia followed, shuddering as the mouth of the sewer swallowed her.

'What's down here, exactly?' Cas asked as they walked. His footsteps echoed off the concrete walls.

'Not what, who,' Sia mumbled. 'Keep your voice down. And walk quietly. We won't go in too far – just enough to keep away from the dust. You'll need to cover your mouth and nose until it passes,' she added. 'Your skinny fingers won't be enough.'

Cas stripped off his shirt, wrapping the material around his face obediently, while she tried not to stare. He was so pale he glowed in the darkness, so clean and gleaming, like a fresh thing. Like prey – or bait. She swallowed, peering into the darkness ahead of them, ears straining. Nothing. They were safe. For now. The radiation sickness made people lose their minds towards the end, made the calm - manic; the gentle - violent.

Sia stopped. 'Here will do. We shouldn't go any further.'

'You didn't tell me what was down here,' he said, keeping his voice low, as she'd ordered.

'Apart from those who work down here? The sick,' she said simply. 'Those too ill to work, those who are a burden on their families. Those who have failed the Trials and have been deemed useless. Those who have become nothing but an extra mouth to feed.' She stopped, unable to help thinking about her mother. How long would it be until she found herself here?

It was a cruel way to die. The radiation sickness could not be cured or treated – but to die alone in the darkness? Sia knew the sewers were swept clean of bodies, but that didn't happen very often. The cleaners must have been here recently, she decided. The air was cool and crisp, clean, but the faint scent of death clung to it, as if embedded in the very walls of this place.

'How long will it last?' Cas asked.

'No idea. Could be an hour, could be a day,' she said. 'You may as well sit. Get comfortable.'

He did as he was told, lowering his body to the ground. 'A day?'

'Worried you won't cope? I bet you've never gone more than a few hours without food or water, have you?' Sia asked bitterly, sinking to the ground. She made sure she sat so she could keep her eyes on him, this strange pale boy who claimed to know what had happened to Sybil. He could be full of shit, she knew that as well, but then how would he know Sybil's name?

'No,' he admitted eventually, then, 'what's it like?'

'You want to know what it's like to starve?'

'If you want to share it, yes.'

'Why? Why would you want to know that?'

'Because then I'll know,' he said, his voice soft, resigned in a way she didn't understand.

Sia sighed, letting her back rest against the curved wall behind her. The concrete was cool; she could feel its alien, icy touch through her clothes. It was always hot in the lower part of the city, it was almost nice to feel cool for a change. 'When you're always hungry, after a while, you get used to it. That gnawing, hollow feeling inside just becomes a part of who you are.'

They were deep enough in the tunnel but still, Sia kept her eyes on the curved concrete mouth. If the wind changed direction, they would be breathing dust. She imagined those particles curling around her lungs and shuddered.

'Sybil,' she said. 'Tell me.'

Cas nodded at her satchel. 'You have the answers; well, some of them anyway. You carry them with you every day.'

Sia swallowed, her fingers tightening on the satchel.

Cas shook his head. 'I know about the ink. If you unroll them carefully, it should be fine.'

'You're encouraging me to risk my life? My job? Whether my family starves or not? And you still haven't paid me,' she added waspishly.

'You risk no more than I do,' he replied simply.

She glared at him. She should leave it, but he was watching her, a challenge in his dark eyes. 'Tell me who you are.'

Cas was silent for a long moment, then he shifted away

from the wall, twisting his body so she could see what she did not before. There, on his shoulder, was a tattoo, not unlike the small nano tattoos everyone had on their wrists. On Cas' shoulder was a capital C.

'That's not a C for cat, is it? You're a fucking Watcher?' The job of Chronicler was not an inherited one. People had to choose it, which meant this kid had chosen to stand by and do nothing while people starved and died and fought each other to survive. 'You—'

'You can shout at me later, Sia. Maybe when the storm is over and we haven't been eaten by radioactive rats or whatever else is down here.'

'Stop that,' Sia said, reaching into the satchel. 'Stop talking to me like you know me.'

'I guess I feel like I do,' he said. 'Sybil talks about you a lot.' He reached into the pocket of his black pants and pulled out a folded piece of paper. He held it out for her. 'She wanted me to give you this.' When she didn't take it, he let his arm drop. 'I'll—'

Sia shot forward, snatching the paper from him.

His eyebrows lifted. 'You can read?'

'Why, can't you?' she shot back, unfolding the paper.

Cas huffed a soft laugh.

'It's too dark,' Sia complained.

Light suddenly filled the tunnel. Alarmed, she tore her eyes from the page to see a small flame dancing on the tip of Cas's finger.

'Better?' he asked. Tiny flames were captured in his eyes, his skin golden, light and shadow cutting sharp lines across his face.

Sia swallowed and said nothing, turning back to the page.

Six words.

I'm not dead. I'll miss you.

A lump crept up Sia's throat. 'What does this mean?'

'She's leaving Symador, but didn't want you to worry,' Cas said softly.

'There's nothing but radioactive dust and death out there,' Sia said, shaking her head. 'Why? If you're her new best friend, why is she doing this? I know she hated being here, but this makes no sense.'

'Sybil never told you she joined the Rebels,' Cas replied. 'Not because she wanted to trick you, but because if it all went to hell in a handbasket, she didn't want you caught in the middle. Her words,' he added.

Sia said nothing. Sybil had always been creeping around at night and, before she vanished, her movements had become even more mysterious. Drop offs in the darkness, hushed conversations with people Sia had never seen before. She only knew because, worried Sybil was Raptor dealing or flesh selling for a quick feed, she'd followed her.

'You're a Chronicler,' Sia said softly, lifting her eyes to Cas. He clicked his fingers and his flames went out, plunging them into darkness again. 'You're supposed to observe and remain impartial. You're neither part of the Select or any Sector really, but you have access to the Fortress. But you're not just watching anymore, are you?'

'No, we're not,' Cas answered. He sat forward, his pale skin glowing. Sia's eyes returned to the tattoo on his shoulder. 'The Imperator has a plan. We don't know what it is yet, but we are going to find out. Beyond these walls are cities, Sia. Like ours. A long way from here. That is where Sybil is going.'

'Why?'

'For answers. The Imperator runs these Trials every year, but why?'

Sia frowned. 'So we can counter the effects of the radiation and return things to how they used to be – with magic,' she said.

'It's easy to believe what you've been told when everyone sings the same song,' Cas said simply. He kept his eyes on her face.

'We've been lied to? Sybil was right,' Sia whispered. 'Those fucking bastards.'

'One man's truth is another man's lie,' Cas replied. He pulled his shirt back on, covering up the C etched into his skin and pushed his hair back from his face.

Sia felt a smile crawl over her face. She slipped the strap of her satchel free of her shoulder and sat back again, stretching her legs out. 'I think they need to redo your tattoo,' she told Cas.

His eyebrows lifted. 'Oh?'

'A big R might suit you better.'

OBSERVATIONS OF THE HEAD CHRONICLER

LIV EVANS

"Petrichor: (noun) a distinct, earthy, usually pleasant odor that is associated with rainfall especially when following a warm, dry period that arises from a combination of volatile plant oils and geosmin released from the soil into the air and by ozone carried by downdrafts."
- Meriam-Webster Dictionary

IN TIMES OF OLD, THERE WERE PEOPLE WHO COULD SMELL RAIN before it came. The good rain. The clean rain. It was described as tangy. Metallic. Full of potential.

Symador smells like that now.

There is a storm brewing overhead.

Dark, angry clouds are swelling. The humid air sizzles with the static of growing tension. Thunder rumbles ominously in the sky and down below, as people who have been holding their breath are finding their voices for the first time. Wind whips around the bodies of those who have been frozen in place, pushing together critical pieces of chaos and forming an unstoppable tempest that will rage until the rain runs out and the earth is washed clean.

The change is coming.

It will start off small, like all good things do. A glimmer of truth, a flicker of possibility, a tiny crack in a facade. People will look up and take notice, and soon these tiny signs will expand into a sense of hope that accelerates so quickly the change arrives before we even notice it has begun.

People are finally seeing what is before them. Others are questioning the world around them. There are even some who go against their longest, dearest held beliefs to spark revolution. To open floodgates that they will have no hope of closing once the truth is unleashed.

This awakening, this perfect storm, has been a long time coming for Symador... but it is finally here. The most recent stories collected by the Chroniclers point to it; and one day, someone will be able to look back and pinpoint where that change began. Where the air started to crackle with potential... when the scent of petrichor filled the atmosphere with promise and hearts with hope.

THE CULTIVATOR

JUDY LIU

THE CULTIVATOR

JUDY LIU

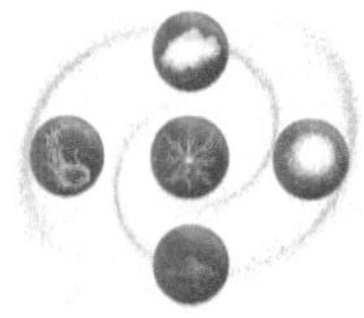

"No! Leave her alone!" a woman screamed. Someone had interrupted Magwei from her nap, and she woke to a rough jerk as a large man tucked her under his arm.

"Mother!" Magwei cried as the sleep wore off. Her mother had wrapped her frail body around the legs of the burly man, clinging with every last ounce of strength her body held.

"Please! Don't take her away." Sobs wracked her body.

"It's protocol," the man spat down. "We've reports that this one holds some magic." Magwei stilled. *Did someone see me the other day?*

"What reports?" her mother shrieked. "I'm a non-magic user! Our whole family wields nothing! My child is not even 18 years old yet. They don't manifest until then - we all know that!"

The man stared unsympathetically. "I've never under-stood how non-magic users produce magic users. You don't deserve that privilege."

"Please," Magwei whimpered. "I didn't do anything wrong."

"Stop all of this whining." The man shook her a bit more than necessary and kicked her mother away. "You should be grateful. If she truly is a magic user, she'll live a better life than what she has here," he gestured at the peeling walls and rusting frames with his free hand. "As for the report, go ask your neighbor."

With that, he stepped out of their small shack, carrying Magwei with him, and that was the last time Magwei would see her mom.

"Token," the lady at the front desk requested.

Magwei fished around in her pockets and pulled a token out. She hoped the rations this time would have some sweets, but she knew not to count on it. The best consumables were reserved for those in the innermost walls. The high class inside the Upper Sector. The strongest magic users.

"Maybe once I pass the Trials, I can move inside," Magwei mumbled to herself. She was turning 18 soon, which was when a magic user's element was fully stabilized and manifested. If she could pass the Trials and prove her value to society and Imperator Vaarem, then her life would be set. She glanced at the castle that loomed in the distance farther inside the city, beyond the innermost wall, and pictured the Imperator sitting on a stone throne.

She wasn't too concerned, though, about the Trials. She had started displaying an inclination toward Earth at a very young age which resulted in the government stepping in to conduct a power check on her. Ever since then, they'd kept her in the Middle Sector to monitor her and hone her skills. She'd been manipulating Earth for years now, and she did her best to not think of her family residing in the Lower Sector.

Magwei slung the bag of food she received across her shoulder and headed back to the Greenhouse. She lived there with several other young Earth magic users, overseen by the Eukaryo, their warden and lead teacher. Lost in thought about her bed of plants, Magwei didn't notice when someone sidled up next to her.

"Thinking about what you'll do if you fail the Trials?" a deeper voice sang in her ear.

"Srijar!" Magwei swung her food bag at him, fully knowing he'd dodge it easily. Srijar laughed in his rich tone before settling his honey brown eyes back on her. She gave a small smile. "You know that's not funny to joke about." She was trying hard to look angry.

"It's a funny joke in this case because you're a shoo-in," he responded. "We all know you're the best in the Greenhouse."

Magwei blushed and shrugged. She knew that about herself, but to hear Srijar say it was another matter. "I could say the same to you."

Srijar manipulated Electricity, one of the more rare elements. Passing the Trials for Electricity was a guarantee into the Upper Sector, regardless of one's skill level wielding the magic.

"I'll see you later," Srijar grinned. "I have to go train, but glad I caught you!" As he turned to jog away, there was a small flash as he hurled a round item directly at Magwei's face. It propelled at such a velocity at close range that Magwei couldn't bring her hand up in time.

Thwump. The item splattered in midair against a large stone that Magwei instinctively manifested to protect her head.

"Srijar!" she exhaled forcefully. The flash she saw was indicative that he had used his magic to launch the item unnaturally. "What in the elements was *that* for? With torque too?" But he laughed and bolted out of earshot. She felt something wet on her face. It was a red ooze that smelled... sweet. She ventured a lick and found it to be a sweet and tangy rasboiberry jam.

Ah. She smiled. Noticing that the stone she'd created and manipulated was still floating in the air, Magwei plucked it from in front of her face, turned it around, and saw a smushed mini tart. She wasn't sure how Srijar procured one since pastries were hard to come by, much less one that had fruit. Fruits were difficult to produce in their irradiated soil, even with magical talents. She scraped the flattened tart off the stone and into her food bag to save for later.

Magwei and Srijar were both well aware of each other's abilities. Even if he knew she could defend herself, she was annoyed he would haphazardly throw something in the streets with extra torque generated by his electricity. If it weren't her, he could have knocked someone over easily. *I guess the rasboiberry tart makes up for it.* Magwei smiled to herself and continued down the road to the massive glass structure that constituted the Greenhouse.

THE GREENHOUSE WAS A LARGE DOMED STRUCTURE MADE OF panels of curved, thick glass connected by an iridescent metal framing. The structure cut quite a contrast to the landscape of the rest of the dry, dusty city made of stones and dirt. The Greenhouse's seven-foot tall entryway was flanked by a guard who checked people's identification to allow entrance. Magwei got through easily, and upon entering, she'd stepped into a miniature compound that thrummed with its own energy. Unlike the outside, it was lush inside thanks to the Earth magic users; the community inside the Greenhouse was self-sufficient.

Magwei had heard that long ago, the high class citizens had petitioned for the Greenhouse to be built in the Upper Sector, given the benefits of food access. However, they found that there simply wasn't enough land in the Upper Sector so the Greenhouse settled into the Middle Sector. The Greenhouse was so massive that if it weren't for the metal framing that cut the view of the gray sky, a newcomer wouldn't know they're inside a glass building. Magwei waved to a few people before dropping by the dorms to store her food and then heading to her plot of land. Instead of manipulating Earth and stones to help build the city, she had always cared more for cultivating soil and growing her plants, and her plot reflected such.

She'd constructed a small hut made of dirt with a tree growing out of the side as a wall support. This was her special space. A space where she could sit and study uninterrupted or to place the plants that didn't want more sunlight. Such plants were deemed useless by the rest of the Earth magic users due to the general climate of the city, but they could thrive in her little oasis, and she liked having a bit of something no one else had.

Magwei approached the knotted tree that made part of the wall. She knocked on it twice and hovered her hand over a section of it before it started twisting as if it were alive. Its trunk seemed to unravel into multiple strands and split apart, revealing a chasm inside where it held Magwei's most prized possessions in suspension. She took out Srijar's pastry, which she had chosen to not leave back at the dorm, and gingerly placed the tart into the space for later consumption. She turned to the rest of her plot, allowing the tree to twist back together and close the space.

Time to get to work. Magwei closed her eyes and felt the tendrils of her mind reach out to Earth, specifically, the plants. Letting her mind run over every speck of seedling, the sprouting roots, and ray of sun hitting their broad leaves, Magwei checked on how all her plants were doing.

With a small smile of satisfaction, Magwei then extended her mind and body beyond the plants and into the dirt. She preferred feeling the plants over the earth because there was a delightful and playful touch to plants, but Earth was a part of her job. Earth ultimately provided for the plants and because of that, Magwei had equally sharpened this skill. Feeling for the dirt was different - it was both microscopic and expansive. It was feeling the soil itself but also what was in it. Magwei sensed for the soil's acidity and presence of mineral nutrients. Usually that manifested as a taste in her mouth which helped her determine if the soil was in good health or in need of something additional. She then sensed for the porosity of the soil and looked for the small organisms that were beneficial.

"Magwei, stop slacking." A lovely voice with a tinge of sneer snapped her out of her trance.

Magwei knew who it was before opening her eyes.

"I'm working with the plants, Bairu. You know that."

"Looks like you're just standing there."

"You know this gets old, right? I don't have to be creating things just to prove I'm actually using magic."

"You know for the Trials, they won't pass you if you just stand th-," Bairu was cut short as she was suddenly pulled to the ground. She threw Magwei an irate look and rubbed her wrist where Magwei previously had a vine wrap itself and wrench her down forcefully. "You know this gets old too, right?" Bairu seethed through gritted teeth.

Magwei shrugged. "I don't know what you're talking about."

Bairu was gifted in the creation of functional and architectural buildings, but she hadn't taken a liking to plant manipulation and hated that someone else was so good at it. For as long as Magwei could remember, Bairu had always had a snarky remark for her.

"Anyway, if you don't need anything, you can leave my land," Magwei added.

"I wouldn't come here just for the sake of it. I'm not *that* bored, especially with the Trials coming," Bairu snapped back. She stood up and smoothed out her pants. "I'm here because you've been requested outside the Greenhouse to clean up some soil."

"Ugh," Magwei tugged on her hair with both hands as

a few seedlings sprouted around her. 'Clean up the soil' was code for cultivating irradiated soil.

"Yeah, I know," Bairu responded with a surprising bit of empathy before switching tones. "Better you than me, though. That's what happens when you're too good at magic," she smirked.

"Thanks, but no thanks for that compliment. Irradiated soil tastes so disgusting," Magwei frowned.

"Now, that's just you!" Bairu put up both hands as if to not equate herself with Magwei. "You're the only one in the Greenhouse who somehow tastes it through your magic. I just feel it and sense it in my head. I don't like it because it always makes me break a huge sweat and gives me migraines," she humphed before turning on her heel and leaving. "The Eukaryo's expecting you, and you know she hates to be kept waiting. I'll see you at the Trials," she called over her shoulder.

Magwei took one last glance at the domed, glass sky and headed toward the warden's office.

STANDING OUTSIDE THE EUKARYO'S DOOR, MAGWEI STOPPED TO smooth her hair and smack some of the dust off her clothes before knocking when she heard a surprised yelp inside. Lowering her hand, she closed her eyes and extended her mind into the Eukaryo's office and beyond the window inside. Magwei felt the sleepy whispers of a hedge outside the window and urged it to grow one of its branches higher. Within a matter of seconds, the branch snaked itself into the office through the seams of the window.

"You know we don't mention them here!" the Eukaryo's vexed voice came across muffled through the bush tendril. Although muffled, Magwei had found that this method of eavesdropping was better than being discovered pressed against a door.

"I wouldn't mention it if it weren't becoming a problem, ma'am," came the steely voice of the deputy warden. Magwei never liked her.

"The Chroniclers? Are they a problem? I thought they were just a bunch of lunatics with good marketing and fear-mongering tactics."

The deputy warden cleared her throat. "I think we shouldn't underestimate them." Magwei thought the deputy sounded a bit... annoyed? Magwei shook her head and got back to listening. "I've heard rumors that we may have a few in the Greenhouse, which is why I'm bringing this issue to you."

"Bah! Impossible. We thoroughly vet everyone, and all the trainee Earth magic users were brought here from a young age during which we carefully molded their minds," the Eukaryo responded. Magwei rolled her eyes. *Sure, we went through their education and are taken care of by the Greenhouse and the Imperator. I wouldn't say they 'molded' our minds.* The Eukaryo was filled with self-importance sometimes.

"You don't think we have unsatisfied students or faculty, who may find it appealing to join the Chroniclers?" the deputy seemed to warn.

"Not within the Greenhouse," the Eukaryo responded succinctly, ending the discussion. Magwei heard assured steps heading toward the door and stepped back right as the deputy opened the door. As she left, she gave Magwei a lingering icy look before sweeping away.

"Magwei," the Eukaryo called. "Are you there?"

"Yes, ma'am!" Magwei responded automatically before stepping inside.

"Close the door, will you?" the Eukaryo requested tiredly.

Upon Magwei carefully shutting the heavy door, the Eukaryo spoke.

"You didn't think I'd notice your plants sneaking into the window?"

Magwei froze.

"You're not in trouble, Magwei. Sit down," the Eukaryo said exasperatedly. "I taught you what you know so of course I can sense when you or any of my students are manipulating Earth."

Magwei dropped into the stiff stone chair in front of the Eukaryo's desk. "I'm sorry! I thought -"

The Eukaryo raised one hand to silence her. "I said that you're not in trouble. I know you probably heard the meat of it all. What do you know about the Chroniclers?" She placed both hands under her chin in curiosity.

"Just... just that they've been around since the radiation has been around," Magwei stammered. *We aren't allowed to talk about the Chroniclers. Is this a trick?*

"And?" the Eukaryo prodded.

"Well, they keep their own history of Symador, right? And maybe even archives of what it's like outside city walls. But they claim to record objectively, hence implying that the Imperator...," Magwei glanced around nervously.

"Implying that Imperator Vaarem pollutes our history,

yes," the Eukaryo finished gravely. A silence hung in the air before Magwei ventured to speak again.

"Eukaryo, why are we talking about them? I thought this was a blacklisted topic."

"Our deputy brought the conversation to us." She sighed. "Anyway, I wanted to tell you that there's nothing to worry about. Focus on doing well at the Trials. There are no Chroniclers here."

Magwei sat in her own thoughts. *Honestly, if they're recording the happenings in the Greenhouse, that's fine by me. As long as they don't get me or my work involved.*

"You're to head to the Ouyang property. They've requested you handle their soils so that they can plant a perimeter of jasmine flowers in their courtyard," the Eukaryo continued. "Dismissed."

"I'll head over now. Shouldn't take me too long since they plan to only plant one type of flower." Magwei stood and headed to the door. *Though if we're talking about resource allotment, then I should be tilling the soils for the Lower Sector so they can grow their own crops, not cleaning the soil for fancy people flowers...* Magwei caught herself. *Though, I guess one of my goals is to become the one of the fancy people inside.*

"Magwei?" the Eukaryo called out before Magwei left.

"Yes, Eukaryo?"

"Good luck and good skill at the Trials tomorrow," she smiled warmly.

MAGWEI STOOD AT THE DARK ENTRYWAY THAT LED INTO THE arena of the Nepenthes, the stadium inside the Greenhouse where the Trials are held. It was named after the long-extinct carnivorous pitcher plant because the arena's round and bell-like shaped walls with an open center area were reminiscent of the plant. All the trainees, though, were sure Nepenthes was more likely named after the plant because of the brutal gauntlet that magic users must go through inside.

Magwei munched on the last bits of the rasboiberry tart she made sure to retrieve before heading to the Trials. She heard her name called on the speaker system and stepped out into the sunlight.

Today, there was a sprinkling of people in the tiered seats lining the arena. The Trials were supposed to be private, but sometimes, citizens of the Upper Sector could pay for entrance. Magwei squinted up at the judge's box where the Eukaryo oversaw the Trials along with other high Earth magic users. She expected to see the Eukaryo's familiar stern but warm eyes smiling down at her, only to find a foreign cold glare in its stead.

The deputy? Magwei scanned the rest of the judge's box but did not see the Eukaryo. She also confirmed that the deputy was indeed in the Eukaryo's center seat.

"Welcome, Magwei of Earth," the deputy spoke into a microphone. "Your Trials shall commence. Upon passing, you will be recognized as a true and official Earth magic user. Upon failure, you'll be placed on a probationary period. Along with our esteemed panel here," she gestured to the others who gave slight nods, "I, the Eukaryo, will be the final judge of that."

The Eukaryo? What happened to the Eukaryo? Magwei's earlier confidence shattered as her mind filled with questions.

"Deputy," Magwei started.

"Eukaryo," the deputy corrected Magwei with a snarl. Magwei ignored her as she mentally reached out, feeling the Earth around her and the roots far below.

"Where's our Eukaryo?" Magwei demanded. Hushed whispers reverberated throughout the stadium despite it only being barely filled.

"There's no need to cause a scene, young Earth magic user," the deputy's voice lilted as she calmed. "All you need to know is that I'm the Eukaryo now. The rest is none of your concern." Magwei felt Earth thrumming for her with orbs of dust forming around her hands. The deputy has stood in for the Eukaryo before if the Eukaryo couldn't make it, but never has she claimed to *be* the Eukaryo. "Magwei, I recommend you focus on the Trials," the deputy's voice was laced in warning.

She probably feels me getting ready. Magwei looked at all the judges and decided she best not act rashly.

I've never fought with my magic, much less with multiple advanced users. The closest experience I have are the friendly spars I have with Srijar... Magwei thought she saw a shadow of a smile cross the deputy's face as she backed down.

"Pass the Trials, and maybe we can talk afterwards. And I can assure you, you'll need all your focus today."

Magwei turned her back to the judges and faced the arena.

"All right. What's first?" *Passing the Trials shouldn't be too difficult. Then I can ask her questions.* Magwei heard some murmurs from the audience, and turned to find the deputy had stood and taken off her coat, a gleaming smile on her face. Magwei's attuned senses felt a surge spread from the deputy down to the arena. As the surge passed under Magwei and passed to the other side of the arena, she felt the hairs on the back of her neck stand on end.

She whirled back around to face the arena and found a thick dust storm forming already. It wasn't just any dust or dirt. It was particles of irradiated Earth with flying rocks. To wield it out in the open was dangerous and illegal because breathing in any large amount spelled certain death.

Where is this soil from? There is no irradiated soil in the Greenhouse to manipulate. Unless... she's creating it? Magwei widened her eyes in horror at the dark Earth cloud. Earth magic users can manipulate what was around and also create Earth, but no one could create something as unnatural as irradiated soil. No one ever thought to because it was barren soil and dangerous.

Is she trying to hurt me? Or is she just giving me an impossibly difficult test? How do the rest of the judges not see this?! As Magwei reached out with her mind to try to settle the poisonous Earth bundle forming in front of her, she realized the deputy had been cunning. The amount of irradiated soil she was using was minute, so with how far away the judges are and with the rocks flying around, they weren't likely to sense this illegal move. Magwei was also more sensitive to irradiated Earth given she'd just worked on it yesterday at the Ouyang's.

Magwei held both hands up to her angry dust opponent and worked to clean the soil, though this was infinitely harder than any cleaning duty she'd done before. These particles were few and moving at rapid speeds in the dust cloud. As she cleaned, she called on roots deep below the Nepenthes. She convinced them to weave tightly together as they traveled toward the surface. She then had a small one more covertly surface and hugged the walls of the judge's box as it made its way toward the deputy's ankle.

If she's bending the rules, then I will too.

OBSERVATIONS OF THE HEAD CHRONICLER

LIV EVANS

> *"If we keep playing by the old rules, we will never change the game."*
> *- Abby Wambach*

IN THE EARLY 21ST CENTURY, A PAIR OF RESEARCHERS* WANTED TO understand the role of curiosity in human behaviour. After experimenting, they learned that humanity's innate desire for answers could drive them to behave in all sorts of risky or unpredictable ways.

The notion that people are always looking for resolutions to uncertain situations is well documented throughout history. Going all the way back to legends from Ancient Greece, where the king of the gods, Zeus, tricked Pandora into opening a pithos (*pithos* is a Greek word meaning earthenware storage jar, but misinterpretations led to people believing Pandora was given a *box*) and releasing all sorts of evils into the world. How did he manage this, you may be asking? By giving her the pithos and simply telling her not to open it. Pandora's curiosity for what was inside led to her doing the one thing she was told not to, consequences be damned.

It should come as no great surprise then, that curiosity has also played a pivotal role in the rise and fall of so many civilisations. Symador is not immune to that impact. Sometimes, it is seen in small ways, where the ripples caused by the actions gently rock the water around it but do little to change the flow. Then, we have tidal waves of consequences that fracture the entire landscape of the known world.

Curiosity and hope are the best foundation for revolution.

The ability to peel one's attention away from the status quo, and to wonder if there are other ways to live, is the first step in implementing a change. The hope that there is something better out there, in the unknown expanse of possibility, can tip a situation over the edge, turns dreams into action. Even if what is waiting on the other side isn't any better, the mere possibility of something better is enough to muster the courage of the human spirit and inspire a person to risk it all.

*Hsee, C. K., & Ruan, B. (2016). The Pandora Effect: The Power and Peril of Curiosity. Psychological Science, 27(5), 659-666. https://doi.org/10.1177/0956797616631733

THE SWEET SONG OF CALAMITY

JP MCDONALD

THE SWEET SONG OF CALAMITY

JP MCDONALD

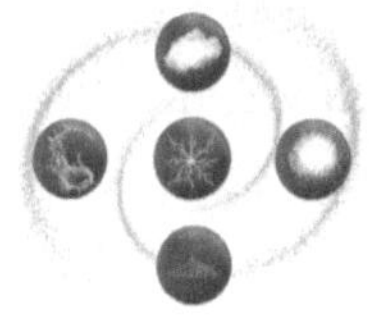

TODAY:

A body traps the wellspring of life. Through arteries and veins the spring flows. Crimson kisses over every internal inch, nicely packaged inside pockets of skin. It is merely a thought to consider the rushing of blood. Like a great secret, it is life, shrouded within until death. At the end, that secret is revealed.

Spewing forth in rivulets. Soaking dormant wells. Splattering walls with whispered whimpers. Spraying high like angry geysers.

I revealed the secret this time. Not death.

It was I who mastered death. Who strutted down Purgatory Road with the cloak and scythe.

Today, I bathed in blood. Blood that looked like mine. It shows that, beneath it all, we are all the same. We harbour vengeance, hope, and despair and cradle the husk of love when it dies in our arms.

Maybe I didn't drain the ocean. But I made the waves

today. That blood red tide has come in and I stand in the shallows with a gluttonous grin.

4 Days ago:

Underneath the city, in a reinforced steel bunker built long ago, I sealed off the magic wielder. Grey wisps of hair crowned him like a halo. Coarse wrinkles webbed along his brow like the roots of a tree. And like a tree, this useless fuck was one in a million. No one would remember him or take notice of where he'd gone. He'd ridden the expiry of his usefulness.

The true curse of life is that we are ephemeral. Our functionality withers like the light in our eyes; expunges like the passion that shrouds our souls.

The man was so old and worn he had already been cast out to live his days meandering through this dead ass city. That was until he became my experiment. Useful after all.

Would he be the final experiment?

When all the toil of my trauma twisted into something tangible?

Useless fuck was tied to a wooden chair. Sable ropes, frayed like the threads of my sanity, bound him. Blood crusted on the side of his head. The initial blow had extracted the life-giving sap from the ancient elm who once stood upon the precipice of the world. Now felled and forgotten. The gag on his mouth was sopping with saliva. Tears coursed down his cheeks like snowmelt.

Scrappi, my talking lizard pet, licked the salty tears at the base of the chair.

"Are you *that* desperate for water?" I scolded her.

She arched her head. The flickering candle-light of the underground made her iridescent scales bloom like rainbow petals. "You serial? No water you give to me." Huffing, she continued to lap at the tears.

"It's pronounced 'serious,' not serial."

Scrappi responded with "bleh" and ignored me.

Her brain had trouble with the subtle differences between words at times and uttered rather simple, short sentences. There wasn't much I knew about how she came into the world. Many years ago, I discovered a collection of hybrid animals who had been experimented on. Robotic claws were gnarled mangroves emerging from the muddy banks of a spiderpede. A forked tongue paired with a venomous hiss of a serpent lapped at the fresh blood of a dispatched squirrel. The bulging eyes of a slow loris, hypnotised prey until their modified scorpion tail sprung like a squall at sea.

They all lived in the tunnel system under the city. I had my first encounter with Scrappi who I had observed in a heated exchanged with a ratroach - which is as disgusting as it sounds. The ratroach and I came to an agreement. I'd let him run his territory in the sewer and I'd add a crafty, thieving lizard to my arsenal. Scrappi agreed to putting an end to stealing snacks from the other hybrids and I became Frankenstein Lizard Daddy.

Unbeknownst to me at the time, she had some truly delectable additions to her lizardness. That being a near fatal injection of platypus venom delivered with a bite from her piranha teeth. I'd seen her kill a raccoon as they fought over a crusty bread roll. She could be as savage as the vengeful thoughts that swarmed my sanity.

"His elemental power is going to burn that fucking chair, you know? And I'll have to fashion a new one from the trash canals," I complained.

"Cry river." Her forked tongue flickered under a petulant gaze.

"Oh yeah, you'd probably drink it all wouldn't you?" I retorted.

She laughed with a bizarre breathy wheeze.

I had to remind myself this experiment was all for a purpose. The glorious big picture was what I needed to visualise. Imagine the vengeance monster satiated, then imagine the glory.

Useless fuck. Well, he would die either way. The potion I had fashioned would poison him or it would do as was intended: activate an increased level of his elemental power so it consumed the entirety of the body and radiate outwards.

A bomb, a vehicle of death, a day of deliverance for the city, for the society that shunned me.

The liquid in the needle was the colour of a crow in pursuit of the murder. It had a gentle dance; a sensual caress of oil in water.

The needle entered skin, the initial prick conjuring animalistic whimpers. Stale, salty sweat filled the air. Anger burned within me as each pathetic weakness exhaled from him.

Magic was power, and power cracked a whip on the barren souls of the ordinary.

But what would I be when I could turn that power against them?

Locks of steel slid into place. The door fastened tight. Reinforced, shatter proof glass was thick. It distorted the view of the writhing fuck on the chair. Scrappi scuttled up my leg and sat on my shoulder.

I held my breath. Holding in all hope. Every dream I'd had of wielding their power rose to the surface and threatened to spill out of me.

Holding. Hold.

Push it down. Push it down like the anger. Push it down like compacted earth, filthy.

Smoke spiralled like a halo. Grey angelic wings sprouted, thickening with each desperate cry. Orange flame shimmered across skin. Bubbling, oozing blood lubricated each orifice. Flames engorged on flimsy flesh. Fire raged. In the glass, my reflection was a beautiful stranger. My untamed hair the colour of burnt chocolate oozed down my shoulders, deep facial scars of yesterday's lament shone with the glow of the blazing corpse. Enamoured by success, I'd never seen myself happy. "Happy Hargrave" I could call myself now. Happy with the image of a burning man reflected in my gaze.

They say the eyes are a window to the soul. My soul was aflame, and my purpose was about to be fulfilled.

The explosion was severe. I flinched. Scrappi slipped down my shoulder into my tattered chest pocket. My heart swelled as pieces of flesh slid down the glass like rancid slugs.

It worked.

After years of letting various concoctions simmer in a

rusty iron cauldron, spluttering with failure, it finally worked.

They would know the name of Hargrave, the Heroic, or Hargrave, the Elemental

Eliminator.

3 DAYS AGO:

Nerves were essential to ensure we did things right. They're within us for a reason. Fight or flight mechanisms provide the desire to soar with frantic fervour or stand with determined roots in the soil. Adrenalin was an alarm clock destined to ring. Sweat gathered like bacteria to dangling cold cuts. My pulse was an angry fist pounding against my neck. My breath ragged, my mouth salivating as the elemental boy of seventeen sauntered away from his classmates and approached me.

Dusty blonde hair like a meadow scorched, lips set in a confident smirk, he walked with the ease of wind tickling leaves.

I watched from the tinted shop window, grates hiding my leering eyes, my skin grimy as I willed the shadows to mask my sinister intent.

Further underground, two bodies lay comatose: the Drexler twins, with a high dosage of *dreamstate*, my own concoction of chemicals that induce coma. They were lying, bound in a dank section of the underground tunnels easily accessed by the sewage connection in the basement of the shop.

Another body lay mutilated within the shop's walls.

There was no life thrumming in veins like bees in a hive.

It had become a corpse. The corpse of robe master, Tyrious Hannon. Scrappi and I had ended his life. A deadly duo of venomous bite and an injection of poison.

I had to remind myself that, because of the death of the shop keeper and robe master, I had to portray Tyrious. I would need to speak to a real person again. My vocal chords were used to singing melodies to frigid walls, darkened by my exile. Spotlights were slithers of sun creeping across cracks. The applause of squeaking rats echoed in the darkness.

Dusty haired Artessan walked inside the shop to see me.

Scrappi galloped toward a crack in the wall and receded into the shadows.

I cleared my throat, readying my transformation into Tyrious.

"My fine gentleman," Artessan practically shouted at me.

The striking power in his voice startled me, but I stifled my surprise by shuffling some robes upon the front desk.

"Artessan, I presume?"

"The one and only," his gaze followed the lines of robes hung high in the store.

"Do you know which robe style you seek?"

He scoffed. "I know nothing of robes. Why do you think I'm here to see the *professional?*" Artessan walked toward the premium section embroidered with elemental designs. He took off his coat. For someone on the brink of manhood he had broad, muscular arms sculpted from physical prowess or simply good genes. I didn't know or care. It did not conjure fear. It made me more resolute. It made me want to show him that I, who many considered the lowest of the lows, would eventually defeat him.

The elementals didn't have to say it, but their pitying gaze was enough to pierce one's pride. I mean, they sauntered around like these manscaped muppets riding the high life, acquiring anything they desired through the trading of magic and through bloodline bias. But did anything trickle down to the ones without magic? No. Power itself was hungry for the weak. It devoured us whole before we realised we were halfway in its jaws.

"Those styles are the most extravagant in the shop so if you want to—"

"Do you know who I am?"

The question startled me. Of course I knew who he was. He was victim number four.

But that isn't what you mean is it? You pretentious little twat.

"I am aware of your . . . stellar lineage," I forced out, hating myself as I did.

"Forget my lineage, I'm carving my own path." He smirked, and it was as if I could smell it. Rancid and festering like fruit caught in the throat of a drain. "Watch this."

Outside the shop window, a young boy drank from a dripping tap. His tongue caught muddy dollops under a scorching sun. Humans needed water and this boy, not of an elemental family, took what he could get. Dried lips blistering like the earth he walked upon, he wouldn't live past twenty.

The tap bubbled and a stream of dirty brown water burst like a blood vessel. The boy fell back, spluttering and choking on the muddy water.

Artessan laughed wickedly.

I eyed him with disdain but corrected it quickly.

"Water magic," he said. "You won't get a more powerful emerging elemental than me." Winking, he brushed his fringe back behind his ear.

"Quite impressive," I forced through gritted teeth.

Artessan handed over chunky pieces of gold. "Just get me the most expensive one, I don't have time to dilly dally with a bunch of second-rate shit."

"Very well, sir."

I retrieved the most opulent coat on the rack.

"Turn around, please, sir."

One rippling bicep sunk into the coat sleeve.

The second arm found its mark.

I pulled the needle from its sheath.

Slammed it into the base of his neck.

He cried out in a soft whimper, falling forward. As he turned to look up at me from the floor, he raised his fingers, but magic didn't simmer or even dazzle with warmth. Magic was trapped inside a vaulted tomb, buried under the weight of vengeance.

Looming above him, I smiled.

Happy Hargrave once more. Artessan's mouth went slack; his eyes crusted over in icy fear. His body became melting ice until he was a puddle of spent arrogance.

Scrappi scuttled across the floor, then crept across his jaw.

"What are you doi—ohhh, yuck." I grimaced.

The lizard defecated into Artessan's open mouth. "Talk shit, eat shit," she croaked, wiggling her tail.

The little lizard had a point.

2 DAYS AGO:

I was a kidnapper, a murderer, a psychopath, and a terrorist.

I wasn't much of a thief.

Scrounging around in the tunnels of the underground and stealing from Scrappi's hybrid animal alumni didn't really count. Nor did the items from yesteryear, with long dead owners unable to sound an alarm when my umbra appeared.

The item was always acquired without a whisper of resistance, and I faded into black with more than what I had before.

On the polished tiled floor of the art gallery, I stood rocking on my heels. My own sweat wafted toward my nostrils, stale and pungent.

This place felt like it was unearthing shiny crystal fragments in a desolate wasteland. Outside, suffering stalked like salivating shadows sucking upon the open wounds of the destitute. Inside, ignorant elementals marvelled at glimpses of the world when it was beautiful. Beauty had long since eroded away, hacked at by the gleaming axe of class disparity. But it didn't need to be that way forever. It *wouldn't* be that way forever, not if I had my say.

My final plan would come together in this art gallery. It

was imperative that if all went well, I would have to add 'thief' to my villainous CV.

I needed a prized object, and it would gain me entry into the gallery of malice, painting everything red.

Artessan was safely subdued in the dungeon. The little shit had the perception of power, but wilful intent often conquers the preening of one's gifts.

Scrappi hid inside my robe pocket as I walked the art gallery halls scouring cracked and worn sculptures.

I was disguised in the same robe Artessan had selected. A fitting facade that helped me blend right in.

Ancient pre-radiation collections lined the walls— colourful splotches on canvas, spray painted walls chis- elled from its original building, textured. I feigned admira- tion for the pieces serving only to remind me that aesthetic beauty was a farce. True beauty was an undiscovered tumour growing within. That was all that mattered.

But could *I* even call myself beautiful anymore? I had been tainted by the affliction, born from the archaic class system I was indoctrinated into.

It had morphed me into a monster.

But there was beauty in monstrosity. A monster raged and ripped and tore so that an equilibrium would be achieved.

Nature is the blueprint of how life should be lived. Where prey cowered, a predator stalked; where a seed pod fell, an insect arrived to germinate. But nature never took more than what it was supposed to. There was a sort of perfection in that.

And here, in the art gallery, vibrancy of colour burned the eyes of a dark dweller. My walls didn't have colour, they had shadows and insects. The drip drops of sewage water were as close to a picturesque waterfall as I'd ever get.

"Why is art exist?" Scrappi whispered, his tail thumping against my left breast.

"I wouldn't know. Seems like a waste of resources to keep this place up and running, to even give a shit about all this junk. But then again, we live underground, don't we? It's not like we care about the colour of the decor."

"Colour comes from inside. That makes a home."

It took me a moment to register what that meant. I realised the lizard was referring to our personalities and the internal quality of who we truly are. If our personalities were vibrant and welcoming, it meant the home was a nice environment. I couldn't help but feel for her. She was born into a world of darkness, with a soul like mine, so allergic to colour it was almost translucent. But did she think I was worthy because I was real? Having seen the elementals wield their power for all the wrong reasons, is that what Scrappi craved? Just someone real, even if real meant dark?

Thoughts in a clouded mind betrayed my focus.

My target had sidled up to me before I'd even realised. It was weakness. I destroyed thoughts blaming the lizard for my introspection. Scrappi stiffened inside my pocket. Long, lacquered nails glinted in the natural light as Marisha stroked the robe with slender fingers.

"That is a fine robe, sir." Her voice was drifting clouds.

It took me a quick second to gather composure and conjure the demon of pomposity. My halo of strength shone radiantly, allowing me to maintain eye contact. My voice of spinning silk twirled in the air. "Fine is in the eye of the beholder."

Marisha's shoulders tightened and her eyes darted to her toes. Bashful meant submission. I already had her where I wanted her.

"Is there a particular piece that has caught that . . . eye of yours?" Her long eyelashes flickered, as if I'd be drawn into the magic of flirtation.

It made me want to peal her eyelids from her face and spit on the crumpled lashes. The hate I felt for all of them quelled any attraction, any carnal desire. Vengeance was my cock and I'd plough her with it. I needed nothing more.

"As a matter of fact, I'd heard about the jewel of the sea."

"Yes of course, a person of your . . . taste and stature wouldn't settle for second rate beauty." She walked ahead of me. Her emerald heels stammered a heartbeat that echoed in the hall. "Follow me, sir."

The large star sapphire jewel sparkled under solar powered halogen globes. Resting on a beige cushion. No glass case. Exposed to the air, exposed to a thief's ravenous fingers.

Scrappi crawled up the back of my neck and whispered into my left ear, "I go?"

I grunted to signify 'yes' and off Scrappi went. She trailed down my leg, squabbling across the floor to where I needed her to be.

"It was said the jewel of the ocean was in the personal collection of Spanish royalty. This one was particularly famous because there are five intersecting lines creating a star, as opposed to the more common three."

I nodded, feigning brainlessness. But I knew what this was, and I knew what I needed it for.

The bell at the front of the gallery rang out and startled Marisha. "Oh, I may have to see to this delivery. Do you mind if I— "

"No, no, no harm at all."

She hurried off down the hall, long raven hair fluttering like falling feathers. No one would be at the door. Scrappi had done her job.

All I needed to do was reach in and take it. It was too easy. Not necessarily laid out on a silver platter, but a beige cushion was close enough. Tense fingers curled around the jewel. My palm was its cushion now. I turned to look for the path of escape, but a dominant force pulled me to the tiles. The earth was angry. The ground grumbled. Dust fell from the roof like summer rain, misting with the humidity.

Tiles cracked, exposing gnarled roots reaching up with wooden talons, clamping onto my ankles. I howled in pain. Serpentine vines wrapped around my legs, choking the blood flow.

I opened my eyes, searching for a way out, but all I saw was her.

Marisha stood there with narrowed eyes, pouting. Vines trailed up her sides sprouting to flowers. Buds opened, releasing perfume that even I could smell from my Earthen restraints.

Marisha seethed, "I knew there was something not quite right about you."

"You know nothing, " I snarled.

Fighting against captivity, my muscles strained. I felt

the welling of pure hatred build up. I wanted to explode and let this bitch burn for her deception. But I couldn't burn her now.

An ember would scorch with the right amount of care. I would add the fuel in careful increments, but I needed to wait. Let the boiling broth simmer instead.

"The authorities have been notified. You'll be spending a night in the cells." She flicked the raven hair from her face and her wooden eyes were dry with disdain.

A cell would feel like home.

Trapped inside a cage, the wild animal rages. The illicit intent festers, eyeing a captor with a golden key. Sooner or later the tide will turn and the key washes upon the shore. Fingers dig into sand like nails raking flesh. The key will be mine. The ripples of rage will meet the ocean, and from there, the squall will drown them all.

THE MIST OF MY BREATH WARMED MY HANDS. THE RUSTED RING of the metal cuffs stained my wrists. Scrappi shook her head. "I cold too." She wriggled her tail in discomfort.

"Stop complaining. Aren't you cold-blooded?"

She screwed up her face and let her tongue emerge like a petulant little child.

Footsteps echoed down the hall and a door creaked open with a tired wail. Scrappi scuttled away out of sight. If anything was to come of this, she would need to aid me.

It was Marisha at the bars, looking solemn. Her anger washed away into the evening exhaustion.

"I've written my statement and I've decided *not* to press charges."

"Why not?" I asked, no hint of grace floating on the surface.

"Because I feel sorry for you." Her dark hair flicked the bars as she turned. The pity in her voice was more fuel for the final dousing of flame. But did being captured put an end to my scheming? Would revenge emerge victorious from the bowels of the earth? Time would tell.

She turned back one final time. "You know, I do remember you, Hargrave. And what happened to you was regrettable and well, disgusting frankly. But robbing something beautiful from my gallery won't replace the beauty of hope...the hope you clearly lost."

I didn't have time to reply, nor would I have known how to respond. Marisha knew nothing of beauty. If she really cared back then, she wouldn't have stood for what they did to me. But she carried on with her life, too scared to fight for something real, walking through echoing halls with flakes of paint for company.

After Marisha's footsteps had long faded, the police-woman came down into the holding area. While being processed, I was drugged and hazy, a lump of meat dragged along the conveyor belt.

A famous Symguard stood before me. She was known as the checkpoint crusader. As the moon illuminated trouble at the checkpoints, she would rule with an iron fist. This was not a figure of speech. Her whole fist was a block of iron and—more often than not—if you crossed her, she would pummel your face until you were mincemeat.

It was evening now, and the excitement was building.

Marisha was nothing to me. Nothing but a pawn in the larger game. Torpena Drusovic, the Symguard, had always been my target and the blockheaded bitch approached me in my cell.

Crooked nose, strong jaw, beady eyes that searched for stars on a foggy night. Fingers turned white as she gripped the bars, then she leaned casually forward against the cell.

"What kinda street rat we got here?" She chewed on a crusty tobacco leaf, then spat brown through a gap in the bars. It landed at my feet.

I didn't answer, just sat there staring.

"Hey boy, I'm talking to ya."

"Rhetorical questions don't require an answer. Besides, it sounded like a personal musing of yours rather than an actual question."

"I seem like the musin' type to ya?"

I looked her up and down. "Not particularly. All you probably have is magic without the brains."

A gust of wind burst from her fingers and pressed me against the stone wall. A carnal fear in me surfaced. The wielding of her power, while I felt so helpless. But deep within my mind I steadied myself in the face of the elemental wrath. *Law enforcement is bound by a code of ethics. Keep pushing her.*

"Magic still gets me pretty fuckin' far, don't it?" she yelled over the howling wind.

Torpena switched the magic off and I slid down the wall, landing on cool concrete.

"Without magic I'd easily have you, you little bitch." I muttered, just low enough for her to hear.

"What ya say, you mangy mutt?"

"You heard me, you fucking bitch. Go on, use your magic again to show how strong you are." I laughed mockingly, threading the needle of shame through her skin.

The key clicked in the lock. Metal scraped as the gate opened. Her breathing was heavy. Her menacing silhouette, bulky standing in the doorway, was framed by blinking lights.

"Don't need magic to break ya."

These brainless fucks were all the same. You goad them enough and they swing their dick or tits around enough to prove a point. If they were more intelligent, it would be over in an instant. Conjure a tornado inside of my body and rip the organs internally until everything that kept me alive was black vomit staining the floor beneath my twitching corpse.

But she needed to exert her power for me to *know* she was better.

Torpena stalked forward, believing me as the prey.

The iron fist cracked my nose, and I saw stars. A second blow depressed my cheek and my hearing flickered in and out. High pitched melodies of pain. I spat blood and laughed as a trio of teeth did the tango across the floor.

"You want this, you freak?"

I looked up at her. "This is all I've ever wanted."

Her fingers curled into an iron fist once again. A snarl escaped the wannabe predator. She only had eyes for me. Which meant that she missed Scrappi appearing on her shoulder. The lizard bit down, drawing blood.

Torpena spun around, her hand knocking Scrappi from her perch. The lizard landed on the cold floor. There was poise in her as she managed to steady her body mid-flight and glide across the concrete, entering a crack in the wall to watch from a safe distance.

"What the fuck was that?" Torpena spat.

"A little present from me to you." Blood dribbled from my mouth as I smiled.

Flat palm against her neck, she stumbled. Her eyes bulged, realising she'd fallen into a trap.

"There was once an animal called a platypus. Its venom could paralyse small animals. A bit of genetic engineering over the years has given my little lizard friend similar potency."

Scrappi inched out of her hole, watching Torpena fall to the ground. Torpena's mouth slackened and she made sounds—a mush of indecipherable words. Her eyes were darting to and fro. Scrappi climbed upon her crooked nose and stared into those eyes as paralysis took hold.

The lizard grinned wide and rasped, "Dumb didilly dumb dumb."

"Indeed." I rose. "Now, don't you dare shit in her mouth too, Scrappi." Scrappi looked utterly forlorn but conceded to suppressing another bowel movement into an open mouthed victim.

I turned to Torpena, "Now you shouldn't be able to move for a solid few hours, which will be enough time for me to get you to the others."

Standing above Torpena, I breathed in deeply, savouring the smell of her urine-stained pants, salty sweat, and metallic blood. Fear was a beautiful scent. A reminder of the true power I held. Elemental magic was inconsequential if one had tyrannous intent. Ruling not with an iron fist, but with a vengeful heart.

I found the sledgehammer in the eastern wing. I dragged it down into the cell. Smashed through the concrete floor into the tunnel I had carved out months before. The same tunnel that linked to the underground system, the lab, and my home. Once I transported Torpena to the others, all I needed to do was patch up the hole, reinforce it properly and reposition the bed on top and no one would be any wiser.

The hero guard would vanish into folklore and the ramifications of my actions would tear a gaping hole in the fabric of society.

1 DAY AGO:

Their words were waves that washed upon the shore. Chaotic and loud and vibrant.

Then, they vanished into the pores of the earth like they had never been uttered.

Gagged once more, they were my audience. Staring at me. Waiting for a spotlit soliloquy. One that might change their fate.

But no, their fate was sealed.

They needed to know, however, that I was not the reaper. Their connections were the very thing that would end them. Their kin composed the song. I was the conductor.

"Five souls, wielding so much power, sit before me. Powerless to someone who is so . . . beneath you." I gestured to myself, bowing my head and recalling the shame. "And you must be wondering why fate has been so cruel, why *you* must be the example of injustice, the product of ridicule. And I profess, it is merely circumstance."

I sat down on a rickety chair and faced them. Their grubby faces were waxed by tears, unabashed and unafraid to spill like a breaking dam. I addressed Artessan first.

"Your father was my closest friend. Wielding the fire power, we would light cauldrons for ceremonies, burn blasphemous books, signal the outer reaches so they could shield from hateful dust storms. It was truly the best of times. Until the waning of my power began."

Those memories, of going from the pinnacle of society to the dregs in an instant, were still painful.

"You won't find my name in any honour roles or medical scrolls for that matter. My name was expunged at the same time my power withered. No one in the history of this world had ever been christened with an elemental power, to have it wane so suddenly."

I scowled. "Your father could've softened the blow but the way he revoked our bond so swiftly, the way his cold eyes turned away each time I tried to seek consolation . . . well . . . it broke me more."

I turned to Torpena. "Your wife banished me from the school and revoked all my rights as a citizen of Symador."

The twins awaited the reveal of their connection. "Your father was the mentor who first alerted the school, first uttered the word banishment, sailing on the wind like a ship in a storm." Scrappi curled into my lap and I stroked her little head. "I was the scared boy that cried rivers at his feet. He had a chance to take me in, but instead, called the authorities and had me expelled to the outer districts to wither in anonymity."

I looked upwards at the cobwebs lining the ceilings. Rodents rode the rollercoaster of brass pipes squealing with delight. "I didn't swear my revenge then and there. Revenge simmers. The longer it festers, the more potent it becomes. It hits the boiling point and flames lace the sky, and with its plume of smoke, I decided to write a new rule: Even without elemental power, I am powerful."

I sighed deeply. The drips of leaking pipes were the tears of fate crying for the souls soon to be expunged from existence.

"Context is not always comforting. In this case, each one of your scowls permits me no grace, no empathy. In the face of my heartache, you are only concerned with your own fate. Faced with death, I expect nothing less. And I can't say it surprises me because empathy has evaded every elemental I've encountered over the years."

Coaxing Scrappi into my trouser pocket, I stood, clapping my hands once with finality. It was time to put an end to them. It was time for the depth of my revenge to reach that boiling point.

TODAY:

Scrappi scratched at my hands, nervous and tense. Sleep had evaded me the previous night. It usually does when the culmination of plans are upon us.

The trains were wrecks on the underground tracks, rusted and useless. I had fashioned a barge that ran along the tracks large enough to carry the horde of catatonic weapons. Their shallow breaths were like the ticking hands of a clock winding down until the end of time.

The barge thumped on metallic tracks—the heartbeat of impending doom. I was sweating but there was a certain euphoria welling within me. Swirling excitement would expel as soon as blood began to drip from slick walls.

"Nerves feel bad," Scrappi complained.

"Being nervous is your body reminding you how important something is," I chided her.

The lizard creature scampered up the front of the barge, and onto my hand. "You 'portent." Her wide reptilian eyes had a child-like innocence attached to them. Tears were like the surface of a lake, glassy and misty with emotion.

I had come to love the creature. My only real companion in this lonely existence. It was the first time she had said anything resembling love or attachment and it surprised me.

I'd put my own emotions away for so long I'd been blind to the symbiosis that had developed. I smiled to encourage calm. "You know, everything will be fine. When the definition of power is changed, the world will never look the same again."

Slowing the barge, I noticed the notch I had made at the bottom of the ladder ahead. It signified this was the spot that opened into the basement of the old clock tower. The clock tower stood in the middle of the town square; a backdrop for the presentation of the new elemental guild inductees.

Thousands of people would be there cheering on their

saviours. Thousands of people would die worshipping false gods.

The needle punctured skin at the throat of the sacrifices. By now, rumours had spread through passers-by lamenting the absence of Torpena, questioning the whereabouts of their top graduate, Artessan. It was all the sweetest overture to a finale worthy of applause from severed hands.

As the final injection took hold, the floor above rumbled with footsteps and raised voices. I stood still, careful not to move.

Scrappi and I needed to get away but couldn't risk being heard or the sacrifices being discovered.

"Everything needs to be just right," the female voice shrieked with stress. "I have a reputation to uphold."

"I understand miss, but when we moved the pieces, they just weren't coping with the heat. I'm so sorry."

"Sorry is not going to make this fucking ceremony look good, is it?"

A silence grew with the shuffling of sombre shoes. "Find something and make everything better, quick smart."

The female slammed the door.

The male's footsteps shuffled listlessly for what seemed like an age. Each second ticked away until the reaction inside the skin of the four elementals would detonate.

Scrappi poked her head out of my pocket. "Go, go, no time," she whispered frantically.

"I know, I know," I whispered in reply.

A crack of light pierced the basement. The male grunted, heaving it open. Light flooded the space.

I shrunk back into shadow. The elementals were out in the open. It would all be over. My plan would be ruined. I stood wide-eyed, my breathing stifled, my stomach sinking, opening gates for the butterflies to enter. I felt like crying, screaming, and letting all the pain out but instead I started to shake, crouching like a powerless hack, waiting for death.

Scrappi, the lizard with half a brain, but a gigantic heart, leapt down from my pocket. As the male walked open-mouthed toward four shackled prisoners strapped to steel chairs, she crawled up his ankle and sunk teeth into flesh. A loud shriek followed as he shuffled frantically, flinging her across the basement careening into a wall.

"No," I bellowed. The final destination was not as important without my companion by my side.

She lay flat on her back. From the distance, I couldn't see the tiny rise and fall of her breathing. I couldn't tell if those bulging eyes were blinking. I turned my back on the man who was now convulsing with Scrappi's venom, and I went to her.

Gathering her up in my palms, she squinted up at me. Eyes like hessonite swirled.

"Are you okay?" My whisper was full of concern, an admission of love.

Her mouth curved upwards. "Little hurt, now okay," she managed.

I placed her carefully on the ground, making sure she was comfortable. My boots thumped against the stone like thunder cracking in the dark.

The love I felt a moment earlier scorched in a searing blast of rage.

My boots devoured his face. Crunching teeth, filleting strips of flesh, a viscous soup of minced brain matter that spread out slowly.

This life was inconsequential in the scheme of things. Yet revenge was a bright spark lit by the fuse of love. All plans could've been squandered with this mess of meat at the end of my boots.

Shadowed ghouls danced on the walls, moaning a final lament for the souls in limbo.

The burning light pulsed under each of their skin, sizzling with a warning. I stumbled toward Scrappi and scooped her into my palms. She trailed up my forearm, to my bicep and leapt into my breast pocket. "Run fast," she croaked.

She need not have uttered words. I wanted to survive this. I wanted to see the power balance shift with the earth as it split, as it rocked with a sudden betrayal. The little man who no one noticed, would make everyone look on that day. On this day.

Bursting out of the basement, my eyes took a moment to adjust to the harsh light pouring in from windows. Where was an exit? I turned to the back of the tower and a rusted metal door beckoned me forward.

I ran toward it, heeding the call.

My hand reached out to grasp a handle, but the door swung back, and I clattered into a woman. Raven hair billowed around us like a curtain catching a summer breeze. It tangled around us, drew our faces close as we tumbled to the ground.

Shock is poignant, but it wears away like the winds of time and her eroding caress.

Her mahogany eyes widened. "You! How did you escape?"

I didn't say a thing, Scrappi launched out of my pocket and bit Marisha on the neck. Her hands sprung to the wound, stemming the blood, and a shrill scream tore through the building.

Picking Scrappi up, I turned my gaze forward and stumbled into a run leaving the wounded woman behind.

The earth grumbled its discontent. My own nerves encouraged me to run further and faster into freedom.

But I slowed, looking back at the paralyzed woman in the doorway. The cacophony of voices told me to run, but a single melody of mercy was loud enough to change a moment.

I turned back, ignoring Scrappi's hisses and curses. Dragging Marisha by the arms, I spotted a wooden cart abandoned in the dusty street. Her dark eyes were wild, and she groaned with tired yelps as I threw her in.

I sped through streets, pushing the cart and dodging the stragglers as they queued up for the ceremony, joining the crowd of people waiting to cheer their future heroes.

The cheer would turn to cries of horror. And heroes would be martyred by their years of arrogance.

Endings are rarely anything of note. I felt the earth rumble. It was in pain. A guttural roar. The plume of smoke thrust into the air. The clocktower burst, raining pieces far and wide.

The explosion was deafening, a loud and catastrophic crack that knocked Scrappi, the cart, and Marisha to the ground, tumbling. A wall of dust came forth like a looming shadow blackening out the sun.

We scrambled into a sewer system underground, throwing ourselves into the trickling water of faeces and urine. Debris flew by overhead.

Marisha was still paralysed; her eyes were wild.

"Why save *her*?" Scrappi spat the question at me, clawing across my cheek.

I touched my own blood trickling off my chin and looked at it in the dark. It was nothing more than a splatter of liquid. It felt so insignificant even though it was the essence of life.

"It was the right thing to do," I whispered, glaring at Scrappi.

"Enemy," she screamed, "She is Enemy!"

"Something stopped me!" The hoarseness in my voice echoed within the sewer tunnels. "It didn't feel right." The anger had diminished; the exhaustion was louder.

Scrappi huffed and started back up the ladder.

She knew me. She knew I wanted to see the destruction first hand. I wanted to see what I had done, take it all in rather than marvel from a distance.

I needed to see that my purpose had been fulfilled.

I knelt in front of Marisha propped against the wall and brushed the hair behind her ears. Her usually rosy cheeks now sunken and grey. "Sometimes an epiphany is realised after enduring a tough lesson. A ray of sunshine that pierces through an insignificant crack.

In that blackness, there is hope. Something that has been elusive for so long." I looked away from her admonishing gaze, as earnest tears tumbled down into the grave of her lap. "Hope is worth building upon, and it's worth giving to people whether it's written in blood or scattered with gold." I bowed my head. "A story untold is a memory's lament. Be a storyteller, Marisha."

She mumbled something and I looked at her again. I couldn't tell if she wanted to kill me or thank me. I guess it could've been both.

"The paralysis will wear off in an hour or so."

I spotted a ratroach watching from near the entrance to their territory. "Whatever you're thinking, it's a no," I said.

"She not fair game?" He growled.

"No mate, you leave her be or I'll be coming for you and your crew."

He didn't say anything but acknowledged his understanding by backing away and fading into the shadows.

I felt conflicted about what I had done.

Not the bomb. There were no ill feelings about the bomb.

But saving someone.

Hargrave the Heroic, indeed.

As I climbed the ladder and walked out onto the street. I told myself that Marisha would tell my story. That was why I had spared her. The story will act as a catalyst for change. If disenfranchised members of society were cobras, my story would be a melody coaxing them to rise.

Scrappi clambered up my leg and hung out of the trouser pocket. I'd make her understand one day, folklore is just as important as the event itself.

Frantic people ran through the fog of debris, away from the blast site. Their tortured cries were ghoulish, shrill and haunting as they zoomed past. Scrappi and I headed toward the harrowing scene, excitement building with the chalky taste of debris clogging my mouth and lungs.

All around me the sweet song of calamity crescendos. The swelling cries were hoarse with pain. Pain of lost limbs, pain of lost souls so vibrant with life not minutes before.

I see all of it, and the carnage comforts me.

The blood of the elementals cleanses my painful past. I am fueled forward into the future as their power will diminish.

When vengeance is realised it is more than fulfilment, more than a sense of completion. It is euphoric. Vengeance is a drug that I've craved, that I've salivated for. And now, as it settles on my tongue, surges through my body, I do not need magic to feel powerful.

I am power.

OBSERVATIONS OF THE HEAD CHRONICLER

LIV EVANS

"The depravity of man is at once the most empirically verifiable reality but at the same time the most intellectually resisted fact."
- Malcolm Muggeridge

BEING A COLLECTOR OF STORIES FROM ALL DIFFERENT WALKS OF life gives one a unique perspective on the concept of reality. Every event that occurs creates just as many perceptions of that event as there are participants.

Not a single recollection is flawless.

Yet people insist on there being a single, definable, immutable truth to a situation. There is a defensive sense of pride that comes along with being *right*. So many people claim their observations are the most accurate, yet so few are true observationalists. They view what they witness through their own experiences, tinted by their biases, and processed by their emotions.

Quite often, whether a person is seen as a trustworthy

observer is intrinsically tied to their level of power and influence in a space. Whether or not they are giving a factual account of events matters less than how they represent such happenings. So, the more a story is told and retold, the more it changes. The recounts shift and morph until they take on a life of their own that is more fantasy than reality.

Even with the way people experience life so differently, there are common factors. Certain agreed upon facts that are taken for granted, so life can continue and there is some level of order in a place.

A shared reality, so to speak.

For the most part, these shared realities and divergent interpretations are the spice of life. After all, if everyone perceived the world the same way, it would be a boring place to live. The richness, the conflict, the heartbreak, and the ecstasy... they're all products of this diversity.

But it would be a lie to assume that all of these differences, these branches of reality, are wholesome and inspiring.

They are not.

Some are more like rotten tree roots that burrow deep into the earth and crack through the foundations of humanity. They wrap their rotting flesh around the tenets of morality and twist them into unrecognisable, reprehensible experiences.

These experiences are poisoned by biases and instead of being processed by emotions, they overtake them, they control them, they putrefy them until the person is no longer able to access reality.

When a person who has broken with reality in such a

way and is convinced that their view of the world is authentic, it can become a justification for all sorts of reprehensible acts. All sorts of evils. Sometimes these people have power, sometimes they do not. That really only impacts the objective reach of their actions, their access to means that can do more physical damage. But the emotional impacts of their machinations? Those are immeasurable.

Even the smallest act of evil can do a hideous amount of damage, with echoes that last for decades. For centuries. For millennia.

As humans, we like to pretend that these things do not occur. We try to explain it all away with reason, or logic, or some other abstract conceptualisation that really doesn't apply.

The question then becomes, how do we measure reality? What yardstick do we use to determine what facts match and what can be disregarded?

The Chroniclers have discovered that these questions are redundant. The quest to determine the actual happenings of any event leads only to endless and unresolvable debates. Instead, we choose to assume that these things, for the sake of argument, *are* real. We choose to look at the impact of these perceptions, how they change the things that come after and reassign meaning to that which came before.

We work instead with how their experience make the protagonist feel. How it drives them to act.

This is an important thing to remember as one reads through the Chronicler's archives and tries to interpret an endless supply of perceptions of reality.

Trying to figure out whether lizards can talk will only lead to headaches. If you're looking for enlightenment, assume truth. Try to dig deeper into *why* someone may be experiencing the world that way.

And ask yourself this: What was the story *really* about?

RAGE OF A DAUGHTER

EA ROBINS

RAGE OF A DAUGHTER

EA ROBINS

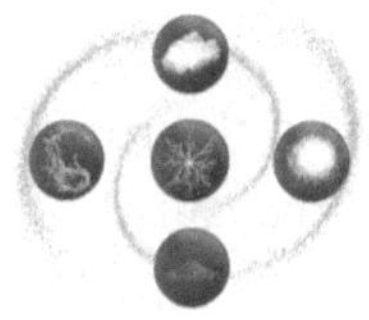

"It's beautiful," Ashani whispered, staring at herself in the dark glass. The mirrored surface had once been part of a large window, repurposed now in her bedroom. Its reflection was dim and distorted, but it was clear the dressmakers had outdone themselves. She touched the silver lace sewn onto the bodice of the gown. "What do you think, Inaya? Do you think he'll like it?"

"Like it?" The image of another pretty, young woman appeared in the mirror. Inaya gently touched the long braid of Ashani's dark hair, a stark contrast to her own loose, blonde locks. Then she smiled. Even in the dingy glass, the expression was radiant. "He's going to fall in love with you for the first time all over again. Imagine, you marrying an earth artificer!"

Ashani felt her cheeks warm. Having shown no predisposition to magical talent herself, those endowed with the skill to manipulate the elements had once made her uneasy and skeptical. There was no way she would have ever trusted someone with the ability to move stone or hold fire in their hands. That is, until she had met Reyan.

Running her hands over the flawless, silken skirt of her dress, Ashani took a deep breath. Within minutes they would head to the party, a celebration of their engagement. Thinking of the moment when she would appear before her future husband, Ashani's heart fluttered.

There was a knock on the room's double doors, and a powerful, masculine voice called to them. "Girls? Are you still in there? Are you finished dressing?"

"Just a moment, father!" Inaya leaned forward, wrapping her arms around Ashani's shoulders and squeezing.

"You look amazing, sister. Reyan is a lucky man," she said. Dropping her hands, she pinched Ashani hard on both of her arms. Then she was gone.

Ashani frowned and rubbed at the pain, grateful she didn't bruise easily. Inaya had always been a little rough, but it had gotten worse in recent months. Some of the previous jabs had left visible marks, and the blonde's usual clever remarks had taken a bitter, spiteful turn. They would have to talk about it soon, but not today.

Ashani smiled at her reflection. She slowly twisted her hips causing the heavy skirt to wrap itself around her ankles before spinning away. Everyone would be envious of the wealth of material spent to make the dress. Unstained, without a single rip in the fabric, the costume represented a small fortune.

"Inaya, my Sunlight! You positively sparkle."

Ashani turned around as a large man, dressed in a fashionable plum-colored cocktail jacket embraced Inaya.

"Father, you're going to crush my dress!" The blonde

brushed imaginary dirt and imperfections from the golden gown she wore. Though her tone was stern, the glint in her eye was playful and her smile full of adoration. She took the man by the arm and turned him toward Ashani.

"Moonbeam," the man said, his face softened with wonder. His voice was so gentle that he sounded almost breathless. "You look just like your mother."

Ashani smiled, knowing he meant it as a compliment. Though she had no memories of her parents, Baig Guli, the man before her, had known them well and often told her of them. Over the years, he had been so kind that Ashani now considered him her adoptive father, and his natural daughter, Inaya, a sister.

As Baig approached, adjusting his purple jacket, Ashani noticed that his thick, auburn hair had begun to lighten at the temples. And though his beard was now speckled with grey, his smile still emanated paternal warmth and affection. He took one of Ashani's hands, lifting it above her head and requesting a spin. She obliged.

"Stunning," he said. Then his brow furrowed. "But it's missing something."

Ashani looked down at her dress, confused. She was sure they hadn't forgotten anything.

When she looked back up, something silver dangled from a chain in Baig's hand. It took her a moment to recognize the Key to the Guardhouse. Goosebumps rose on Ashani's arms as she realized what he was offering.

The pendant was a symbol of Baig's position as Commander of the Guard. Overseeing all defense preparations, patrol rotations, and authorization of weapon distribution in the fortress, his was a rank of great power and authority. The key meant Ashani would someday assume Baig's title, and with it all the responsibility and reward it entailed.

As Baig lowered the necklace over her head, Ashani looked at Inaya. She found her adoptive sister's eyes narrow, her lips pressed together. The blonde's jaw flexed as she clenched her teeth.

Ashani understood her anger. They had both spent their lives training for the day Baig would allow them to join the guard. While they had both been accepted into the ranks without question, it had been generally accepted that, when the time came, the key and Baig's position would pass to Inaya.

"I've spoken with Imperator Vaarem," Baig said, lightly touching the pendant and drawing Ashani's attention back to the gift. "He supports your appointment as my official successor, and sends his blessing for your marriage."

Ashani found herself unable to speak. Baig had chosen her over his own daughter. The leader of their community had supported the decision. She felt the weight of her future descend on her shoulders, thrilling and terrifying. Already emotional from the excitement of the day, a tear slipped down her cheek.

"You've made her cry!" Inaya stepped between her father and sister. Her hands flapped around Ashani's face like the wings of a bird, trying to dry the tear. "Do you know how expensive this make-up is?"

"It's alright," Ashani said, sniffing. "It's just a lot."

"Of course, it is," Inaya took Ashani's hands in her own. The compassionate smile on her face made it clear she'd recover from Ashani's unexpected promotion. "Congratulations, sister. You're going to be an amazing commander. But, wait." Inaya's face crumbled, as if she'd eaten something distasteful. "You're going to be my boss."

Ashani laughed, grateful for the humor.

"Well, I'm not sure how I feel about that," Inaya said, playing up her concern even as Baig gathered both girls into his arms.

Heedless of their nice clothes, Ashani leaned into the embrace, grasping at the last moment of quiet before the party. She had known marrying Reyan would change her life, but it was from this moment that nothing was ever going to be the same. She closed her eyes and breathed in the familiar, calming scent of her family.

Inaya was the first to pull away. "We should really get go—"

A sonorous boom silenced her and the floor shook. The dark mirror rattled ominously, and a small vial of perfume on the dressing table crashed to the floor. The bare bulbs hanging from the ceiling swayed and flickered.

"What was that?" Ashani asked, her heart racing. She gripped Baig's arm. "Father, what was that?"

"I don't know," Baig said. "Are you both alright?"

When they had confirmed that they were uninjured, Baig went to the door of Ashani's room and looked into the hallway.

"Nothing seems amiss...wait."

Ashani suddenly heard the faint sound, as well. "Is that someone screami—"

There was another loud rumble, similar to the first, followed by a second reverberation. Ashani reached out, steadying herself on a nearby table while Inaya clung to a bedpost. Dust fell from the concrete ceiling.

"What on Earth is going on?" Inaya asked.

"Stay here," Baig said. His face had gone oddly pale and there was a wild quality to his eyes that Ashani had never seen. It occurred to her that he might be remembering the Hargrave Attack, a madman's revenge that had claimed the lives of many in the upper sectors. The assault had killed her parents, and made Baig a widower.

"We're coming, too!" Inaya said.

"No!" Baig said, his tone desperate, but commanding. "You will stay here!"

Baig raised his hands and closed his eyes, silencing Ashani's immediate argument. He took a deep breath and released it slowly. When he spoke again, his voice had become calm once more.

"Please, my sunlight, my moonbeam, stay here. Stay together. I'll return shortly."

Exchanging a look, both girls nodded.

When Baig had disappeared into the hallway, Inaya turned to Ashani. "We're not actually staying here, are we?"

"Of course not," Ashani said. "Come on."

Deep within the fortress, the residential wing was persistently gloomy. Fragile electric bulbs, rare and costly, were reserved for the private chambers of the elite. Ashani and Inaya stepped around small tables piled with flickering candles.

Within moments, they had reached the first of several common rooms, lit by stinking oil torches. Here the fortress had once had windows, but they'd been covered long ago, boarded and sealed with cement to protect from the sands and radiation that had long covered the world.

"Oh! Wait a minute." Inaya released Ashani's hand, stopping mid-stride. She gestured back down the hall. "I have a small medical kit in my room. It might be helpful."

"You have your own kit?" Ashani asked, frowning. They had both taken the emergency response course mandatory for all guard, but it was unusual for any single resident of the fortress to have their own medical kit. The resources required were rare and preciously guarded.

Inaya shrugged, already heading back to the residential wing. "Better to be prepared, right? You go on. I'll be right behind you."

The decision made for her, Ashani continued alone toward the source of the disturbances. Dust slowly began to fill the passageways as she approached the Grand Entry Hall. She entered the massive room cautiously.

To her left, a set of double staircases rose to the second floor of the fortress. They would have been mirror images, but only the one on the left was serviceable. The flight on the right was missing a large portion in its middle. A disfigurement that stood as a monument to the violence of the past, reminding all of the struggle and sacrifice needed to keep Symador a peaceful and productive city.

Across the room, massive wooden doors allowed admittance to the fortress. The wall above them was made entirely of windows. Broken over time, many of the panes had been repaired with glass scavenged from ruins in the wasteland beyond the city's walls. The kaleidoscope of mottled light that was emitted was always grimy, filtered through years of settled dust, but it never had such a gritty quality. A thick haze of dust particles swirled through the room. Ashani could hear people yelling, though it was muted and seemed far away.

Covering her mouth with her arm and plunging into the billowing cloud, she quickly crossed the room. On the far side, there were several sets of double doors that opened into the ballroom, the place that had been prepared for her engagement party. As Ashani approached, the dust grew thicker and a sense of dread buried itself in her belly.

Seeing the outline of a doorway in the shadows, she rushed forward. Just as she was about to enter the ball-room, someone emerged from the dust, their arms covering their face. They ran directly into Ashani. She staggered away, almost falling.

"Hey! Careful!" Ashani said, rubbing her shoulder. "Wait. Who are you?"

The stranger didn't answer. He simply stared at her with pale blue eyes, rimmed red. His expression was slack, as if in mild surprise. Dust clung to his face. His hair, poorly dyed an uneven blue, was cut in the short, shaggy style of the lower city. His clothing, badly sewn and hanging off of him as if it had been made for someone larger, confirmed that he did not belong in the fortress.

"Who are you?" Ashani asked, repeating her question. "Why are you here?"

Before he could answer, a tall woman stumbled out of the ballroom. She held her hand pressed to her side. Her hair, similar to the young man's but dyed pink, was covered in small pieces of concrete. "Bijan! Get away from her!"

"What's happened?" Ashani asked, watching as the man hurried to the woman's side.

The woman gasped as he slipped under her arm, closing her eyes and clinging to him as her knees buckled. She was evidently in a great deal of pain.

"I can show you to the infirmary," Ashani said, deciding her questions could wait. It was a guard's duty to help the injured. She approached them with her arms out, ready to help support the woman's weight. "It's not close, but I can help you."

"Stay away from us," the wounded woman said, glaring fiercely at Ashani. "We don't need help from lying prigs like you."

Ashani took a step back, her brow creased. Having done nothing to offend these people or to be so rudely insulted, she simply gestured toward the exit. She would do nothing more to hinder their departure.

The woman looked at the blue-haired stranger, and then jerked her head toward the entrance, hidden in the dust. Without another word, they hobbled away, becoming phantoms in the haze and then disappearing.

Ashani stared after them, wondering if they had been hired for the party. She hadn't expected anyone from the lower city, but it wouldn't have been the first time the fortress had utilized a cheaper workforce. Pushing the strange pair out of her mind, Ashani turned and passed into the ballroom.

The concentration of concrete particles in the air made it difficult to breathe. Covering her mouth with her arm, Ashani tried to suppress the coughing she knew would only make the itch in her chest worse. She squinted into the swirling cloud, unable to see much beyond her own feet. Someone was speaking nearby in an urgent tone, but she couldn't make out what they were saying.

Tripping over rubble, Ashani wondered if her presence was about to become more of a hindrance than a help when she felt a breeze on her cheek. The gentle wind fluttered the fabric of her skirt as it grew stronger, scattering small pieces of loose debris against her ankles. The dust was being driven toward the end of the room, gathering in a condensed orb of grit and sand hovering between two of the fortress's air artificers. The pair were pale and sweating, using massive amounts of energy to bend the wild element to their will.

Ashani's arms dropped to her sides as she took in the revealed devastation. Boulders of concrete, torn from the walls, lay strewn across the marble dance floor. The crystal chandeliers had fallen and glittered in shattered heaps, their electric bulbs eviscerated. Tables that had held food and drink were broken or overturned, the costly refreshments ruined. Delicate paper decorations, arranged only the day before, had settled like confetti over everything. Worse than this destruction, small groups of people, dressed in ruined finery, knelt weeping above others who lay unmoving on the ground. It took Ashani a moment to recognize Reyan on the floor. His mother kneeled above him, holding his hand to her cheek as she wailed.

Despair wound itself around Ashani's insides and squeezed. She couldn't breathe. She clawed at her neck with trembling hands, trying to loosen the invisible rope around her neck. She stumbled forward, falling to her knees. Her vision blurred, growing dark at the edges.

Suddenly, someone large was kneeling next to her. Their strong arms surrounded her body, pressing her tightly to their broad chest.

"Shh, it's alright," Baig said as he held Ashani. "It's alright, Moonbeam. It's alright. I've got you."

Ashani closed her eyes and sobbed.

"I know, Moonbeam, I know. But, we can't do anything for him, now. Let's get you back to your room."

"Reyan..." she said, unable to say more.

Baig turned, keeping himself between Ashani and the gruesome sight as he lifted her to her feet. She held tightly onto his arms, looking up at his face and seeing his own deep grief. She wondered how long the wrinkles had been so sharp at the corners of his eyes.

A brilliant white light flashed above Baig's head, causing Ashani to shut her eyes. She felt him jerk upward and for a moment, it seemed as if they were in the air. The heaviness of her body lifted, and she felt a moment of weightlessness. Then they hit the ground.

Ashani's head cracked against the hard marble floor, sending a lightning bolt of pain down her spine. Something heavy landed on top of her, knocking the air from her chest. Then everything grew quiet, calm, and dark.

"Hello, Earth to Ashani. Are you listening?"

Ashani blinked and turned toward Inaya, unsure how long she'd been standing at the window, staring at the stained and pitted glass. They had brought her another round of painkillers. The strong drugs worked quickly to dull her physical suffering, but they fogged her mind and made it hard to focus. It was a numbness she welcomed.

"I was saying, they gave father and Reyan and the others a beautiful vigil," Inaya said, lowering her eyes to the board in her lap. She sat in Ashani's bed, a piece of charcoal in her hand, sketching as she spoke. "Imperator Vaarem noted your absence. You should have come."

Ashani looked back at the sealed window, letting the accusation roll over her and away. She knew Inaya was right, but she had found the idea of leaving her room, of seeing the sadness and blame on the other resident's faces, more than overwhelming. When they had come to escort her to the service, she had locked the door.

"Are you in any pain?" Inaya asked without looking up from her art. "You don't need anything, do you?"

Ashani shook her head and raised her hand, almost touching the bulky cotton dressing that covered her shoulder. She wasn't yet used to the emptiness where her right arm had been, but the amputation had been clean. The doctor had promised that the occasional sharp pains she sometimes felt in a hand that no longer existed would pass.

"They spare nothing for my comfort," she said.

"Good. That's good. I told them to take care of you," Inaya said, her tone distracted. "Can't lose you, too."

Ashani swallowed the sudden, hard lump of emotions in her throat. Even drugged, there were some feelings that pierced the intentional emptiness. Guilt had particularly sharp edges.

It had been a third, unexpected explosion that had knocked Baig and Ashani across the ballroom floor. The doctors had said that she was lucky she hadn't felt the shrapnel shred her arm before she was knocked unconscious. They said she was lucky Baig's body had protected her from the worst of that blast, and the next two. She had wondered if theirs was a special, uncommon definition of luck.

After the attack, Ashani had spent days sleeping, waking in pain only to weep uncontrollably, lost to her sorrow. Eventually, the medical attendants had taken pity on her, smuggling her stronger medicines to ease her misery.

"What do you think?" Inaya asked, raising her drawing to show Ashani the sketch. "I think it's one of my best."

Ashani stared at her own likeness. Inaya was right, it was one of her best. She had perfectly captured the drug-induced emptiness in Ashani's eyes, the pallid glow of her sickly skin, the bulk of the white-cotton dressing piled on her shoulder. Around the image's neck hung the Key to the Guardhouse. Ashani touched the pendant, warm on her chest. Before she had had the strength to get out of bed, Imperator Vaarem had personally come to visit her, offering his condolences and then bittersweet accolades on her elevation to Commander of the Guard. He had assured that her duties would be waiting for her when she felt well enough to assume them.

"Is there any word on the investigation?" Ashani asked, shaking her head to focus her mind. This was something she needed to hear and remember.

Inaya's lower lip jutted out in a childish pout. She lowered her art, gazing at it as if to find the imperfection that had warranted Ashani's disregard.

"Nothing," she said, still squinting at the drawing. "They can't seem to find the vagrants you saw."

Ashani remembered pale blue eyes, badly dyed hair, and a stranger's hateful name. She had given this information to the guard. They had promised to bring the criminals to justice.

"What is taking them so long?" Ashani asked, a touch of annoyance in her voice. It had been little more than a week, but she expected a quick resolution. She needed it. There had to be a reason she was still alive when so many others hadn't survived.

"You know how the guard works," Inaya said, touching charcoal to paper once more. "They had to get all the paperwork done on the attack. Then they had to ask other survivors if they saw anything. A few did, so you're not crazy, which is a relief." She chuckled, but her amusement seemed hollow. "They've gotten the signatures and made the initial sweep of the lower city. I'm sure they'll find something soon."

Ashani wasn't sure if it was the painkillers, or if Inaya had meant the explanation to seem both impersonal and disparaging. A quiet cold bloomed in Ashani's belly, an anger the drugs couldn't quite silence.

"It's not enough," Ashani said. She balled her hand into a fist against her thigh.

"You could always do it yourself, miss Commander of the Guard," Inaya said.

Ashani heard the mocking tone in her sister's voice, but the suggestion didn't seem unreasonable. She *was* Commander of the Guard. It was only logical that she should be out searching for those that had committed this act of terror. As if it had been waiting, the fog in her mind suddenly rolled back revealing a plan. Instead of blindly scouring the lower city with the guard, she would speak to Baig's personal informant. They were sure to have the information she needed. The answer was so simple.

Images of a man with blue hair, and a tall woman with a bitter face flashed through Ashani's mind. They wouldn't be able to hide. She would find them, and they would be punished.

In her chest, a calm rage unfurled its petals. It tingled in her fingertips, demanding vengeance and whispering a stranger's name.

"Really, I'll be fine," Ashani said, moving past the guard at the gate. She knew his face, but his name was buried in the part of her mind that was still hard to access. Even on a smaller dose of painkillers, there was still so much she couldn't recall. As Commander of the Guard, she would have to do better.

"We'll need to document your departure," the guard said.

Ashani waved her hand, dismissing the concern in his voice. She understood the departure procedure and she had made her decision.

"I'll be back by dark."

Leaving the guard to his duties, Ashani emerged on the far side of the inner wall. From here to the outer wall, the lower city of Symador spread out in predetermined sectors, each ruled by their own people. The fortress guard, called the Symguard by the populace, patrolled the city regularly, keeping an unsteady sort of peace. Everything beyond the outer wall was considered lost. Irradiated sand dunes spread out in every direction to the very ends of the Earth. Very few people had ever braved the wastelands, even fewer had ever returned.

To Ashani, anything outside of the fortress was bleak and cheerless. Each of the city's sectors had always looked the same; shoddy buildings covered in red sand, streets and alleyways covered in red sand, residents in protective masks covered in red sand. Though the fortress was considered by some to be claustrophobic and dreary, it was generally free of radioactivity and considered the safest location in the city. Ashani adjusted the heavy mask over her face and moved into the lower sector.

Halfway to the outer wall, exhaustion caused her to slow down. She had to focus to lift each foot, her legs stiff and heavy, and a persistent throbbing had begun in her shoulder. She realized her morning's painkillers were wearing off. Soon she would be in real pain.

Sidestepping into an alley, Ashani crouched down, feeling in her pocket for the tin of medicine she'd smuggled from Inaya's room. Knowing the medics would never freely supply her with a few days' worth of the drug, she had snuck into her sister's room searching for the contraband emergency kit.

She had been shocked to discover Inaya's "little" kit was fully stocked. Not only had there been enough clean dressing to bind Ashani's shoulder thrice over, but there had been two full tins of painkillers and three of radiation medicines. Taking a tin of each, Ashani couldn't help but wonder how Inaya had come into possession of so much and why her sister might be keeping it secreted in her room.

Popping open the lid of the painkiller tin, Ashani used her forearm to pull her mask off her face. She dry swallowed the pill. Then, exchanging the container for the other in her pocket, she swallowed two more pills. These would help keep whatever radiation she was being exposed to from making her sick. Both tins back in her pocket, she unscrewed the cap from the canteen on her hip and took a long drink. The long days of survival training for the guard were paying off. She had come prepared.

Refastening her mask, Ashani sighed. Adjusting to life with one hand was frustrating. The smallest actions took more of her concentration and were far more complex than they had ever been. Before she could convince herself it would be easier to return to the fortress and let the guard handle the questioning, she moved back onto the main street, continuing toward the outer wall of the city and this sector's street market.

She saw the queue before she saw the food depot. A long line of people, most not wearing any sort of face protection, stood with their heads down, slips of paper clutched in their hands. While Ashani had never had to worry about her own meals, the poorest in the city could only exchange their coupons for food once a week. It seemed a dehumanizing practice, but one to which the city had become accustomed.

Ashani passed through the nearby market quickly, her eyes scanning the left support beams of each wooden stall. Finally spotting the mark she was looking for, she approached the vendor, keeping her eyes on the odd collection of items on the seller's table. Ragged-edged books were piled next to scraps of stained cloth. Small bits of metal, cogs and screws, sat in chipped ceramic bowls. Shards of broken glass as long as a forearm glittered in the early morning light.

"Looking for something specific?" the vendor asked, tilting her head and considering Ashani. "I might have it stored away."

"Information," Ashani said, looking up at the short, dark woman. "About a young man."

The woman chuckled, a sound like the grinding of stone on stone. "Information? I don't deal in information. Only scavenged goods."

Ashani bit her lip and reached into the fold of her jacket, pulling out the pendant she still wore around her neck.

The woman's thick eyebrows slowly rose. She clearly recognized the Key to the Guardhouse.

"Where is the old man?" the vendor asked, looking around Ashani as if she were searching for Baig.

"Retired," Ashani said. She knew her voice sounded cold and hard, but it was better than the trembling she feared would become evident. She shifted her weight, focusing on the feel of her boots in the sand and turning her mind away from thoughts of her father. "I'm in charge now."

The woman looked at Ashani's jacket, the way the right arm hung empty from her shoulder. She ran her tongue over her front teeth making a grotesque sucking sound.

"Look, girl, my agreement was with the old man." The

vendor lifted her hands, flicking them at Ashani in a shooing motion. "I owe you nothing."

Ashani felt her face go hot under her mask. She had been foolish, thinking Baig's informant would work with her for nothing. Her heartbeat quickened as she thought of returning to the fortress without the information she needed. That was not something she was prepared to let happen.

"What if I owe you?" The offer was made quickly.

The woman paused, mid-flick, and slowly lowered her hands. "What are you offering?"

"What do you need?" Ashani asked.

The woman sucked on her teeth again, and began to nod. Her eyes narrowed in consideration.

"Medicine," she said. "Anti-radiation drugs."

"Anti-radiation... you must be mad."

The woman shrugged, and turned away. There would be no negotiation. The conversation was over.

Ashani took a deep breath and reached into her pocket. Her hand closed around one of the medical tins. She pulled it out and found it to be the correct container. She set it on the vendor's table.

The woman had turned around at the sound of the tin, her eyes widening when she recognized the medic's seal on its lid.

"His name is Bijan," Ashani said. "He has blue eyes, blue hair. He's about my age. I need to know where I can find him."

The woman sucked on her teeth and then, lightning fast, reached out and snatched the medicine from the table, tucking it into an invisible pocket.

"Boy lives with some other strays in the tunnels," she said. She was watching Ashani with suddenly sharp and curious eyes. "You'll find the tunnels on the far side of the market, down an alley marked with a white stone."

Ashani turned away, moving in the direction the woman's hand had suggested.

"Pleasure doing business," the vendor called out. "Come back any time!"

Ashani wondered if Baig had ever paid so much for the information he had bought from the woman.

The alley was harder to find than she expected and she walked past it twice before recognizing the small white stone set into the wall. Making her way quickly between the buildings, Ashani didn't realize she had been followed until the man said her name.

Ashani turned, barely stepping away in time to avoid the knife in the man's hand.

"They do train you well up there, don't they?" the man asked as he advanced, giving Ashani no time to recover and run. His arm went wide, slashing the air where Ashani had stood.

Already panting, Ashani knew that she had reached her physical limit. This was a fight she had no chance of winning. She raised her hand, showing it was empty.

"I don't have much," she said. "But, it's yours. There's no reason to hurt me."

The corner of the man's mouth lifted in a cool sneer. Without a response, he lunged.

A line of fire opened on Ashani's thigh as she tumbled away. Exhausted and off balance without her arm, she found herself sitting in the sand unable to rise. She growled in frustration, her vision blurring with angry tears. She had been so stupid, leaving the fortress before she had fully recovered.

"What do you want?" she screamed at the man.

Still smiling, he seemed amused. He leaned down and grabbed the side of her mask, jerking it up and off of her face. Ashani grimaced as the man leaned close, sliding his hand into her hair and pulling her head back, exposing her throat.

"Just doing my job, chicken," he said. "Nothing personal."

Ashani closed her eyes and felt the gathered tears slip over her cheeks. This wasn't how it was supposed to end. She was Commander of the Guard. She deserved a better death. Baig and Reyan had deserved better deaths. The thought caused her to sob.

"What the—"

The man above her grunted and the knife lifted from her throat. Ashani took a shaky breath. She heard the approach of footsteps and the thud of something heavy hitting the dirt. She opened her eyes and struggled to her feet, wincing as she put pressure on her wounded leg.

Two men had ambushed the would-be murderer. In between his attacks, the pair were making use of the openings he gave them, taking turns striking him while they spoke to each other in calm, easy voices.

"Watch his blade!"

"I'm watching! Ooh, bad timing."

"It's just a nick, looks worse than it is."

Each time the man with the knife advanced, they

would dance away laughing. It almost seemed as if they were enjoying themselves.

"On your right!"

"Appreciated. We had about enough of this?"

"Yeah. Should check on the girl."

"Alright, you go on. I'll end it."

Ashani watched in amazement as one of her rescuers smoothly disengaged himself from the fight, setting his hands in his pockets as he walked toward her. Behind him, the other fellow continued the fight.

"Are you alright, miss?"

Recognizing the man approaching her, Ashani felt the breath leave her chest. Her cheeks suddenly felt flushed and she could hear her heartbeat in her ears.

"You," she said.

"Yeah, me," the man said. His hair was lighter than she had remembered, but the blue of his eyes was the same pale. A smile flickered across Bijan's mouth. It was a wary, amused expression. "Have we met?"

A coldness raced over Ashani's skin as if she had been hit by an icy wind. She drew her arm back and punched him.

Bijan took a step backward, but not from the force of her hit. Overbalanced, once more, Ashani had overcompensated and almost fallen. He had caught her.

"Everything alright over here?"

The man who had stayed behind to fight her attacker appeared, his amber eyes open wide in confusion and curiosity.

Ashani growled and pulled herself out of Bijan's steady grip. "This man is under arrest!"

She knew it was a mistake as soon as she said it.

Bijan and his friend exchanged a quiet look, and then began to laugh.

"Arrest?" the man asked. He ran a hand back through his russet-colored curls. "He's a scoundrel, alright. But, begging your pardon, on whose authority might you be arresting him?"

"And what for?" Bijan asked with a smile.

"Mine," Ashani said, pulling the Key to the Guardhouse out from where it had shifted under her shirt. "For the recent attack on the fortress. You'll answer for what you've done."

The two men went quiet. They, like most residents of Symador, recognized the sigil of authority. Bijan had gone pale. The other man, larger than Ashani had first noticed, stepped toward her, his expression grim. Ashani took a quick step back, scanning the ground for something to use as a weapon.

Bijan placed a hand on the other man's chest, halting him midstep.

"We didn't do that," he said. There was softness in his blue eyes that might have been called sadness. Ashani saw the gentleness as a sign of guilt, a clear confession.

"Didn't... Didn't do it?" She threw her arm wide, noticing that the chestnut-haired man flinched. "I SAW YOU!"

Frowning, Bijan stared at Ashani. Then he sighed deeply and shut his eyes. "I remember. You were the girl outside the ballroom."

"I didn't see her," the other man said, folding his thick arms over his chest and looking down at Ashani.

"You'd already gone, Tavish," Bijan said. "It was when Alma found me. Before the last blasts."

His gaze dropped to Ashani's missing arm and his expression softened further.

"It doesn't matter!" Ashani said, almost yelling, trying to hear herself above the hot pounding of blood in her ears. "If you were both there, then you are both under arrest. You will come with me immediately to the fortress. You will be held for your crimes. You will confess. You will be punished."

The man called Tavish was shaking his head, but Bijan spoke.

"We didn't do it," he said, again. "We were invited."

Ashani almost choked. "Invited?"

"An upper city girl found us in the market," Tavish explained. "Said if we fancied some free food and drink, we need only come to the upper gate and give the guards a password."

"She said we could take as much as we could carry," Bijan added.

Ashani covered her face with her hand and then rubbed at her cheeks. The story was ridiculous. No one would have invited people from the lower city to her engagement party as guests.

"You're lying," she said.

"We're not," Tavish said. "The guards heard the word, and let us in. No one stopped us."

"Why would we just walk in to blow ourselves up?" Bijan asked. "We lost friends up there. Good friends."

Feeling like someone had punched her in the gut,

Ashani looked up into Bijan's blue eyes. He seemed so earnest and his point so valid.

"The girl with pink hair?" she asked.

"Alma," Tavish said. "She's still in a lot of pain. There were others who didn't make it."

Others. Other attackers. Other innocent people killed in the fortress. Ashani lowered her head and closed her eyes. She felt light headed, a bit like she might be sick. She wanted to believe that none of what they were saying made any sense. But, somehow, it didn't seem completely illogical. She felt herself sway.

"Woah," Tavish said, reaching out for her even as Bijan took her arm, keeping her from falling once more. "Bijan, look at her leg. She's wounded."

"Help me sit her down," Bijan said. "Over there, in the shade."

They lowered her onto the sand and, before Ashani could object, Bijan tore a strip of cloth from the bottom of his shirt exposing some of his stomach. He began to bind the cut on her leg. Startled by the sudden act of kindness, Ashani simply stared at him.

Trying to distract herself, Ashani looked over at the man who had attacked her, the man Tavish and Bijan had fought. He was still lying facedown on the ground. For a second, in her mind, he was Reyan on the marble floor of the ballroom. Her stomach turned, rejecting the memory. She averted her eyes, staring instead at her boots.

"Is he...?" She couldn't bring herself to ask the question.

"Ah, well. He won't be bothering you anymore," she

heard Tavish answer. "Which reminds me. He had this on him."

"Who was he?" Ashani asked, looking up as Tavish handed Bijan a piece of paper.

"No idea," Bijan said, handing her the paper. "But, it looks like he was after you."

Ashani's hand began to shake. She took a single shaky breath, and then another.

"What was the password?" she asked, unable to take her eyes off the image on the paper. "The one you gave to get into the fortress."

"Something about the sky," Tavish said. "Sunny. Starry. Cloudy."

"Sunlight," Bijan said. "It was sunlight."

Ashani curled her fist, crushing the portrait. Inaya had done it again. She had captured Ashani's perfect likeness, down to the blazing fury in her eyes.

ASHANI OPENED THE DOOR TO INAYA'S ROOM WITHOUT KNOCKING and limped inside.

The pretty blonde was laying on her bed, discolored paper and charcoal in her hands. Drawings of Baig and Reyan in various stages of completion were scattered around her. She began to gather them as Ashani approached.

"You're back!" Inaya said, a too-bright smile on her face. "Any news?"

Ashani snatched a half-shaded picture of Reyan from the

bed. His kind expression, so perfectly rendered, almost caused her resolve to falter. He would have never understood the consuming rage in her heart. He would have cautioned her to compassion and warned her against the confrontation. He had been a good man. Ashani wiped the tears from her cheeks with her forearm. She set the drawing down.

"You can keep that one, if you like," Inaya said as she climbed off the bed and set the other pictures on a small side table. With her back to Ashani, she checked her hair in a tall, dark mirror, the twin to Ashani's own.

"Why did you do it?" Ashani asked, watching her sister in the mirror.

Inaya's reflection frowned, her brow furrowing in confusion. She turned around. "Excuse me? Do what?"

"Why did you kill them?"

Inaya's eyes widened slightly, but her surprise was quickly replaced by an expression of concern. "Killed who? I think the radiation has gotten to you, sister. Please, lay down here. I'm going to go get a medic."

"No!" Ashani stepped into her sister's path, blocking Inaya from her exit. "No. I talked to them, your lower city scapegoats. I know you let them into the fortress. Why did you do it?"

Taking several steps back, Inaya raised her hands as if to protect herself. "Ashani, you're scaring me."

Ashani reached into her pocket, pulling out the portrait Tavish had taken from the assassin. She thrust the paper at Inaya.

"A man tried to murder me," she said. "He had this on him."

Looking at the picture, Inaya lowered her hands. She pressed her lips together, and then she smiled.

"I knew I should have paid for two killers," she said. "But how did you get rid of one? You're so..." Inaya waved her hands, gesturing to the whole of Ashani. "...banged up. Though I guess it doesn't really matter." Her voice took on a melancholy tone and her expression became sympathetic. "Since you've contracted radiation poisoning on your little excursion. Oh, my poor sister. Such a terrible way to go."

"What do you mean? I don't have radiation poisoning." Even as she spoke, Ashani understood. An overdose of anti-radiation pills would cause similar symptoms to the beginning of radiation sickness. Inaya had more than enough in her secret medical kit. "You're planning to murder me? I'm right here!"

Inaya shrugged and approached Ashani, a sickly-sweet smile on her face. "Third time is the charm."

It was Ashani's turn to back away. She bumped into the larger table in Inaya's room, the one her sister used as a vanity. Closely set glass bottles clinked together and a small tin of loose powder fell, spilling across the floor.

"Did you know you were all father could ever talk about?" Inaya asked, ignoring the wasted cosmetics. "Ashani, so beautiful. Ashani, so smart. Ashani, with the best marks in training. Ashani, catching the eye of handsome, talented Reyan. Ashani, the new commander. You had EVERYTHING!"

"You've hurt so many people, Inaya," Ashani said, reaching back until her hand came in contact with something heavy. It felt like a small metal block.

"You made me do this!" Inaya screamed, grabbing Ashani's shirt and jerking her forward. "All you had to do was share *something*."

Ashani swung, driving the small jewelry box into the side of her sister's face. Blood splattered across Ashani's hand. An image of Baig from the night of the attack flashed through her mind. His face was covered in blood, his eyes already sightless. Ashani's felt herself go cold. She screamed and hit Inaya again and again, driving her sister back.

Reining in her wrath, Ashani lowered her arm, gasping for the air she didn't know she needed. Inaya stood with her head down, holding her shredded cheek. She began to laugh.

"Really, Ashani?" She asked without looking up. "You're going to beat me to death?"

Inaya looked up, her eyes wide, but not in pain. Though her face was torn and blood dripped from her jaw, hers was the wild gaze of the deranged. She grinned.

"Do it," she said. "Ashani, so perfect. Ashani, one-armed. Ashani, sister killer! Do it!"

Ashani struck her once more.

Inaya fell back into the dark mirror, shattering the thick glass. She slid to the floor, amongst the glittering shards, her arms and upper body spotted and striped in red. Some fragments remained lodged in her skin. One, no larger than Ashani's thumb, had pierced Inaya's forearm, near the wrist. It sparkled in the dim light as blood pulsed from the wound. It would be only minutes before she was dead.

Ashani dropped the jewelry box. The metal clang of it

striking the concrete floor sounded as if it were very far away. Her anger, too, felt distant, though not dissipated. This act of vengeance would not bring her the satisfaction she desired.

"You have taken everything from me," Ashani said, heading toward the door. She would summon the medics and save her sister's life. Then, she would confess her actions to the guard, and reveal her sister's loathsome crimes. They would both be imprisoned for their offenses. "Turns out, that is something I am very willing to share."

OBSERVATIONS OF THE HEAD CHRONICLER

LIV EVANS

"It is not the most intellectual of the species
that survives; it is not the strongest that
survives; but the species that survives is the
one that is able best to adapt and adjust to the
changing environment in which it finds itself."
- Leon C. Megginson paraphrasing
Charles Darwin

ONE OF THE MOST CONSISTENTLY ASTOUNDING THEMES IN THE
annals of the Chroniclers is the sheer adaptability of
humanity. For a species that can be selflessly kind at best
and utterly destructive at worst, we have an incredibly
innate ability to change to suit our environment.

Or, in some cases, to change our environment to
suit us.

There were reportedly other animal species that were
capable of the same feat, but always at a much smaller
scale and with far less collaboration. This habit of ours is

what allowed us to spread over the earth, to drain it of its natural resources, and to turn what was otherwise a perfect planet for hosting life into a radioactive wasteland.

And that's only covering the impact on the planet.

The conversation around adaptability would be incomplete without looking at the nature of the human spirit. At what the intense need to survive does to the relationships between humans.

Back in the days referred to as 'prehistoric', homo sapiens relied on each other as a means for survival. Strong clan units were able to gather shared resources that allowed them to weather extremely difficult living conditions. Rejection from a clan was tantamount to a death sentence.

As millennia passed, even the mere thought of possible social exclusion was enough to trigger panic in a human brain. This sense of threat, an ever-present worry that one's clan-mates may abandon them for even the slightest infraction, was enough to cause people to seek out others they could ally with. Great divides were created, and tentative balances of power were struck and restruck over the years to the point where those who were able to adapt to a changing social landscape survived, and those who did not were forced to fight for scraps in the putrid gutters.

History has taught us that one of the greatest threats to adaptability is complacency. The idea that the things we think are right just because we think them. That we know the nature of the world around us so completely that our plans are impervious to change and interference.

But even the most self-assured folk are vulnerable.

When humans no longer need to fight for their survival

on a daily basis, they forget to look for incoming threats, and they don't see their own potential extinction coming, even though the signs were there all along. It follows, then, that the fittest to survive are in fact the ones who remain vigilant. Those who ask questions, who dare to look deeper, who are the most adaptable, even if they are not necessarily the ones who hold power.

SYMADOR 2223

KATIE CIVITELLI

SYMADOR 2223

KATIE CIVITELLI

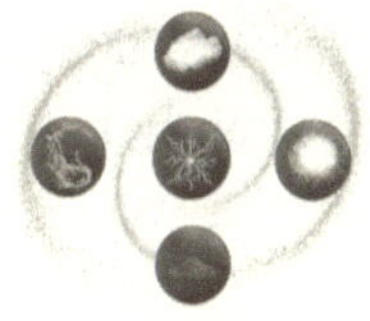

"Happy Birthday!!" they shouted around the small, rickety wooden table as Ophelia blew out a single candle in the center of a small square ration, an extra for her birthday, hoarded by her brother, Leon. The ration was supposed to sustain him for three days, the second one bought with his token the other four days. However, he decided that it was alright to go a little hungry this week, as it was Ophelia's eighteenth birthday.

Eighteen was a largely celebrated birthday in Symador, however, in the lower sectors such as this one, it seemed more of a punishment to reach this age than it did to celebrate it. Twenty was the year that magic users, known as the Wielders in some sectors, were sent for the Tests, a round of ability testing overseen by Imperator Vaarem from atop his castle on the Watcher's Hill. Ophelia's smile did not meet her eyes as she gazed at the ration that Leon had saved for her and a sad pang struck her heart at the thought of him hungry. Leon had always been there for her, ever since she was a child. She had been born with the ability of Fire, though in this part of the sector, magic abilities were to be hidden from the Guard until the age of eighteen, when the powers were at their full potential.

Tomorrow. Tomorrow would be the day she travelled to the center of their sector to compete in the Tests with the other eighteen-year-olds whose power had surged. Wilson had the power of electricity, and if he passed the Tests, he would most certainly be put to use toward the richer sectors of even the Watcher's Hill working at keeping what little lights and gadgets survived the war in working condition. Some who passed the Tests would join the Guard, an elite force in charge of keeping peace throughout the walled city and keeping in those who dared try sneaking out to the toxic air beyond. Most of the Fire Wielders were used for agricultural ---, making sure the crops and fields were tended properly when brush needed to be burned and eradicated, though some Fire Wielders were recruited to the richer sectors, keeping Symador's natural heating and water lines warm and sterilized.

Tomorrow, she would meet up with Wilson and Anika, a Water Wielder, for their Tests, though she did not think that she would sleep at all that night—and she was correct.

Ophelia was rushed from her house by the Sector Guard and ushered through the waiting crowds, her family following swiftly behind. She spotted Wilson and Anika standing toward the outskirts of a ring drawn in the dirt beneath their feet. Ophelia took her place in between them, earning a nod from Wilson but a sneer from Anika, whose hands were shaking. She and Anika had never really been friends, in fact, Anika tried to drown her once when they were young when a boy their age chose to sit with Ophelia rather than her. It was then that people started to notice Anika's fascination with water, and before long, small signs emerged of a growing power.

"Wilson Edderson," the moderator announced above the crowd, who instantly fell into a hushed silence as Wilson took his place in the center of the ring. Ophelia looked around at the Guard, something seemed different this time around in the Tests, though she could not put her finger on why.

"Power?" the moderator asked. Wilson glanced at Ophelia, then at Anika, before taking a deep breath.

"Electricity," he projected, earning a nod from the moderator.

"Begin now."

Wilson stared at the ground, muttering something that seemed like a chant to the elements. His hands crossed in front of him as the sparks began to dance off his fingers and around his wrists, growing in size. Ophelia had witness him do small things, but never had seen this magnitude of power come from him, though if she were honest, none of them had really shown their powers until recently anyway.

Lightning struck the ground around him and he was quickly swept up in a large ray of luminescent white and purple and silver dancing around him.

"Enough," the moderator announced, making Wilson's

sparks calm in an instant. She stared at him for a long while, the crowd so quiet you could hear a pin drop on the ground.

"Anika Dennon."

Anika's hands shook more fervently as she sighed, replacing Wilson in the center of the ring. He was out of breath by the time he reached Ophelia once more, his power taking much of his energy along with it.

"Power?"

Anika looked straight ahead as she answered, though Ophelia noticed the fear behind her eyes.

"Water."

"Begin."

It was magical to watch as Anika lifted her arms above her head, drawing the water particles from the air into giant waves above her. The water seemed pure and blue, not like the drinking water they had here in the sector, which was contaminated. She twisted and morphed the wave into different shapes as she manipulated the droplets together.

"Enough."

Anika dropped her hands, the water splashing around her, though never touching her person and walked back to her original spot.

"Ophelia Maleus."

This was it, the moment she had been dreading. Wilson moved a finger across her wrist, as if to wish her luck. They had never been close friends, but they had never been enemies either, and in that moment, it was exactly what she needed. Ophelia took her place at the center of the ring, her family watching with anticipation at what she could do.

"Power?"

"Fire," she answered, her voice as firm as she could make it, though still shaky from the nerves that fought to break free.

"Begin."

Ophelia took two deep breaths and snapped her fingers, a small flame emerging from the tips. It danced as she moved it over her knuckles before opening her hand and making the small flame into a blaze. The audience awed at the sight, making her confidence grow as the blaze grew and grew. She never worried about losing control of it, as she and Leon practiced in secret on how to control the flames.

"Enough," said the moderator as Ophelia stifled the flames back down to embers at her fingers and walked back to her position in the line.

The moderator faced them then as she placed her hands behind her back. She was a tall woman with gangly features and a stern face, her dark hair pulled back in a tight bun.

"This year, the Tests and Trials in each sector have been modified to find the ones who will be recruited into our new elite guard which will be made up of five members of each elemental power. Lucky for you, each of you exhibited more power than your other competitors combined, which means each of you will be chosen. You will gather your belongings and we will leave tomorrow morning first thing to the base the Watcher's Hill."

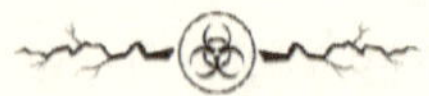

THE NEXT 24 HOURS FELT LIKE AN ETERNITY AND AN INSTANT flash all at once as Ophelia and the others boarded the train bound for the sector paced at the base of the Watcher's Hill, each giving one final wave to their families before the moderator slammed the door shut. The night before her mother held her tightly, reassuring her that everything would work out in the end and that she would make the family proud, though Ophelia did not feel pride at being chosen for this endeavor; it felt more like a daunting curse instead.

The richer sectors were something to behold as they passed through each, moving further and further away from their poor little homes on the outskirts of Symador, closest to the lead walls surrounding the city, protecting each of them from the radiation outside. The sectors gleamed in the artificial sunlight produced by the Fire and Electricity wielders that did not get recruited to enhance the other areas of the city. Their combined power shifted and created the artificial sun used to warm the richer sectors, while their home was covered in skies filled with dust clouds. They were each amazed as they took in the bright colors and sights, and if Ophelia was honest, a bit jealous at the way the other side lived.

"To think they have no idea that we live in rotting homes while they live in luxury. The Imperator disgusts me when I see stuff like this," Wilson murmured next to her, and she felt a slight pang in her chest at the remark.

"It's not his fault, this is simply how the society

works," Anika snapped beside them, her eyes glued to the glittering sector before them.

"He sees everything, Anika. You're really going to tell me he can't do something to change it?" Wilson snapped.

"Ok, ok calm down everyone," Ophelia chimed in, her hands outstretched as Anika turned to face Wilson from her position on the chairs against the train wall, "We need to stick together. We have no idea what is going to happen to us here so let's just try to keep politics out of conversation, alright?"

Wilson stood rigid for a moment, then nodded as Anika huffed out a sigh, conceding as well. They were strangers here and if they were going to survive whatever was awaiting them, they needed the numbers—especially with two other Magic Wielders that they had never met.

Exiting the train was more overwhelming that Ophelia figured it would have been as the three, who normally tried to stay apart, huddled together as they walked through the masses waiting to greet them. Guards on either side of them kept the hoards back as the moderator pushed forward in front of them, leading them to the training arena to mee the other two magic wielders from the richest sector.

The arena was vast as they took in the sight of the empty court, the open gymnasium stretching out as far as they could see. There were obstacles for each wielder's specific power, Ophelia noticed, as she stared at her own not too far from her: a pyramid made of the thickest ice a Water Wielder could create. Each obstacle, meant for training, seemed to have a small sign next to it with a specific element etched into the glass specifying who the training exercise was for.

"Attention!" the moderator screeched, bringing Ophelia back to the present moment as Wilson nudged her to pay attention. The other two wielders came forward—one male and one female—as they stared at the new recruits with disdain.

"From the outer sector—Wilson, electricity; Anika, water; Ophelia, fire," the moderator said as she pointed to each of them, then turned to the two more seasoned recruits, "From the inner sector—Agatha, earth and Elijah, air. You will be the members of our Elite Guard, assuming you can grow your powers and your strength in time. Start your training. Dismissed."

Ophelia took in the richer members carefully noting Agatha's long brown hair and olive skin as she glided away with a scoff. Then she turned to Elijah, who she was surprised to see taking her in as well, though his dark eyes showed a sense of judgement. He was tall with tanned skin and dusty blonde hair ruffled along his face as if he were in a constant windstorm of his own making—which would make sense, Ophelia thought to herself.

The obstacles made for a difficult time as Ophelia tried her hardest to melt the giant ice block in front of her, failing to complete the task within the amount of time she was given. The ice was thick, its inner layer vast as she had to melt the entire structure within five minutes or less, though to her it seemed impossible. To her surprise, she was not the only one who was having difficulty with her task. Each of the magic wielders in the room were failing miserably as their obstacles could not be achieved within the amount of time the moderator set. Agatha, especially, was having severe rages, storming out of the room every so often to cool off when it came to building the exact plant covered formation needed in the exercise.

Ophelia could feel Elijah's eyes on her as she looked around the room, meeting them with an intense stare before rolling her own and looking back to her task at hand. She took a few deep breaths, centering herself as she searched for the source of her power deep within. A small fire blazed within her as she urged it forward, pushing it through her fingertips as the flames flew toward the giant blocks of ice newly added to the obstacle in front of her. She could feel the flames burning her as she threw them harder and harder, trying with everything she had to melt the ice within the five minutes she was given, though it was all in vain. Breathless, ears ringing, she stopped to drink some water from her small canteen beside her. The sound of slow clapping behind her brought her out of her fog and she scowled as she saw Elijah coming toward her.

"Nicely done, red," he said, a smirk crossing his perfect face as his hair fell to his forehead.

"The sarcasm is not needed, thank you," she snapped, taking another sip from her canteen.

"I meant it. You're the only one here so far who has been able to make a dent in their elemental task. You mostly melted the block whereas I have not even been able to contain a small tornado. So I meant it, nicely done. Although, you could probably use some assistance."

Ophelia glanced at him, a quizzical look crossing her face.

"I'm pretty sure we are supposed to do this on our own. Plus, I'm not sure how your powers would help me in melting the blocks."

"Try me," he replied, a playful look gleamed in his eye.

With a sigh, Ophelia conceded, summoning her flames once more as she hurled them toward the block of ice. With one swoop of air, Elijah blasted his winds toward her flames, growing them larger and stronger by the second as the oxygen in his winds fueled their warmth.

Oxygen. Of course, why did she not think of that?

Within four minutes, they had successfully melted the block of ice in front of them, each allowing their powers to work in tandem as they slowed them to a stop.

Shocked, Ophelia looked to Elijah, who smiled at her with a warmth that filled her core with the same heat that flew from her fingers each time she called it forth. The sensation startled her as they stared for a moment too long, Elijah's eyes suddenly growing a bit wide as they turned away toward his own obstacle.

Ophelia watched as his winds swept through his obstacle, the tornado flowing through him a sight to see as he initially controlled the winds. Though as the five minutes dragged on, Elijah soon lost control once again, drenching Agatha in mud as her own Earth powers mixed accidentally with Anika's water.

"*Dammit Elijah*, learn to control your powers," Agatha snapped, stomping off to the changing rooms at the very end of the arena as Elijah's face burned a dark crimson. Ophelia slowly approached him as he turned his gaze away. Was he...embarrassed? It was a simple mistake; none of them were strong enough or old enough to completely control their powers yet.

"She's overreacting. Don't let her get to you," she said, her words gentle as his face burned deeper.

"Maybe it's fine for you to be an amateur, but from our sector, it's not. Just leave me alone, lower born," Elijah snapped, his words knowingly slicing through her as he looked at her face. There was a moment of regret that flashed through them as he took in her hurt expression, though it was only a moment before he stalked the other way toward the male changing rooms.

Wilson and Anika stood beside Ophelia as she watched him leave.

"Screw him, Phi. The richer sectors only breed assholes," Wilson said as Ophelia's shoulders straightened a bit. She seemed to think that the only reason Elijah seemed to snap at her the way he did was because Agatha had embarrassed him; it looked to Ophelia he did not take kindly to embarrassment, though his comment struck a chord inside her. What had he meant by their sector not allowing amateurs?

THAT NIGHT, AS EACH OF THE CHOSEN ONES ENTERED THE LARGE dining hall for some much-needed dinner, Ophelia could not shake the foreboding feeling creeping its way along the walls as it filled the silent room. For a dining hall, it was incredibly quiet, she noted, as each of them carried their food trays and sat at the long wooden tables spanning the length of the echoing room. Forks clanked down on the steel of the trays as they ate in silence, Wilson and Anika sitting side by side as Wilson beckoned Ophelia over to their table with a hand gesture. Agatha sat alone at the far table toward the exit doors, silently glaring down at her food as she took small bites. Ophelia looked toward the opposite end of the room where Elijah sat, alone with a decrepit book in his hands, his eyes scanning each page as he lost himself in the story. She glanced to Wilson before continuing straight until she reached Elijah's table, placing her tray across from him and taking a seat.

Elijah's stormy eyes lifted as she took her seat, his brows arched in a quizzical look, asking a silent question.

"What?" she asked, stirring her gravy with her fork as Elijah closed his book and placed it beside him. Ophelia looked to the words on the cover and smiled. *A Tale of Two Cities* had been one of her favorite stories as a child. Not many from the poorer sectors learned to read, though Ophelia's mother had insisted each of her children be taught at young ages.

"A Charles Dickens fan are you?" she remarked, taking a bite of her potatoes as Elijah's face twisted into a surprised smile. "It was the best of times, it was the worst of times, it was the age of wisdom, it was the age of foolishness..." she recited.

"You can read," he replied, his words in the manner of a question, though she knew it was not an actual question but more of a remark.

"My mother insisted," she said, briefly looking up to see him watching her, "She was lucky enough to know herself. Us *lower born* don't always have the luxury of opportunity."

Elijah winced at her pointed words to which she smiled before turning back to her food.

"I'm sorry. You did not deserve to be spoken to that way," he said, "I was...angry, though that is no excuse. You have as much right to be here as we do."

Ophelia placed her fork back down on the tray and looked to Agatha, still hyper focused on the food in front of her. She noticed Wilson watching her, his expression concerned.

"I accept your apology, though what did you mean by 'not allowed to be an amateur'?"

Elijah sighed, "From the time we start exhibiting signs of power, our families rely on us to achieve perfection. They work us however they must so that when the Trials or Tests come, we will be chosen to represent our sectors and secure our family's positions in office or in wealth. To be out of control is to be weak and it is unacceptable."

His eyes darkened as he spoke and Ophelia noticed the same look evolve that had crossed his features earlier that day when he had snapped at her.

"Well, if it hadn't been for you and your control, I would never have accomplished my obstacle," she said, her voice like a calm in the storm that raged in his eyes as she gently placed her fingers over his, "I do not think you are weak, Elijah."

He held her gaze, then, as his finger brushed the top of her own. A sense of warmth coursed through her, the same as she had felt the moment she had met him; this warmth was different than her fire, it was...

"Phi," Wilson said behind her as Elijah pulled his hand away from hers, snapping her back into reality, "Anika and I are going to train, the moderator wants us all in the arena this afternoon. You coming?"

Ophelia looked once more to Elijah, the storm in his eyes no longer visible.

"In a few minutes," she replied, her voice straining to break free as Anika shoved Wilson forward toward the doors.

"Your boyfriend is touchy," Elijah mused, though his words had more bite to them than mirth as he watched Wilson and Anika leave the room.

"Oh no, he's not—he's been my friend since childhood. He's just incredibly protective, like my brothers," she replied, her face burning.

"So never any...?" Elijah asked, earning an intense eyeroll from Ophelia as he chuckled.

"No, never. And there never will be. We will always be just friends," she snapped, then asked, "Why do you ask?"

She held Elijah's stare a beat too long before he cleared his throat.

"No reason," he rasped, "Mere curiosity of the way those in the poor sectors live."

His words hit their mark, earning a glare from Ophelia as she stood and grabbed her tray.

"I should get to training," she snapped, tossing her tray into the bin as Elijah followed on her tail.

"Ophelia, I didn't mean it like that I just mean..."

"What? You mean what?" she said, whirling on him as he stopped short.

"You intrigue me."

Her skin felt like molten lava as they stood in the dimly lit hallway, his eyes boring into her own. She could not tell if she were angry with him or intrigued as well as their faces rested only inches from each other.

"Arena. Now," the moderator said over the loudspeaker, breaking their eye contact.

What was happening? What was this sensation between them? Ophelia knew that if she studied this more thoroughly, she might not like the answers...then again, she also might.

THE ARENA LOOKED THE SAME AS IT HAD THE LAST TIME SHE HAD set foot inside, besides the fact that the obstacles were now placed side by side as if one followed suit with the next. Ophelia stood by the others, her hand nearly brushing Elijah's as Wilson looked on with sheer annoyance before turning back to the moderator. Her face was her normal shade of white; the chill emitting from it had hardened in the last 24 hours or so.

"I have a message from Impetrator Vaarem," she started, Ophelia holding her breath as the stone-like woman spoke, "There is a threat amongst the city of Symador. As trainees who have been selected for the Secret Guard, you are now responsible to gain control of your powers and work as a team to defeat this adversary in one week's time. Train and learn control. Begin."

As the moderator stood at the back of the arena, her eyes fixated on each obstacle in front of the recruits, Ophelia stepped up to the one she figured had been designated for her: a small pool of water built to withstand her flames. She wondered if this were another exercise where they needed to work together with their powers, as her ice blocks had been with Elijah's wind. She looked toward Anika, her whirlpools soaking the earth beneath Agatha as the two girls argued, their voices rising higher until the ceiling above them shook from the vibrations. Wilson struck the ground between them, a warning to stop.

"What is the problem?" he snapped as Elijah and Ophelia walked toward the irritated group.

"She's out of control," Agatha barked, pointing a long finger at Anika as she scowled, "You lower borns need to remember your place."

"And *you* need to learn to work as a team, Agatha," Ophelia retorted. Agatha turned her icy gaze toward her then, scoffing.

"Elijah, let's go," Agatha ordered, yet Elijah only moved closer to where Ophelia stood.

"*Elijah.*"

"She's right, Aggie. We are a team and we need to learn to act like one," he said, his voice was quiet and yet pointed as Agatha scoffed once more.

"I don't need this. I don't need *you.*"

Agatha spun on her heels, exiting the arena as Anika nodded to Ophelia in thanks, the first kind gesture she had ever received from her in all their years growing up together.

Training went on as expected throughout the week, each member working on their solitary obstacles, each member failing to combat each time. The moderator, never far from the arena, watched in disdain as the members failed to improve their strengths at every turn. The next training exercise had been mannequins propped up on strings, all representing the terror and threat the new guard still knew nothing about. The exercise honed in on their combat skills and reflexes, Ophelia getting beat down try after try as she tried to learn the strategy of their movements.

Elijah had been keeping an eye on her each day, walking past with tips to use during her combat lessons each time he would finish with his own. He trained with her after hours in the arena, their powers growing stronger together as they learned to work in tandem, soon gaining Wilson and Anika in their after-hours practices as well.

Ophelia had explained to them how she and Elijah had realized the obstacles are meant for more than one of them to enhance their powers, to teach them to be more of a team and work together if they were ever going to defeat this threat. Since they only had mere days to complete their training, which Wilson repeatedly informed the moderator was incredibly unfair, they had to at least try to get along or face possible banishment back to their homes, or even worse...death. The four worked expertly together, learning the strengths and weaknesses of each power as they flowed through the obstacles and training exercises, all except Agatha, who had refused I numerous occasions to come to after-hours training.

There were three days until they would stand up against whatever threat had infiltrated Symador, fully aware that they were on their own as their unit was kept quiet from the rest of the guard handled by Imperator Vaarem, and though they were each doing incredibly well under the pressure, Ophelia knew that there were significant weaknesses among them. Their combat training was subpar at best seeing as none of them were trained fighters and had only just turned eighteen not long before the tests had come to their doors, Ophelia's birthday only one day before.

Throughout the training they had to endure as part of the secret guard, Ophelia had grown a new kinship with Anika that had never blossomed back home in their sector. Ophelia was not sure if it was simply because they were far from home or if they had one day been destined to become closer, though she simply accepted their newfound friendship with open arms as they threw their trays in the trash and exited the dining area. Today, however, the arena looked quite different as the sentient robots with which the new guard had been training with all stood in a line at the very far end of the arena. Each of the guard waited as the moderator walked toward them, Ophelia noticing the ominous way her tight face seemed to tighten further as she looked to each one of them, the look of worry mixed with disdain. They had all been trying their best during training, making progress as the week went on, though it seemed as though it was not enough for the moderator and possibly not enough for the Imperator. Whatever threat this was in Symador, the five of them seemed unworthy to fight against it.

"What's going on?" Elijah asked, placing himself

beside Ophelia as the others stood to the opposite side of Anika.

"We don't know, but the robots are all in a specific fighting formation," Anika answered, looking up to the moderator's newly placed podium.

"Earth. Fire. Water. Air. Electricity. Each of these elements are possessed by the members of the Secret Guard, all training to defeat a new threat to Symador by order of the Imperator. These five individuals have succeeded in small progress, though not enough to survive the threat coming against them. I require more time for their training of the extinction of this project altogether. What say you?" she bellowed, confusing the members as four individuals revealed themselves from the shadows of the wings in the arena. They looked as though they were Symador's council members, though being from a lower, poorer sector, Ophelia had never laid eyes on them until now.

"Let us see what they can do," one of the members replied, his voice monotone and deep.

"Begin," the moderator announced as the robots began to move toward the new guard members.

"What's happening?" Wilson asked, his voice raising in confusion as he looked to Anika and Ophelia.

"Our training has come to its end," Agatha replied strongly, though Ophelia could sense the hint of fear in her timbre, "*Fight.*"

At Agatha's command, they sprang into action, doing their best to connect to their powers against the obstacles in front of them, the obstacles all much larger and more threatening than they had experienced in the previous week. They fought side by side, even Agatha, as best they could. This set of obstacles, Ophelia realized as she looked to the other's faces, could potentially kill them. By extinction, the moderator had not meant sending them back to their homes, but to eliminate them for good. Her fire swarmed in tandem with Elijah's wind, creating bursts of waves against the robots as Agatha and Anika's powers created mudslides, trapping each robot. Wilson's electricity bounced off the mud, electrocuting the ground beneath and short circuiting their machinery.

"Ophelia! *Fire. Now,*" Agatha screamed as Ophelia's fire blasted toward her, the minerals from the ground melting into ash flying toward Elijah's wind, pushing each of the robots back and covering their faces with ash and smoke before Wilson's lightning bolts charged at Anika's waves and destroyed the remaining robots. By the end, each of the members of the guard were gasping for breath as their powers retreated into themselves.

Ophelia could not tell if the moderator was pleased or infuriated at their success, though there was something off about the way she held herself.

"Well done. The program will continue, and they will fight the threat. This discussion is over," another council member chimed in, this time the voice was high, like small bells ringing in the wind.

The moderator simply nodded and walked back through the wing opposite the council members before disappearing into the dark.

"What was that all about?" Ophelia asked Elijah, whose hand smoothed over her back as she tried to catch her breath from the exertion. She was not used to using her powers this intensely and the strain was enough to make her body convulse.

"It seems the moderator feels we are ill equipped to handle whatever threat is upon us. I wonder why," he said, saying the second part more to himself than to her.

"Something is going on and I want to find out what it is, what exactly this *threat* is against Symador where they speak of it to no one except to us, and even so they barely even tell us what this evil could be," Agatha snapped.

THAT NIGHT AFTER DINNER, OPHELIA'S BONES ACHED FROM THEIR training session earlier in the afternoon, if training could be what they could even call what had happened to all of them. She remembered the way the moderator's face twisted as the council deemed them each worthy of keeping their ranks in the secret guard, and she wondered why exactly the moderator would be disappointed with the news considering this was part of her job. Was the threat really that intense that she truly thought they were not ready? Even after their display today, which had surprised even them?

A knock at the door focused her thoughts back to the present moment as she reached to thrust it open. Who could be at her door at this hour? Ophelia was in no mood for visitors as she looked to see Elijah standing there, his arm balanced against the metal doorframe, exposing his muscles in the dim light of the hall. He looked like the gods of old in the stories her parents would tell her; the gods from myths and legends passed down through the apocalypse and beyond. His hair fell over his forehead as his lifted his head to smile at her, her body warming as it responded to the movement.

"Oh, hi—did you need something?" she asked, trying to make her voice seem more nonchalant than the surprise that flitted its way into her throat.

Elijah ran a hand through his hair.

"I—well—I actually came here to ask you something," he stammered, a light blush caressing his cheeks as his dark eyes gazed at her. Ophelia made a motion for him to continue; she did not want anyone to come into her room, though with Elijah, she decided she may have to make an exception. His eyes flitted to the inside of her room as she stepped aside, closing the door behind them when Elijah took a seat in a nearby chair.

"I overheard the moderator talking to one of the council members just before they left. I hid in one of the alcoves as they were speaking, and she said something that caught my attention. Something isn't right, Ophelia." His hands were clammy as he spoke, his fingers ringing their way around each other; something was clearly bothering him.

"Since our positions were approved by the council, they granted she allow us one day off in the city tomorrow before our meeting with the Imperator."

"What meeting?" Ophelia asked, her brows quirking with confusion. No one had said anything about a meeting, only the training timeline before they fought the threat against Symador.

"That's exactly what I thought," he agreed, "No one this entire time has been forthright with us. What even is this threat? The moderator seemed annoyed that we passed those insane training regimens earlier today. Something is up and I do not trust her. So, I—" he paused, sucking in a deep breath, "I was hoping you would come to the city with me tomorrow and help me do some digging."

Ophelia's breath caught in her throat. None of this made any sense. Was the moderator trying to put them all in danger? No one knew about this secret guard except those in this building, the council and Imperator Vaarem. So, who could they trust? Who else knew what they were up to in this above ground bunker? Though the thought of spending an entire day with Elijah made her heart flutter in her chest, Ophelia could not help but feel validated and nervous all at the same time. Elijah suspected something amiss as well as she and she was terrified of what they might uncover if they dug too deep.

That was a chance they had to take to get to the bottom of this.

"Yes, I will go into the city with you tomorrow, of course," she smiled. They sat there, then, in an awkward silence for what seemed like eternity until their eyes met. His face was so beautifully crafted, she found herself hearing a song her mother had taught her that was passed down through the family from the old days before Symador had been created, it was called "Angel Eyes", she wondered what it would feel like to kiss him. The thoughts startled her though she did not turn away from his gaze as he rose from his chair and slowly walked toward her, stopping mere inches from her face so their breath intertwined. Soon, her aching limbs felt light, as if she could float right out of the room.

She had always dreamt of having this reaction toward someone, though she had always thought it would be someone from home, like Wilson. From their body language, however, it was entirely more than she could have imagined.

His winds carried her lightly toward the wall it seemed and she had not even realized, though she saw that he was...shaking.

"Are you alright?" she asked, touching his arm to calm the movement.

"I'm fine, I'm just...I'm really nervous. There is something about you, I felt drawn to you the moment I saw you that first day," he said, "But if you say no then I will walk out this door and try nothing. I meant it, your friendship is important to me."

Elijah went to pull away, to put space between them as she hesitated, though Ophelia found herself pulling him back toward her and closing the space between them with a single kiss before looking into his eyes once more. Elijah's smile grew as he leaned in once more, this time their lips filled with passion as he lifted her from the floor and drew her legs up around his waist, never breaking away. Her heart soared as their kiss deepened, her hands running through his hair as he held her in place. She knew that this was a fleeting moment, as they would come to do bed checks soon enough, but in this moment, she felt calm and cared for, something she had not felt since before her birthday—when she was still safe. Elijah released her and dropped her legs back to the floor as they both took staggered breaths.

"Wow," he said, earning a laugh from Ophelia. The bed

check alarm rang out in the hall, startling the two as they parted. "Until tomorrow?"

She smiled, "Tomorrow."

Elijah ran his hand through his hair once more and gave her an awkward smile as he walked to the door, moving back only briefly to plant one more kiss on her.

"Tomorrow."

THE NEXT MORNING OPHELIA FELT LIGHTER; EVEN THE DANK halls and the disgusting breakfast of oats and wilk could not sully her mood as she sat beside Anika, this time Agatha joining them. Agatha had been more cordial to the group after yesterday's exercise and had even smiled once or twice. Wilson had decided to skip breakfast, Anika reported, and go straight to the arena to work on his fighting skills as to not be caught off guard again.

"Why are you so chipper this morning?" Agatha asked as Ophelia stirred her oats; she could not help but smile at the girls.

"Oh nothing," she said, her voice high and light.

"Alright, tell," Anika said, her eyes wide with anticipation.

"Well, last night right before bed check, I—" Ophelia stopped mid-sentence as she watched Elijah stride into the dining hall. His hair fell over his forehead as he swopped it back with a hand, grabbing a tray of food placed out for him. Ophelia felt her heart skip beats as he walked by the girls, gently gliding his hand across her back, the sensation sending shivers across her skin, as he passed and sat at his usual table with his book in hand.

She turned back to the girls, who had both stopped eating to stare at her.

"What. Was. That?" Anika asked, her smile growing wide as she spoke, the same smile crossing Agatha's face.

"Elijah may or may not have come to my room last night to talk and we ended up making out after talking..." Ophelia spewed, her eyes never leaving her bowl.

"*I knew it*," Anika squealed.

"He truly did come to talk about something, we just got a little...caught up."

The girls began to laugh as Ophelia stole a glance toward his table to see him smiling as he stared at his book. She finished her breakfast, excusing herself from the two girls as she left the dining hall with Elijah to venture out into the city. The moderator had announced the day off over the loudspeaker earlier in the morning and if each person so chose, they were allowed to venture into the city to explore a little of the life in the capitol. Elijah grabbed Ophelia's hand as they made their way through the busy streets to do just that—explore and find what exactly the moderator was hiding. Elijah had tailed her as they saw her leave, staying a decent distance away as not to be seen. They stopped behind a nearby electrical station, the guards outside parting to allow her to pass through the doors.

"We have to get in there," he said, earning a nod from Ophelia.

"Get in where?"

Ophelia squealed as she and Elijah jumped in surprise to see Anika, Agatha and Wilson behind them.

"What are you three doing here? I thought you chose to train today," Elijah snapped.

"You two looked suspicious so we followed you, then noticed that you were in turn following the moderator. Why?" Agatha asked.

"She's up to something, something doesn't add up. Did you know we are meeting with Vaarem tomorrow to discuss the threat?" Ophelia asked. Each shook their heads in response. "Well, apparently we are and there is something that has been off about her ever since yesterday with the council."

"Alright, so how do we get in?" Wilson asked. It seemed to Ophelia's surprise that none of the other members had questioned anything she had just said, making her believe that she and Elijah were not simply being paranoid in their perceptions. The group watched as the door closed behind the moderator, discussing amongst themselves how to use their powers together to get past the guards. Once the plan was finalized, each of them diving into action to distract the guards as Anika dampened the locking mechanism and the door popped open.

"Let's go," she yelled as she turned to see the guards incapacitated. The five ran through the maze of dark hallways lit only by a small, thin light above them spanning the length of the corridor before them. Small sounds echoed from the throughout as the five guardsmen slunk along the wall single file. Lights of blue, white and purple lit up the corridor, startling the group as they pursued further.

"What *is* that?" Ophelia asked as the group moved closer to the sounds, her hands sliding along the wall beside her and they inched further in to the mysterious underground.

"Oh no," Wilson whispered, cursing under his breath earning questioning looks from the others as he sighed, "It looks like...electrical lights."

"*What*? But how could that be?" Agatha snapped, her whisper-like voice deafening in the corridor.

As the group moved toward the opening of the balcony looking over the room below, the group was horrified at what they saw below. Lined against the walls of the underground room, seemingly soundproof by air wielders that no one recognized, were clear, what looked to be plastic-like material cages, with—human beings inside of them.

"They're electricity wielders," Wilson breathed, each of them looking on in horror as they watched at least fifty electricity wielders of all ages standing in their clear cages as other wielders looked on, as if guarding them...or guarding the world *from* them.

"What *is* this place?" Ophelia asked before a hand fell on her shoulders, earning an audible gasp.

"Come and see," a sharp voice urged behind them. The moderator stood firm, her hand gripping Ophelia's shoulder tighter as she moved each of the guard toward the edge of the balcony.

"Long ago, when the secret guard was created after the city became secluded, five members of each element were put to the test to determine if they were strong enough, though it was all a rouse. The council, teaming with the Imperator, decided that a guard with superior control and abilities was not enough to keep the population under control. With fears of an attack hanging in the air, they all created a serum that, if given to each member, it would enhance their ability to control their powers and the people of Symador.

"The serum backfired on those born with electricity enhancing powers, creating uncontrollable monsters needing to be contained. The rest who had taken the serum succumbed to its abilities and were able to keep the electricity wielders at bay."

"Why are you doing this? Why are you helping them control us?" Elijah asked, the group keeping a barrier around Wilson, who had gone pale.

"I wanted to stop them, to cancel the program. So please, stop them, before it's too late," the moderator said, her normally icy voice calm and serene as the floor below began an uproar, flashes of light bursting all over the room, startling the group. The electricity wielders below had broken through their cells, unleashing their powers on their now controlled peers, the latter charging everything they had at the contained, orders being barked at them in fear from scientists hidden in the corners of the room below.

"We have to destroy it. All of it," Wilson whispered, the group staring at him in awe as color returned to his face, "I know what they are capable of. They will all destroy Symador in their wake."

Ophelia looked to her friend, her eyes wide with terror as Wilson sighed.

"It's the only way, Phi."

They were out of time as the fighting grew more violent below them. As the group moved to leave, they each looked back once more at the moderator's face, now calm as she nodded to them, a farewell.

The group stood just outside the building as not to be seen as they each locked hands and dug deep inside of themselves, remembering their training.

"After this, we can never come back here," Agatha said, a tear escaping her eyes as they all exchanged knowing looks. However, there was no other choice. As their powers moved as one, they collapsed the building holding the secret underground lab, everyone inside perishing under the rubble. They had saved Symador and kept its secrets, though this place was no longer safe for them.

Agatha had swiped gas masks and suits made from a strange type of fiber from the lab just before escaping, stealing enough for each other them in case of an emergency; Ophelia was impressed by her quick thinking. Returning to the training compound, they gathered enough food as Anika purified some water for each of them and suited up to sneak under the walled city. Elijah had heard rumors of a sealed underground tunnel that led outside of the walls and into the radiation filled terrain. Though uninhabitable, there was nowhere for them to go inside Symador, for the Imperator could see everything within the walled city.

"Will we survive?" Ophelia asked him as the group walked their way toward where Elijah had heard the tunnel could be located.

"I don't know. But if we die, then we die together," he responded, taking her hand in his as he led them down the dark underground hallway, hoping that it contained a way out.

OBSERVATIONS OF THE HEAD CHRONICLER

LIV EVANS

"My daughter, there are times of moral danger when the hardest virtuous resolution to form is flight, and when the most heroic bravery is flight."
- Charles Dickens

THERE IS A GRAVE MISCONCEPTION AMONG HUMANKIND THAT THE bravest acts involve standing one's ground and fighting, even when facing certain death.

Recorded history is full of tales about these righteous saviours, about these heroes. Rightfully so. Their spirit is not to be diminished based on the outcomes of their decisions, as they often allow others to achieve great things thanks to their sacrifice.

History, however, rarely acknowledges the quiet and unique bravery involved in flight. In retreating to live. In surviving to face another day. There have been many words for people who abandoned a cause, and so few of them are complimentary. Deserter, defector, absconder, betrayer, traitor, whistle-blower, refugee, delinquent.

It does not do to compare the two groups, however. That would not pay appropriate respect to either sort. They are both mentioned here to point out that there are options, in hopes to illustrate that neither is right or wrong, some are just more conventionally valued than others.

Cowardice and courage are often viewed as two opposing sides of a sliding scale. The more one leans toward either side, the less they have of the other. This perspective does not fit with the records of the Chroniclers. The stories I have read indicate that the difference between the two is merely a matter of perception. It is a face value judgment we use to make logical shortcuts. It is far easier to assume either quality than to dive into the reasons pivotal decisions were made.

Next time you see someone cry cowardice, remember the stories in this archive. Consider the tales of people who chose not to act, even if it meant disaster for another. Ponder the accounts of others who decided to act even if they knew it meant they would never be able to do so again. Try to suspend judgment and imagine the *why*. Consider all the knowledge and life experience that led up to that moment, and the endless threads of possibility that existed thereafter.

When you look deep enough, you will find that many things once thought of as cowardice were actually supreme acts of bravery. Acts of defiance of circumstances, resistance against an incompatible regime...

There is bravery in facing death head on, but there is also great courage in taking a stand against it and saying "not today", knowing full-well the struggle that will follow.

THE SILENT WATCHER

EMMIE HAMILTON

THE SILENT WATCHER

EMMIE HAMILTON

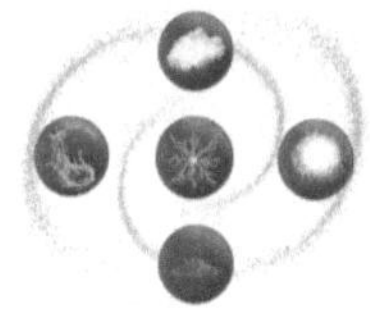

IN THE HEART OF THE LOWER DEPTHS, I AWAKEN TO THE SOUNDS of dogs scrapping outside my thin, plastic tarp wall. They whine loudly, no doubt fighting over the deformed bones of a pigeon we were forced to cook last night. Mama held off as long as she could, but it had been nearly seven days without anything more than a stale piece of bread and cold broth. She has four children to feed.

I lay in bed, wondering not for the first time why we are starving while a mile away, children are waking up to eggs and fresh vegetables free from the radiation and chemicals we have grown accustomed to in the Lower Depths. I feel the anger swell within me as I come to the same conclusion every time I allow my mind to wander in this direction.

Magic.

Mama does not possess magic, so we do not belong anywhere other than the dregs of society.

A sharp squeal sounded followed by a whimper and

silence. One of the dogs is the victor. If Mama heard, that means we will have something new to eat tonight. If anyone else living in the makeshift tarp city us non-magic users have been forced to dwell in heard, there will be more fighting and probably more death.

I raise myself from the thin mat placed on the ground. The heat is nearly unbearable and the sun has not risen yet. I unzip the opening and peer into the darkness. All is silent, except for soft cries from a nearby tent, and a baby screaming in another. These are common for me to hear. We are all starving, all wasting away from sickness. Our shanties lean against the outermost walls where the radiation poisoning has seeped through minuscule cracks. There is no medicine for people like us.

My eyes take several moments to adjust to the hazy darkness, but once they do, I walk to the side of my tent and find the misshapen animal with its neck twisted at an awkward angle. Its coat is greasy with dirt and grime, and it is still warm to the touch. I feel my way down its body, my fingers running over each hard ridge of its ribs, until they find two growths that don't belong on the body of a dog. They are bony and stick out like tiny stumps of unformed branches. They serve no purpose and will provide no extra meat for my siblings and me, but Mama might be able to find a use for them.

There are chunks of fur missing in some areas and my fingers sink into a hot, squishy patch of exposed skin. A faint *pop* sounds as I wrench my fingers free. Something sticky clings to my skin and I bring my hand to my nose, retching at the scent.

The dog is diseased and I just popped one of its sores. A

slight panic threatens to rise. If I have any abrasions on my own skin, I will become infected as well. And now that I've released the toxins into the air, we are all at risk.

Groaning inwardly, I lift the animal from the ground, surprised at its heft for being all skin and bones. Sweat prickles at my temples as I begin the half-mile walk to the incinerator. With any luck, Melba will be tending to the machines tonight.

My muscles shake with the effort but I try to stay silent as I hold the dog away from my body. It shouldn't take this much effort, but the pigeon wing I had last night was hardly enough to sustain me for this type of rigorous activity. I count the steps to distract myself from the threat of passing out.

The incinerator's hulking shadow grows closer, the sounds of the gears shifting and fires crackling faintly in the air. It runs every hour of the day, turning diseased crops, animals, and the deceased into ash. Melba usually works the night shift. She has enough power running through her veins to work the machine alone, allowing others with electric magic to properly rest for the day shift.

Melba is one of the lucky ones. When she turned eighteen, her elemental magic emerged and when it was her turn to take part in the Trials, she outlasted everyone else. She could have left the Lower Depths and chosen a more extravagant lifestyle, but she stayed behind. She still gets an increase in her rations of food, and she is lucky enough to have a partner with water magic, so she can have purified water whenever she wants.

I reach the gated enclosure and ring the buzzer. After a

moment, a woman's voice crackled through a speaker. "Who is it?"

When she hears no response, a red light flicks on, indicating the camera is in use. I take a step back so she can see what I'm holding.

"Kai? Is that you? Hold on."

The gate clicks open and I wait for the opening to get large enough to walk through. The urge to drop the animal was strong. At this point, I couldn't be sure I hadn't inhaled the toxins on the way over. The air is sprinkled with ash that melts like metallic snowflakes on my tongue and the blanket of humidity clings to my skin without a breeze to carry the disease or the stench of it away. I am grateful to have an empty stomach, otherwise, I might have emptied the contents of it along the way.

Struggling the last few steps, I make it to the side entrance, where Melba waits for me. She is tall and slender, with cropped black hair that sticks out at odd angles as if she had been electrocuted. A dim spotlight over the door casts shadows on her face, accenting the frown that mars her lips.

"Not another one," she whispers. "Shit, it's leaking. How long has it been dead for?"

Her dark eyes bore into mine and she reads the silent plea on my face. She holds her gloved hands out. "Give it to me, I'll take care of it."

I shake my head violently. Despite her overabundance of protective gear and my lack of it, I don't want her touching the animal. Melba notices my alarm and furrows her eyebrows.

"This isn't the first animal you've brought to me, Kai.

You know it's my job to..." her voice trails off, eyes widening with realization. "It carries the disease. Are you certain?"

My knees start buckling, and she quickly moves aside, allowing me through. I had only been inside once before when I brought her a bird with leaking pustules. Then, I was able to contain it and she quickly disposed of it without a problem. This creature, however, is much more of a danger to us.

Melba scoots past me, careful not to touch me or the animal, and leads me down a dimly lit metallic hallway, revealing a set of steps leading down.

If I could make a sound, she'd have heard me whimper, but nothing short of a broken exhale leaves my body. The stench quickly overpowers the narrow staircase and I silently urge Melba to hurry.

"You can leave him here," she says, pointing out a conveyor belt next to the landing. The space is tight with the three of us, and I stumble on the last step, scraping my ankle against its sharp edge, nearly dropping the animal. "Careful! If that toxin gets on us, it will be disastrous."

My heart quickens when she says this. It has gotten on me, and in fact, it feels as though it's snaking through my veins, infecting my blood. No, I can't think like this. It only landed on my skin. There was no way for it to seep inside.

My knees bump against a table, the cool metal a relief to my sticky skin. A fly buzzes near my ear. My hair drips down my neck. My stomach clenches, either in hunger or disgust. I can't tell the difference anymore. I place the animal down and immediately the belt activates. I jump back, not wanting my clothing to snag on the metal.

Melba is resting her hand against a plate embedded in the wall and sharp bursts of blue light crackle from her fingers. I watch as her power sends the conveyor belt through an arched opening and into the fires beyond.

It is stifling down here. My tongue is dry and scrapes against my mouth as I desperately will my body to produce something other than sweat to quench my thirst. Our water ration ran out yesterday and it strikes me that I can't remember when I last had a drink. I lean against the wall for support as I climb the stairs, my legs feeling like they are weighted down with bricks.

The groan and click of gears slows down and I hear footsteps patter on the stairs behind me. "Hey, Kai, you alright?"

Being mute has its obvious disadvantages, such as being unable to communicate the way others can or expect me to. I've learned how powerful body language is, and how energy is manipulated based on movement. It is how I know that Melba reaches her hand out and hovers it over my shoulder. It is my own personal superpower, even if I am not like the others.

I keep trudging up the stairs until I finally reach the hallway. The room spins and dark spots dot my vision, so I press my back against the wall, letting the cold metal seep through the thin fabric of my shirt. I blink and Melba is standing next to me.

"Shit, you look terrible Kai."

She grabs my arm and wraps it around her shoulder, helping me stand straight. We walk down the hallway but before we reach the door, Melba veers right, dragging me with her. We stop outside an archway and Melba shifts her positioning to allow her hand access to the lock. She holds her palm out and a flash of green light lights up the space so briefly, I think I hallucinated it.

"We're almost there," Melba pants next to me. I feel sorry for her being so close to me. The stench twists my insides, the heat presses against us, and there is no breeze. She must wish for death rather than help me for a minute longer.

Melba lets out a long whistle followed by two shorter bursts. The wall in front of us slides open, revealing a waiting room of sorts. We step in and the sound of gears shifting clangs through the dark space. I feel myself being lowered and marvel at the sensation. There should not be technology like this in the Lower Depths.

"Talc is down here," Melba says, referring to her partner. "There are no cameras. Do you understand what I'm saying?"

Her meaning is clear, though I have no way of telling her. We are entering a secret area, accessed by forbidden technology, and Imperator Vaarem has no way of finding out. I look at her, the double vision making concentrating on the right image more difficult, and nod once.

The platform we stand on jars to a stop. Melba holds tighter to me as I lose my balance. Another door slides open and Talc runs in, grabbing my other arm, and between the two of them, I am led to a chair and they force me to sit.

A cold glass is placed in my hand and my head rolls to the side, attempting to see it clearly. I lean closer marveling at the liquid. There is no blue hue, no trace of dirt or other particles floating in it. This is not water afforded to the Lower Depths.

"It's fresh water," Talc says. Condensation clings to the glass, allowing it to slide easier when Talc pushes it to me. I try to look at her but the room is spinning and I cannot find her eyes. I cannot see the deception that could lie within them.

The temptation overwhelms me and I try to lift the glass but only succeed in tipping it over. Grief like I have ever known consumes me and if I had any liquid in me, tears would slide down my cheeks.

"Damn it, he's worse than I thought," Melba says. Her voice lowers. "Get the IV."

"But-" An unrecognizable voice protests. There are more people here, wherever here is. I should be worried but can't seem to bring myself to feel much of anything.

"Now, Luca." Melba's voice is sharpened ice. "We can spare one."

A cloth rubs over my cracked lips and it takes me a moment to realize it is drenched. I eagerly open my mouth, willing any ounce of liquid to make its way onto my tongue. Talc places another cool cloth against the back of my neck. I shiver against the sensation, welcoming it.

A flurry of activity piques my curiosity so I glance to the spot where Melba stood just a moment ago and see a blur of bodies rolling a pole with a bag attached to it. Melba changes her leather gloves for a pair that looks like latex. Where did they get latex gloves? There are no factories left, no one is manufacturing anything new. Anything within a one-hundred-mile radius has already been raided, with the better items going to the Upper Crest

District and Imperator Vaarem. How did Melba get her hands on those?

"Open your mouth, Kai," Talc directs me. I heed her request and am immediately rewarded with more liquid squeezed onto my tongue. She finally makes eye contact with me, and I stare into their navy depths, drowning in them as much as I wished I was suffocating by the Pacific in this moment. "You're gonna feel a pinch in a few moments, okay?"

Just as she says that, I feel a break in the skin on my hand as something tears through me. My eyes widen in panic. I just carried a diseased dog, touched the toxins and have not cleansed myself. I should not be here. I should not be anywhere. I cannot tell them not to touch my hands. Shouldn't Melba know to warn them?

A minute later, I feel an odd sensation run through my veins, circulating their path throughout my body. I wonder for a moment if they are drugging me until I realize Melba said something about an IV. I remember learning about them. Hospitals used to supply them for their patients. They are hydrating me.

"You probably need about three of these things," Melba says, pointing at the bag swinging lightly on the pole beside me, "but we can't spare any more, not since we don't know what's happening in the coming days."

"Should we really be saying anything about...you know...?" I recognize the voice belonging to the one Melba called Luca. "We're already breaking a lot of rules, here."

The room has stopped spinning and I glance over in his direction, finally taking stock of where we are. A small group of people sit on a couch on the far wall, watching me curiously. Two have the same blond curly hair and face structure and I realize they must be siblings. The third person is a small boy with bug eyes and a stoop to his spine. As he reaches up to wipe the sweat off his forehead, I count three missing fingers.

Just behind them along the metallic wall is a sink and what looks to be an old microwave from at least a century ago. There are a few dishes scattered about and a small door that says Restroom.

"He is mute, it isn't like he can tell anyone." Talc juts out her hip and places a hand against it. "Plus we have known him for years. We can trust him."

The boy with missing fingers speaks up and I realize this is Luca. "Just because he's mute doesn't mean he's dumb. I'm sure there's plenty of ways for him to communicate."

I decide I don't like this Luca person, but he's right. I don't need my voice to speak or words to convey a message.

"Kai knows how to keep a secret. Right, Kai?" Melba asks, her eyes imploring me to agree with her. I nod my head once. If there is anything I can do, it's keep a secret, but I somehow feel like I am agreeing to more than that.

The two on the couch stand in unison and approach the table I am sitting at. From this close, I see that neither of them have eyelashes, making their piercing stares that much more penetrative. I shift uncomfortably in my chair and grimace as one crinkles their nose when they catch the scent of sweat and disease all over me. My ankle stings with the reminder of the scrape I endured a few minutes ago on the stairs.

"The sun is almost up," the one who crinkled their nose said. "Weekly ration distribution is starting soon."

"You should go now just in case...something happens," the other said, their voice barely a whisper.

Tova removed the needle from my hand and helped me to my feet, handing me a fresh glass of water. I down it quickly, barely giving myself a moment to enjoy the fresh taste of clean with no chemical tang marring it.

Melba gently grasps my wrist, the only place that appears relatively unmarred. "You need to be home by the seventh bell, Kai." She opens the door and ushers me into the chamber, pressing a button to close the elevator door. I hear the whirring of machines in the walls. As the door slowly closes, Melba bites her lip and repeats, "The seventh bell, Kai. You must be long gone by then. Understood?"

The door shuts and I feel the floor beneath me rise. In a moment I am alone in the hall to the side entrance door, though I have a feeling cameras are on me. I try not to think about who might be watching me as I leave.

The sun is a brilliant crimson as it rises over the outer wall. I estimate that it is about six in the morning just as the bell starts to ring. I groan inwardly. There is probably already a line for our weekly rations, which means I am unlikely to be out of there before the seventh bell. I had hoped to have time to change at least, but I will have to make do.

The ten minute walk from the incinerator feels like an hour. I have walked this path countless times in the past few years since Papa died and it has been up to me to get our rations. Today is different, though. It could be the little sleep or the dehydration sickness but I am certain it is something else.

Thick humidity and the lingering scent akin to burnt plastic turn my stomach. My shirt sticks to me and the scent is overwhelming. I remove it and stick most of it in my pocket, leaving the bottom to hang out. I used to be worried about the way my ribs stuck out but everyone in the Lower Depths looks like this, or they soon will if the system doesn't change anytime soon.

Sweat slides down my legs, stinging the cut to my ankle. I make a mental note to check it when I am under the safety of my tarp. People get strange about open wounds.

There is commotion in the line for weekly rations and as I get closer, I see the reason. The tank has less water than usual, and the crates of food are half of what is typically given. I cannot fathom the reason for this. More people have died in the past two weeks so there should be plenty of resources. If anything, we should be given more.

The look of disappointment on Mama's face almost stops me from entering the line altogether, but I have siblings to provide for, and I cannot wait longer to grab what is ours. The shouts at the front escalate and I start to worry about the time. I can't be sure what will happen after seven bells, but I know to take Melba's warning seriously.

Flies swarm around my face and stick to my skin. I can feel their wings twitch as they try to save themselves from the unknowing trap I set. Nearing the front of the line, I search for Lorna, a sweet older woman who helps pass out the weekly rations. She is nowhere to be found, replaced by militia men - citizens from the Upper Crest who are paid to protect the Imperator. What are they doing here?

Shouts break out and the person in front of me is pushed and falls backward. I hold my arms out to catch him, realizing too late that he is covered in sores. Jump back quickly and he slams to the ground, but not before clipping me in the ankle. The same one that I had injured before.

"Get back in line," one of the militiamen shouts, pointing a weapon at the crowd before him. "Next person to fall out of line gets no rations for the week!"

"You can't do this!"

"Where is Imperator Vaarem!"

"We need clean water!"

A movement grabs my attention and I see Luca slip through the mob and slide behind the militia men's stall. Briefly, he catches my eye and shakes his head at me, though whether it's to tell me to get out of there or to keep quiet, I am not sure. Probably both.

But I will not leave without this week's supply. We have no water, no food. The burden of my family's survival rests on my shoulders.

Just then, the bell strikes with a resounding clang echoing in the courtyard. I notice a few people in line exchange a look before peeling themselves away from the line. It's something I might have missed if I weren't mute, but being a silent watcher had its benefits.

I still don't have my rations for the week and now the bell has rung three times. Four. I elbow my way to the front, snatching an old plastic container and bag of food. Shouts of "Hey!" and "Thief" follow me.

But I am no thief, only desperate to survive.

The fifth bell echoes when I hear the imperator's booming voice over the chaos of the mob now fighting over each other to get to the militiamen.

"Silence," he says. It takes a few moments before everyone realizes who is speaking to them. The imperator steps up onto a platform behind the stall. He is wearing long dark pants and a cape around his neck. His shirt was unbuttoned. His skin is free of dirt smears and his hair is brushed - *brushed* - back from his forehead. The fabric of his clothing has a sheen in the dawn, no doubt a special material to keep him cool. Those from the Lower Depths don't have access to anything like that.

The sixth bell echoes.

Luca sprints from behind the water truck and though I know the Imperator is the cause of us having no food, the cause of us dying from radiation poisoning, I drop the rations I just took. As the seventh bell rings, I tackle the Imperator to the ground.

A gust of wind slams me just as a blast shakes the land. The pain in my ankle spreads up my leg and I wonder for a moment if I broke it. The shrill explosion renders me deaf until a slight piercing ring is the only thing I can hear. Dust is thick in the air.

Imperator Vaarem lays on his back, his breath heaving through the dirty air. He probably isn't used to something so unclean in his lungs. I'm disgusted with myself. This man is the cause of thousands of deaths, to our illness and suffering, all because we do not possess the magic that others do. Because magic makes us worthy to live a more comfortable existence, according to him.

Melba warned me this would happen and now I have let her down because I followed some instinct or sense of honor that I didn't know existed for this man.

"You knew." His gritty voice grates me. I shake my head, determined to end the shrill noise but he mistakes it for denial. "Don't lie to me, boy."

He sits up, eying me with disgust. I don't hesitate to do the same to him. His eyes linger on my ankle and I follow his gaze until I notice thick black lines coming from the gash on my ankle and running up my leg. Panic sets in.

The disease.

Breathing heavily, I try and fail to stand up. "Don't move," the Imperator's voice cuts through. He cocks his head at me and a look of recognition comes over his face as his eyebrows raise in surprise. "I know you."

This time I do shake my head, though I don't know why. He has spies everywhere, probably hidden cameras. He knows who everyone is, which makes it worse that he knowingly allows so many people to suffer.

"You are the boy who cannot speak. The one who holds all the secrets."

There's no point in denying his claim so I remain silent.

"I can heal you, you know. We have the means in the Upper Crest. I have my own healers at my beck and call." The thought of that disgusts me. He can heal the disease, the one that is a blight on the Lower Crest, but he has chosen not to. For months—years— he has let us live like this. The Imperator continues. "You tell me who planted that bomb, and I will help you. A life for a life."

The refusal was etched all over my body, from the tightness of my limbs and the way I looked away from him.

Screams and chaos rang in the air and a pool of blood slowly trickled its way toward me. The imperator did nothing to see to his people and instead keeps his gaze on me.

"You will die, Kai Slaigon. You will die, and then your mother and your five younger siblings will follow. And it will be on your shoulders, because you are not agreeing to the very generous offer I made." He paused a moment as if considering who he speaks to. If his words affect me at all. "Ah, I know...I'll heal you, and I will increase your rations to twice a week."

My eyes shot over to him, wondering if he is telling the truth or only saying what he thinks I want to hear. And I do —I desperately want to believe.

"All you have to do is tell me who is behind this. Decide now, Kai. You truly only have moments left."

He is right, I know he's right because my vision blurs and nausea strikes me. Militia men run to us, pointing their guns at me and surrounding their Imperator from harm. Idiots. If they could see what state I'm in, they'd know I'm the least threatening person in the Lower Dephs.

Rations. And he can cure the disease. I don't want to turn on Melba and the others, but I'm terrified to die and leave mother and my sisters to fend for themselves. Dread fills me as I know I am about to turn traitor and give away information I never wanted in the first place.

Slowly, I rise to my feet. "Help him, help him," Imperator Vaarem impatiently orders. Rough hands grab me and force me to my feet.

I look at the horizon, scanning the crowd for any sign of Melba, of Luca, or the twins with the strange eyes. It is a risk, not knowing who else is involved in this rebellion, but it is either risk their wrath or die. Finally I nod once and point to a sprawling dark shadow in the distance, its chimneys spewing ash into the air.

The incinerator.

OBSERVATIONS OF THE HEAD CHRONICLER

LIV EVANS

"Both of us victims of the same twentieth-century plague. Not the Black Death, this time; the Gray Life."
- Aldous Huxley

So few things in life are simple.

So few things are what they seem.

Imperator Vareem and those in his employ are clever like that. They know how to control people. They know what makes them vulnerable. They know how to wear them down.

The concept of brainwashing was formulated back in the 20th century. The idea was that it is possible to reprogram the way a person felt, thought, and behaved. Whilst it could be seen in extremely evident, polar changes, later research showed just how coercive and subtle those shifts could be.

With a mixture of indoctrination, threats of violence,

isolation, degradation, and sporadic kindness, even the most headstrong of people can be manipulated. This can occur in any type of relationship, from an intimate level to a civic one.

Symador has this system mastered.

They have created a regime that is nigh unquestionable. Their truth is absolute, their power unshakeable. Every time someone dare doubt their purpose, they are swiftly reminded that the one true goal of the walled city is to protect them. The act of questioning, of defying, is seen as a coup against not only oneself, but the very world in which one lives. Rebellion, then, is tainted as a selfish, foolish act.

There are repercussions for people who do not comply with Symador's regime. There is the outright violence: executions, assassinations, imprisonment, torture—for the person themselves and, perhaps more potently, the people they hold dear. Once someone has seen enough violence, the rulers don't even need to carry it out anymore. The mere hint of it is enough to have most people quaking. In Symador, violence wafts through the city, a sharp tangy scent on a breeze that catches one's attention and has them on high alert, even if they don't know why.

The degradation varies by location but never in intent. Those of the upper echelons are forced to serve unquestioningly, to dedicate their lives to uphold the tenets of a regime that is more important than their humanity. They are reduced to marionettes, their faces painted with crimson smiles that slash through their independence and dull the hope in their wooden hearts. The lower dregs are not exempt from this either, although their degradation is clearer to see. The way people are forced to live, to beg for the very basic things to sustain life, is a constant drag on the human spirit. It weighs heavily on their shoulders until they believe they deserve it. That it's just their lot in life. And then, right in the middle, you have people who yearn for higher positions yet feel they're not allowed to complain about their own because others have it so much worse. They still struggle, but they form the opinion that a little hard work and dedication is all that is needed to progress. They do this to protect themselves from the true nature of their reality. Progress is rare, and it is easier to pretend it is attainable than to accept it was never meant for them. It is far easier to hate yourself than to hate the invisible cage you are trapped in.

But none of this would work without a fine dusting of kindness. Without the light. Without the false sparks of life and hope. It is seen in the joy of the trials, the spectacle of parades, the whisper of a better future, and the false veneer of progress. These moments allow citizens of a hellish cityscape to believe that maybe, just maybe, they can tolerate their lot. The dark moments are worth wading through when the sweet ones like these exist.

This is how Symador changes people. *This* is how it shapes them. This is how it gets the most aspirational souls to roll over and allow themselves to be brutally trampled. How it can turn lovers into enemies and friends on friends.

This is how Symador wins.

THE HUNTSMAN, THE MOTH AND THE DRAGONFLY

VICTORIA JADE MOSS

THE HUNTSMAN, THE MOTH AND THE DRAGONFLY

VICTORIA JADE MOSS

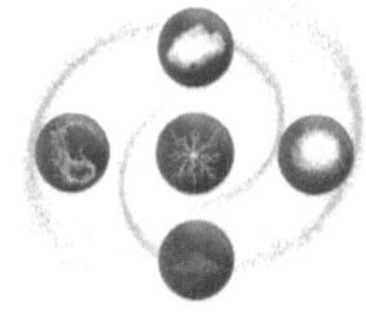

THE MAN WAS GOING TO DIE. THAT WAS NOA'S FIRST THOUGHT. Her second was she just may be in the blast radius. Positioned in the rafters of a musty workshop cloaked in shadows and cobwebs, Noa surveilled her target. He was no expert alchemist; that was clear enough by the highly volatile chemicals he left unstoppered, set carelessly beside accelerants. *Idiot.* Either he didn't know any better or wanted to blow himself up. The latter would save her the hassle. The ramshackle shed she was crouched in was once used to formulate and produce radiation medication for those destined for the grim life in the outermost regions of Symador. Lack of ingredients and humanity from those of influence saw to its closure. Enter ill-intended opportunists. Drug labs were nothing new in the Lower Sector, but this particular chemist was the creator of a lethal strain of Raptor that had been circling and was responsible for more deaths than any other opioids combined. One hit and even the most hardened users were prone to a fatal overdose. A serial killer who fancied himself a mad scientist.

It had been going on for months, yet no one—including the government—did anything to stop it. Until now. But not for free. The Vanguard had been hired by a tailor from the Upper Sector whose son died overindulging in one of the slum's pleasure houses. The tailor was a wretch of a man with few people skills, which was a polite way to say he was a fascist swine. He also had enough money from dressing the richest of the Select—and offered an amount so appealing—The Huntsman, the crew's boss, accepted the job without blinking.

From intel gathered by Moth, the Vanguard's ears, Noa could recognise the contents of each vial and flask. She also knew exactly which one needed only the slightest encouragement from the proper element to reduce this derelict shed and her target to cinders.

She grew tired of waiting for his own negligence to spark a combustion. *It would have been a more poetic end,* she had thought, *for him to become a splattered mess of blood and gore in his pursuit to kill others.* But she would happily play the middleman.

A bead of sweat had rolled from the man's craggy face, his gloved hand trembling as he lifted a vial to add it to the mix. So, he had some idea of how dangerous the ingredients were, after all, if he was nervous. Noa smiled. Let the last emotion he feels be one rooted in fear. Spearing her power into the substance, she allowed her magic to become familiar with it. The feel, the weight, density, how it recoiled from the reactive ingredients. But that's precisely what she wanted: a reaction. A big one. So, she pushed back, isolating those molecules and oxidising the substance. It was a dance, reducing the hydrogen and forcing the oxygen to accept the electrons. Anticipation was an iron knot in her chest, but she kept her breathing steady. Calm. Noa didn't often work so intimately with the individual atoms. Her lip was a veritable chew toy. She split her concentration between the brewing explosive and constructing a shield, completely encircling herself in a protective bubble of solid air.

A strange sensation tugged at her magic; she pulled her focus back to the flask, which was teetering on the edge. Too much. She had given it too much oxygen.

Her eyes widened. "Oh shit."

The workshop exploded. The world was nothing but a shaking, burning blur. Like a comet, Noa was engulfed in the blast, sent plummeting through the air, debris slamming into her barrier with such velocity her teeth gritted, straining to hold it in place.

The ground was fast approaching. A breath before collision, she threw out a blanket of power. Catching herself on a cushion of air, Noa curled up, covering her eyes against the blinding glare as a wall of flames rolled over her shield, a blazing orb-shaped wave of red and orange. Sweat formed on her brow from the intensity of the heat. The inferno pummelling against the surface like an invading army. She briefly wondered how fire-wielders dealt with the sensation all the time. But she held out, weathered it, until the inferno had subsided.

She dispersed her magic, landing in a crouch, chest heaving, ears ringing, sweat a second coating on her skin.

That was one way to burn some calories, she supposed. *And a body.*

Noa straightened, brushing off her palms as she took in her handywork. Spot fires still burned, the rubble a mess of twisted metal and charred remains. Plumes of white billowed, smothering the surrounds. With a thought, Noa stole the oxygen from the remaining fires and then sent the smoke upwards in a funnel until it reached high enough to disperse into the night sky. The locals didn't need to breathe in any more pollutants, and she sure as hell wouldn't be the reason they had to.

A minute passed. Then another. Still, the smoke kept emerging, showing no sign of lessening. Whatever was in those chemicals, it was producing an unusually excessive amount.

She had to get back, had to give her report and follow up on a lead for a new job. Besides, her magic reserves were getting dangerously low. She probably wouldn't have anything left to regulate her air supply for the walk to the Compound. *But the smoke...*

She couldn't let it spread to those unsuspecting people who lived nearby. So, Noa sat down, the ground rocky and hard beneath her, and continued playing chimney. Until there was no sign of dangerous smoke left. Until her magic was as barren as the world beyond the walls.

THERE HAD BEEN A TIME, LONG AGO WHEN CIVILISATION HAD BEEN different. Better. Of course, things were never perfect, and there were always those who cared for none other than themselves. But there was a time when humankind gripped onto compassion more tightly than greed. But the scales tipped. Technology rose, and the cost of living soared higher than the metal structures built to pierce the brilliant canvas of the sky. And life as it had been became unattainable to all but the 1%. Humans had spread like a plague, taking and taking and leaving too much in their wake. A funeral procession of waste. Consumerism and waning resources hacked at that once coveted thread of compassion until it frayed—until it snapped.

Like the earth itself was punishing them for their war on nature and each other, for the abominations too many of those in power became and the havoc they wreaked, radiation rose, and man fell.

And though the walled city of Symador looms, a corrupt beast riddled with devastation, humankind continues. But they may never stand again.

Chenoa Haines didn't glance up when a presence appeared on the other side of the timber benchtop she was carving a nonsensical pattern into with her hunting knife. "Seat's taken."

"The Dragonfly takes flight at dawn to the crimson tree."

She paused mid-gouge, recognising the code. Noa waved a hand, offering the vagrant to sit. Keen eyes marked the state of the woman. It was an effort not to grimace. Even with the stench of spilt ale, unwashed bodies of the other patrons, and refuse wafting in from the street that had coalesced into one rancid creature of poverty, she could smell the woman.

Dammit, Fly. The girl could never turn a client away, no matter how destitute. But they weren't in the business of working for free. In this deplorable excuse of society, they, too, have to survive. The least she could do was hear her out, and then track down Fly and squish her beneath her shoe.

"My son," the woman croaked. "He filled in for a Runner friend of his, didn't come home. I don't have much, but I've saved three rations. Find him, they're yours."

Surveying the woman, Noa noted the slight sway of her outreached hand as it grasped the paper tokens, the raspiness to her tone not just from pollution but hoarse from dehydration. For three weeks, a mother had starved herself to the point of passing out all to have some currency to deal in.

They didn't usually take jobs for rations; it seemed a bit redundant. Not that the Vanguard were saints or bound by any real code of honour, but taking from people in need was something even they refused. Granted, not all crime factions worked that way, but there was more than one reason they were the city's most prolific crew.

In a flash of movement, Noa swiped the tokens, inspecting their authenticity. In a past job, they had dismantled a counterfeiting ring that thought distributing forgeries throughout the lower sectors would help ease the rate at which people died of starvation. But the fakes were too easily discernible to the Symguards, and any caught with them were hanged. Even those unaware of the fraudulence. That's what happened to those with good intentions: a quick drop and a sudden stop.

"For which sector?"

Silence was the woman's response. Not exactly helpful.

"I don't have all day, lady." It was true. She was due back at the Compound just after dawn and still had to scout the Western Quarter.

"Upper."

Noa snorted a humourless laugh, the sound empty as the Western Wastes. No wonder she didn't want to answer. "The Huntsman isn't reckless enough to take jobs in the Upper Sector. And certainly not for stale bread and potatoes."

Standing, she dug out her knife from the timber and tossed the papers back down. "We're done here."

Turning to leave, she was stopped by an iron vice. Nails, like the frigid, death grip of a corpse, dug into her arm hard enough to break skin. The deep-sunken eyes of the woman bore so desperately into her own that it almost stirred some feeling in her chest. Almost.

Digit by digit, Noa removed the woman's hold, sharpening each word. "The Huntsman doesn't risk their life or that of their crew for scraps, lady."

The stagnant, dust-clad air beckoned Noa to the streets beyond when a strangled sob escaped the woman. Facing her, Noa's eyes traced the image of the distraught mother, barely more than rag and bones, useless to her missing child. There was that thing again—a tiny, pathetic flop of a heart long done caring. Chin raised, Noa's expression turned to ice. "This is Symador; everybody has a sob story, just as they have bellies to feed."

A BREEZE MOVED LIKE AN INVISIBLE RIBBON THROUGH FINGERS, the skeletal trees rustling under Noa's ministrations, radiation forced upwards wherever her wind travelled. She often worked to cleanse the area she was in—whenever she could spare the energy. But she had work that needed her magic and focus. In a meditative state, she had unfurled her power, stretching it across the landscape like a blanket of silk, each thread connecting her to the very fabric of the atmosphere. Of life. All was still this time of the morning, the hazy smudge of sun not yet tainting the horizon. There were far too many vermin scuttling about, but Noa had learned to tune such things out, focusing only on larger life forms.

There was a sudden stirring in the air. Her eyes snapped open, zeroing in on the commotion at a nearby roadside. A slight girl slipped from the stormwater run-off and tumbled down an embankment. Following after her was the dead weight of an even deader man. By the looks of his garb, he'd been a Carter. From her perch on a precariously constructed roof, Noa smirked, "Attagirl."

She sent a breeze her way, helping shift the corpse from where it landed atop the struggling girl. Whatever the guy had done, Noa was sure it was deserved. The taste of liquor seeping from his pores was strong enough to have her spooling her power back into herself. Considering the early hour, it was a safe bet he was no upstanding citizen. There were too many lowlifes and not enough policing protecting those society deemed dispensable. Lowlifes that would not think twice about harming a disenfranchised girl. So, Noa waited for the girl to clamber back to the top of the embankment, waited till she had disappeared from sight before dismounting and taking off in the direction of the Compound. Not sparing a second thought to the corpse left to bloat and fester in the blistering heat soon to greet them.

Just another day in paradise.

THERE WAS A TIME BEFORE NATURE BECAME THE PERVERTED mockery it is now when it was pure, utterly captivating in its beauty, even more so in its wildness.

For generations, stories had been passed down through Noa's family, the only thing of value they had considering the abject conditions in which she was born. Beneath a threadbare blanket, huddled together under a wooden table with uneven legs, her mother would tell her how the world had once been. Painting a picture so vivid and dazzling, it was the surest way to calm a scared child during a dust storm. Especially one who felt the panic in the air and tasted the fear of others, their screams woven into each gust. A child whose magic had awoken a decade before it was supposed to.

An anomaly, a miracle, her mother would whisper, barely audible over the riotous storm outside. *Born with the song of the wind in your heart.*

By her next birthday, Noa was an orphan. The thing

that made her blood sing, the reason her soul soared, was also why her mother's voice was a memory so distant she often mistook it for the wind itself. During the first few years surviving in the contaminated streets of the Lower Sector, she would spend her nights dreaming about what it would have been like to exist in a time when the air was clean. What it would be like to taste the salty air tumbling from the spray of an ocean wave as it broke, a rising and falling mass of liquid sapphires and emeralds, each drop of seawater a gem humankind would never see again. Or a summer-scented breeze racing through meadows at a mountain's feet, carrying the sweet fragrance of wild-flowers and untold secrets of hidden valleys and unchartered canyons.

Mostly, she wished to know the change in the air before it rained. That, she was told, was one of the most underappreciated treasures of nature. How it seemed as if the very essence of the world shifted, the change both subtle and profound. A veil of unmistakable aroma that every living creature innately recognised. Petrichor. Soil would exhale the scent of minerals, rising in tendrils to greet the coming rain.

It was crisp, fresh and filled with the promise of nourishment, clean water. It was life. It was hope.

Now, it only rained ash.

And hope was a starving mother begging a mercenary who could barely remember her own—pointless.

"FLY, REPORT." FLY—SHORT FOR DRAGONFLY—STRAIGHTENED. Tasked with being the crew's eyes, Noa felt, sometimes, she saw too much, like every micro-movement or expression any of them made exposed more than they wanted.

However, The Huntsman and Bull were really the only ones who kept to themselves, hoarding their secrets and vulnerabilities like the Select did clean water. With skin carved from the darkest hour of night, aiding her in blending seamlessly into shadows, she was the best damn spy around. Dragonfly's greatest asset, though, had nothing to do with appearance and everything to do with her ability to see all and be seen by none. Even through curtains of pollution and the constant blanket of dust that suffocated Symador, her vision was razor-sharp.

Dragonflies were once known to have the greatest number of lenses per eye than any creature, eyes which covered nearly their entire heads, granting them close to 360-degree vision. They died out long ago, as most animals had.

Gathered in the Compound common area, the members of the Vanguard crime crew suppered. Most of the food courtesy of Bull and his earth-wielding powers, which he used to cultivate the greenhouse. The rest was because of the lucrative business The Huntsman had established.

Fly swallowed whatever she'd been chewing. "The Butcher was killed."

The sound of eating ceased, everyone stopping to stare.

"Bullshit," Raj blurted, mouth agape.

Fly gave a confirmatory dip of her chin. The room

erupted in howls, cheers echoing off the warehouse's rafters and cocooning them in a cacophony of celebration.

Jett jumped onto the long dining table, stein raised to the room like an offering to gods everyone had forgotten, just as they had been forgotten in turn. "Shall we toast the demise of the oh-so-legendary assassin?"

More hollering and laughs answered.

The Huntsman cleared their throat. Just twice. A quiet but pointed sound, two shots of a gun with a silencer. It was all that was needed. Everyone returned to their seats, carrying on with the meal.

A hand gesture from The Huntsman had Fly continuing her report. "Was a shameful death. Two sewer boys caught him in the middle of a job—broad daylight—saved the girl, killed him easily enough."

"Anything of note about the girl?"

It was Moth who replied, having gleaned the intel from her own adept sleuthing, "The new Commander of the Guard."

"Bet ya it was Big V that took out the hit. Don't think he'd be too chuffed with a girl running his mob."

"We don't deal in theories, Raj," said Noa, ignoring the ridiculous nickname he took to calling Imperator Vaarem.

The Huntsman went on, "And the explosions, are they related to the ones last summer? The attack on the Guild?"

"Family squabble among the Elite, the latter the work of a madman."

Three explosions, countless wounded, some dead because of a family feud? It nearly made Noa glad she didn't have one. Apart, she supposed, from the sorry bastards surrounding her now. Using a hunting knife, The

Huntsman carved a chunk from an apple, popping it into their mouth. "The Roster?"

On the topic of possible jobs, Noa shot daggers at Fly, who pretended not to see it. They were all required to source work. The boss would then divvy it up between them or assign roles in a joint job, where multiple skill sets and bodies were needed.

At this point, they were a well-oiled machine, although Noa preferred to operate alone. When the whole crew was together, things could become... chaotic. They did the job perfectly, but the horseplay commenced the instant they were off the clock. The most guilty being the twins, Raj and Jett, who both had a mischievousness about them that no amount of training or misfortune could purge from their systems. They had been that way ever since Noa caught them trying to pilfer her little store of food she had managed to scrounge up when she was fourteen and living on the streets. A knife to Jett's throat, a few vicious threats of dismembered body parts, and they became fast friends. It was the last time they tried to eat any of Noa's food, but not the last time she held a blade to them.

"A bunch of Raptor addicts are causing trouble for a few Middle Sector merchants. Said they'd pay top dollar for someone to return the favour."

"Are they under Vaarem's employ?"

"Of course not, Boss. I know the rules." Jett hardly concealed the hint of hurt colouring his voice.

It was one of the only laws this lawless lot followed, one of The Huntsman's few requests when they found each member in whatever horrid excuse of a life they'd been shackled to and inducted them into the Vanguard. Raj often joked how they were trophies The Huntsman collected and turned into canny criminals; little insects stuck in their web. Huntsmans, of course, didn't weave webs, but Raj also thought rocks were just eggs that never hatched and then calcified.

"Take Bull. Get it done." Bull, the crew's muscle, gave a barely perceptible nod, never really one for words. The twins started up on how best to execute the mission, but Noa decided to take her leave.

Heading for her room in the warehouse attic, she collapsed onto her bed, the timber crate frame groaning under the weight, exhaustion gnawing at her, oblivion beckoning. Noa tried to sleep, the quickest way to recharge her magic, but every time she grew closer to its embrace, she was bombarded with the image of a vagrant woman crying for a son who never came home.

When Noa's power started stirring, showing signs of its existence, she feared it. Feared what it could mean and the depth of the well that continued to expand with age. It would only bring about bad things; she was sure of it. For years, she had seen teenagers leave their boroughs and suffer the trials. If they had magic, it meant they were of use to society and were put to work. Different work than those without. Work that usually took them away from their families, and that was what Noa truly feared the most. So, she repressed it, as long as she could, ignored the call of her name when the wind blew, how it made her heart grow wings to feel the whispering of midnight breezes when it seemed the whole of the world was asleep, and it was just her and the dancing air, begging her to join it. Even as it grew so strong, it broke free of the confines she'd built whenever she became angry, sad, or excited. Any magnified emotion of a child.

Destruction would lay in its wake. Busted furniture and plates of pitiful food splattered against the walls. Once frightened, Noa had recoiled so far into herself that she drew all the oxygen in the room with her. She hadn't even realised what she'd done until her mother dropped to the floor, wheezing and clutching her throat. Noa ran away that night. She had made it to the Western Wall when her mother had caught her and held her so tightly she felt the impression of her arms for years.

You are my wind-weaver, her mother whispered, such love in her voice—her heart. *Do not fear it. Nurture it, protect it, treat it with kindness and respect so it may one day save the world.*

But Noa was no hero. In fact, some days, she had the urge to rip the air from everyone's lungs and watch as they asphyxiate at her feet. Just for living, for breathing while her mother no longer did. Because Symador took anything sweet and kind-hearted and smothered it with starvation, prejudice, disease and grief until it was nothing but an empty shell. One better suited for survival. Not living but surviving. That's all Noa's ever done since.

THE NEWS HAD ARRIVED A FEW DAYS LATER, THE BIGGEST JOB TO come about in years. Moth and Fly had caught murmurs of it from rival crews, the buzzing of deals in the making.

"A package?" The Huntsman confirmed.

"Of extremely high value, enough for them to pay a king's ransom for its swift and discreet delivery." Fly shared a conspirator's smirk with Noa. Swift and discreet, their specialty.

"Contraband?" Jett asked, casting aside his playing cards, the possibility of law-breaking finally garnering his full attention.

"It doesn't matter what, not for that price," said Moth. On that, they could all agree.

"Hit the streets, secure us the job."

At The Huntsman's orders, the Vanguard dispersed.

WAITING BESIDE AN IMPATIENT RAJ, NOA'S TEETH GRINDING WAS surely audible. They were the first two to arrive back at the Compound, and it was taking all her control not to swat him over the head at his incessant shifting. His bouncing knee had hit the table more than once, but still, his fidgeting continued.

"What. Is. The. Matter." She realised the question sounded more like a threat. Raj didn't seem to care.

"Just nervous, I need a new gig. Something else to think about."

"Why so desperate for distraction?"

"No real reason."

Lie. Noa could taste it on the air. And for all his skills, deception wasn't one. Raj had been more reserved, his antics few and far between ever since his run-in with the

Raptor addicts, so she asked, "What happened in the Middle?"

His gaze snapped to hers, surprised that she had been able to guess the connection to his mood. It was no guess. Noa had only lived this long, thanks to her magic and astuteness. "I knew one of them. She used to leave food out for me and J whenever she had earned extra tokens. Clean as they came. But the woman I saw the other night, she's...." He shook his head, his mess of curls falling forward as his shoulders slumped.

She waited for the emotion to pass, for him to continue. "I asked what the hell had gone wrong for her to end up like that. She wasn't one to just try it or chase a high. Said her little sister had gone missing, then her father hanged for trespassing when he went lookin' for her."

He didn't need to say more; it was a story too typical in the Lower Sector. When their pain became too much, when they became so desperate for a moment's reprieve from their impoverished lives, they turned to something they might never have considered before: drugs. And it was only too easy to become addicted. But Raj had mentioned earning extra tokens. Only magic users had that opportunity.

"What element did she have?" Past tense. Because Raptor completely muted powers. It was one of the main reasons Noa always turned away from such vices, even when she had been homeless and took to staying in drug dens for shelter, sleeping amongst unconscious bodies of those riddled with the substance. To lose touch with her magic was unimaginable. An existence not worth maintaining, not without that part of her.

Again, Raj was taken aback. *Now it was just becoming insulting.* She shot him a glower, and his lips twitched, "Fire, nothing too special in ways of strength."

If the woman was a wielder, her sister would likely have been as well, but they wouldn't know until she was tested. That was how it worked ninety-nine percent of the time. Noa had been the exception to the rule. The thoughts fell away as the others returned.

Fly was last to enter the room, out of breath and frustration heavy on her brow. "The Marauders got it."

"What." Everyone straightened at the pure wrath coating The Huntsman's word. They didn't need to have air magic to feel the storm brewing.

"Apparently," she said, apprehension trickling into her demeanour, "the client had stakes in that drug lab we blew up."

We. Noa bristled at the accusation, even if the Dragonfly didn't really level one. It was no group effort destroying that lab. Which meant they lost the job because of her. A sudden squall picked up outside, her power rising with her temper. It wasn't only the implication that angered her but that someone other than the chemist she'd killed was responsible for that abomination of a drug; worse, they had profited from it.

The Huntsman, however, didn't comment on it. "The Marauders are a mid-level crew at best. To win this bid will send a message that they are moving up the rank. We cannot allow that."

Jett picked up on the thread, mischief alighting his face. "Devilry on the mind, Boss?"

The Huntsman's smile was a thing of nightmares. "Let

us show this client the true cost of his greed."

THEY WERE GOING TO STEAL THE PACKAGE. WAS IT OUT OF SPITE? Mostly, but also to send a message. The Vanguard were the most notorious crew in Symador, and keeping that status meant keeping them fed, clothed and untouchable by those who would wish to harm them.

Amid the smog that shrouded the Eastern District of the Lower Sector, the members of the Vanguard littered the shadows, waiting for the signal to strike. Their intelligence, courtesy of Moth and Fly, had pinpointed this narrow alley as the smugglers' chosen route. Not the worst decision the Marauders could have made, but it was far from the smartest. At least it made their job easier.

The muted light from the oil-lit lamppost cast reflections on the graffiti-covered walls of the buildings. All in varying degrees of disrepair like the rest of the slums. Windows were covered with an array of odd materials, whatever the locals could find in junkyards. Very few had glass panes left, but nothing truly stopped the dust from breaking through or the radiation. A sudden stirring in the air, like the crack of a whip, came from the south. Noa gave a two-part whistle, alerting the others that Moth was in position.

Clad in a dark, form-fitting suit, she was indistinguishable in the night, her heart thundering with anticipation. Down the alley, the low creaking of hinges and clopping of hooves on dirt grew louder. Their targets getting closer. The Marauders were riding in heavily modified carriages designed for speed and security, mirror-image to those utilised by the Imperator, perfect for the operation because no one would dare trifle with them. No one bar them. She was, admittedly, mildly impressed by the resourcefulness, especially for a mid-level crew.

The package was believed to be a cache of contraband weapons the Select had been sourcing and hoarding for protection against the growing dissonance among the lower sectors. At this point, it didn't matter what it was. This was about principle. Moth signalled the approaching convoy's position.

As the first carriage came into sight, Noa, still invisible to their eyes, sprung into action. Darting nimbly across the rooftops, she used air to keep her footsteps featherlight, a silent wraith in the night. She tossed a palm-sized glass canister and sent a slither of air to steer it directly into the carriage's path. It was a new invention, filled with the substance the assassinated chemist had in his possession, now with the exact measurements and level of oxidisation to create the perfect smoke bomb. Another rotation of the wheel had the smugglers driving straight over the canister. The glass shattered. Instantly, the alley filled with thick, obscuring mist. Noa quickly coaxed the fog to surround only the rival crew before it could get out of control.

At the sound of a second whistle, the rest of the Vanguard launched their ambush. From either side of the street, vines thick as rope snaked over the ground, tangling around the spokes of the wagon, growing in strength and size until they were as inescapable as iron chains. Until the Marauders were nothing but lambs set to face the slaughter.

Spooked by the smog, the horses bucked and reared, fighting to break free of the binds. Yells from the smugglers joined the braying as they emerged from the carriages in search of the threat, only to drop where they stood. Like phantoms rising from the smoke, Raj and Jett were poised with tranquillising darts, firing with the accuracy of any sharpshooter. Where they aimed, a body dropped. It wasn't fatal, just a concoction of sedatives the Ratroaches had come across in the sewers, then bartered for an extravagant price.

Chaos reigned, the Marauders struggling to understand what was happening and who exactly was attacking them. The Vanguard didn't give them the chance to figure it out. Taking advantage of the confusion, The Huntsman and their crew closed ranks, advancing from their nooks to incapacitate the remaining men with a brutal sort of efficiency that struck fear into most. Even the Symguards knew to look the other way when they crossed paths.

Lowering herself from the rooftop on a current of air, Noa landed on the street, falling into step beside the Moth and the Dragonfly as they finished their task of releasing the horses. They exchanged glances, adrenaline setting their gazes alight. Moth flashed Noa a wink, and for once, she allowed herself to feel the thrill, the triumph, and even the camaraderie. But the mission wasn't over. Where the women stepped, the smoke split, skewing around them as they headed to the back of the middle carriage—the one carrying the package. Raj and Jett were already there with the Bull. Jett's pale face was set in a frown as he rubbed at his palms.

"What's wrong?" Fly asked, of course, noting the same thing.

Raj was smiling. "Those smoke bombs worked a little too well."

"I tripped," he grumbled, holding up his hands, both torn up and beaded with blood. Noa snorted a laugh, the others sharing jeers at his expense.

"Bolt cutters," The Huntsman ordered from their position in front of the wagon's double doors. Bull obliged.

"Ready the cart," they said to Moth. Without a word, the girl disappeared. The sound of metal on metal filled the alley, and a moment later, the doors swung wide, revealing a single wooden crate. It was smaller than Noa had been expecting. If it indeed contained weapons, it wasn't much of a haul.

The twins weren't disheartened. "Can we open it now?"

"Yes! Can we, Boss?" Jett parroted, all woes of wounded hands forgotten.

Like children, they were. Noa couldn't stop her eyeroll, but The Huntsman gave a single nod. One after the other, they jumped up into the back and began trying to pry open the timber crate. After struggling for a few minutes, they seemed to realise what everyone else already knew. A crowbar was needed. *Idiots.*

"Bull, some help?" said Jett.

The Huntsman turned to the sound of Moth returning with the cart, one the crew designed themselves with Noa's air magic in mind. *Who needed horses when you could ride the current of the wind?*

Grunts of effort turned to shocked inhales when the lid

finally came loose, and Raj muttered a curse. Any feeling of victory dissipated like the smoke Noa sent skittering away, for when they cracked open the crate, an unconscious body was inside. The body of a young girl.

THE BULL HAD BROKEN ONE OF THE CAPTURED MEN IN ONLY three hours. Noa would be impressed if tonight's turn of events hadn't plunged her right back into that icy abyss inside of her, where any sort of traumatic situation became secondary to herself. It was like her mind was no longer wholly present. She was detached from everything. It wasn't a skill so much as a coping mechanism she didn't know how or really care to shake.

The young girl lay sleeping soundly on a cot, the crew gathered around like sentries. Seated on a stool, Noa watched her, listening to Bull relay the information. Every harrowing detail.

A slave ring. That's where the girl was going. The job was supposed to be an ongoing arrangement since the last trafficker had been caught. Which meant that not only had this been going on for some time but that they had no intention of stopping.

"What's so special about her?" Moth voiced. "This was a big operation for one girl."

It was true, and why would the Select want a malnour-ished kid from the Outer Sector who was sure to develop radiation poisoning before adulthood? She would be nothing but a strain on their resources. The answer came as a nightmare took hold of the girl, the child whimpering as the ground began to shake, a minor earthquake enveloping the radius around her.

Bull fell forward a step, half in awe, half like he heard a summons no one else did.

"Earth-wielder," he breathed, staring wide-eyed, with more emotion than Noa had ever seen him show in all the years she'd known him. The shaking picked up, rattling the furnishings, items falling from their nooks. Everyone looked to Noa to do something, but it was Bull who moved. Still seeming to be held in a trance, he dropped to his knees, a behemoth looming over the tiny child. With a giant hand he pressed his palm against the floor. A flurry of energy lit the air. Magic. Noa's responded in turn, rising to the surface of her skin begging to be let free. A cracking noise filled the space, fractures spider-webbing through the Compound's concrete surface, and where the gaps formed, vines emerged. Green and luscious. Teeming with life. Like she sensed the power even in slumber, the girl's eyelids fluttered open. Staring up at the Bull, not with fear but curiosity, the shaking subsided and she pushed upright on the cot, studying his show of magic. When the young girl glanced back to the man on bended knee before her, she reached out a hand, wordlessly opening her fist to present a purple flower.

The breath that came from Bull was that of wonder. The bloom wilted before their eyes, the violet shade blackening. A grimace of displeasure formed on the child. She couldn't hold the magic, Noa realised. There was a flutter in Noa's chest, a flicker of... something, seeing the frustration and determination on her little face as she tried again and again to conjure the power. Nothing happened.

Discouraged, she stared at the greenery with longing. Suddenly, blooms burst from the vines, the Compound now a field of wildflowers at her feet, the young wielder gasped, a smile bright as the sun had once been, shinning up at the Bull. And he—a man who learned the language of torture from an abusive father and had then chosen to use it on others like him—smiled back.

It took only a day to find the child's parents. Plural. A rarity in the slums. She may have been poor and a touch too thin, but she was well-loved. Noa had stayed behind while the others had been dispatched to learn about any of the fallout from last night and uncover more about the abhorrent Ring.

Nothing had felt quite the same around the Compound, like an invisible but definite shift had taken place. Noa was at the table, staring absentmindedly at the cracked foundation on one side of the common space still sprouting flowers. No one had commented on the fact the Bull had kept them in perfect health. There had been a change in him too. Maybe all it had taken was a young earth-wielder to look at him with wonder in her eyes for him to realise precious things still existed.

Every time Noa reached out with her senses, her air magic rejoiced at the feel of velvety petals, drinking in the perfume the flowers exhaled. Of its own accord it would dance around each bloom, sending a pulse straight through her blood as if her powers were alerting her of its finding. Life, life, life! It seemed to sing.

Noa reeled her magic in. Muzzled it. Either The Huntsman didn't have the heart to have it removed or simply didn't care about the literal change in scenery taking up their living quarters. Noa wasn't sure.

She had been so deep in her thoughts, she had missed the start of the conversation.

"—all come into their powers substantially early. Prepubescent magic users," Moth was saying.

"And you're sure of this?" Jett questioned, a seriousness about him that was as rare as the stolen children.

"It's the only pattern that fits. We would need more time to uncover the Ring to see if it's exclusively gifted children."

"There had been rumours of it over the years," Fly mused, her expression growing distant. "It's so rare that no one ever connected the dots. They must have informants in the slums to look out for signs of emerging magic."

"Molly," Raj rasped. That must have been the name of the woman he used to know. "Her sister was taken."

Pain flickered over his brother's face, he clapped a hand on his shoulder.

"The client I sent you," Fly said to Noa. "The missing boy. I suspect he was a wielder."

"Why?" *And why the hell didn't you mention that?* She wanted to add but didn't. If she hadn't turned away the woman, she would have found out for herself.

"She had been spotted multiple times asking people for help, always mentioning how special he is and that he couldn't be alone." It might have sounded like words any mother would say but Dragonfly saw more than anyone. She would have seen enough to come to that conclusion.

Noa's gut tightened uncomfortably. *We all have a sob story*, she had told the woman.

It was quiet for a moment, everyone absorbing what this truly meant. Jett, never one to let silence linger, said, "It would feel good to get our hands on the miscreants running that thing."

"Aye," Raj added, a smirk twisted with savage intent on his mouth. "Love to hear them scream."

The promise of death glinted in the Bull's dark eyes as he grunted in agreement, as if imagining all the unspeakable things he would take his sweet, sweet time doing to the monsters who had gone out of their way to create more suffering in a world already full to the brim with it. To children no less.

"You mustn't like it," Moth said a bit carefully to Noa, the only one of them who would broach the subject, or any topic remotely personal with her. Was it fear, or perhaps respect? Noa never gave it much thought. Maybe she should have.

The room had quieted at the suggestion, the fact that it was actually a question. She knew Moth was referring to how it could have just as easily been her snatched from her home, from the loving embrace of a mother and forced into slavery. Before she had mastered her magic, before she was strong enough to squish them against a wall like a mosquito or cause their lungs explode. When she was vulnerable. Forced to use her gift as they willed it, as a tool. The most sacred, innermost part of her, no longer her own but someone's else to defile. The thought alone had her stomach turning, had her conjuring magic to her fingertips as if she could hold its hand.

"No," she said simply. Then tilted her head, a challenge issued. "Are you suggesting something, Moth?"

The girl casually picked at her nails, ignoring the shift in the air, in the tone of conversation. A shrug. "Maybe."

"Spit it out, or drop it." The Huntsman's voice was a whip, evidently tired of skirting the truth. Especially one of this magnitude.

"Maybe I don't like feeling a coward. Maybe returning only one kid tonight made us one."

"We're mercenaries not vigilantes," Fly said, a cringe contorting her features, though Noa wasn't so sure which title caused it. For the first time, she wondered if the girl liked doing what she did, or if she was only here for the same reason most were: survival.

"Think it's time to branch out," was Raj's vote. The Bull, the crew's ever-silent presence, nodded his choice, violence still wafting from him in waves. It brightened though, when he glanced upon his flowers.

"Could do with some change around here," Jett seconded, bringing his cup down on the table.

Five yeses. All eyes turned to her, the dinging of Jett's metal stein ringing out—church bells harbingering a new era—as he drawled, "So Huntsman, what say you?"

Chenoa Haines, thief, orphan, wind-weaver and crime lord took one last sip of her drink and then returned the eager looks of her crew, their gazes glimmering with something not seen for an age in this part of the city—hope. *Shield it, nurture it*, a voice whispered to her. Her mother's voice. *So it may one day save the world.* There was a stirring in her chest, this time she did not stifle it. And The Huntsman said, "Looks like we've got some work to do."

OBSERVATIONS OF THE HEAD CHRONICLER

LIV EVANS

> *"Fate whispers to the warrior, 'You cannot*
> *withstand the storm.'*
> *The warrior whispers back, 'I am the storm."*
> *- Unknown*

IT'S SO EASY TO FALL INTO THE TRAP OF BELIEVING THAT THERE IS only one way to live your life.

The breadth of circumstances around a person act to convince them that theirs is the only way to exist. That everything in their life has primed them for their situation. Any attempt at change is seen as futile and, often, these efforts fail because they believe they will. It isn't that they are incapable of progress, merely that they believe they are.

So, humans fall into patterns.

They then internalise these patterns and use them to justify all sorts of things. In some cases, this can be helpful. It gives them the ability to get through the drudgery of their daily life, knowing that everything is as it should be.

What they are doing is okay, because they have little choice in the matter.

Many of the most heinous atrocities happen when people give in to this complacency. When they absolve themselves of responsibility because, well, that's just the way the world works.

Change is possible, though.

Humanity demands to be felt.

Habitual denial of one's internal drive to do better can only last so long. For some, the foundation of habit just needs the right kind of shake to work it loose.

As the surface starts to crack, new life begins to sprout through. Resistance, as they say, is fertile. The wild, chaotic beast that is the human spirit will fight, even in the most extremes of circumstances. It will rear up when it is violated, calling for help and demanding change until it is heard. Sometimes, these calls are subtle. Other times, earth-shattering.

But all it takes is one crack to shatter a mould.

A GLIMMER OF TRUTH

DANIELLE HUGHES

A GLIMMER OF TRUTH

DANIELLE HUGHES

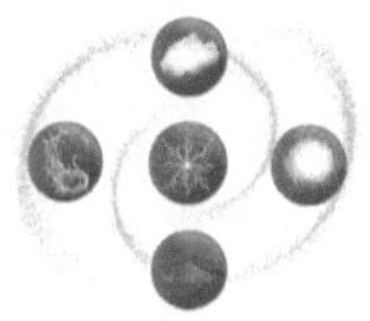

SYMADOR - 10 YEARS AGO

MOLLY SAT IN THE CHAIR BESIDE HER WINDOW, AND LIFTED HER favourite chipped tea cup to her lips. Her aged and weathered hands trembled slightly as she blew the steam, before taking a sip. She smiled as she watched her eight-year-old granddaughter, Julia, playing catch on their small terrace with the boy from next door. She observed Julia send a spark of electricity after throwing the ball up, causing it to jolt higher into the air. Caleb clapped and begged her to send it higher again. Molly tapped on the window and shook her head, telling Julia to stop. Julia rolled her eyes but stopped using the magic. It was unusual for a child as young as Julia to show signs of power. Most children didn't show any ability until they're at least in their teens. But Julia had always been a smart girl and an early developer. Crawling, walking, talking, reading, counting; she did everything before the expected age.

Molly turned back to the jewellery repairs she was

working on, her way to bring in extra money. Between fixing old family heirlooms, broken clocks and watches and small gadgets, Molly was able to make a meagre living for herself and Julia. She also made and mended clothes for those in the lower sector, who weren't as fortunate. It had been hard since her daughter, Sara, had passed away, leaving Julia behind. But the small allowance paid to her by the Fortress where Sara had worked when she died, barely helped keep them going. Molly picked up the brooch she was repairing - a sapphire stone, set amongst pearls. Both extremely rare and valuable since the devastation of the meteor and radiation flare. Molly felt proud to be trusted by people to repair their precious belongings. Many would seize the opportunity to steal something so prized and sell it for cash, or food. Not everyone in Symador was as fortunate as them to have a small, but safe home, and enough money to pay for extra rations, and the things they needed to get by.

A knock on the door startled Molly, causing her to nudge her cup and slosh the tea. She made her way over as something was pushed underneath. The white corner of an envelop poked out from under the door. Molly turned the handle and peered out, but no one was there. She bent low, cursing her aching knees, and retrieved the envelop. It had nothing written on the outside. Molly slipped her finger under the sealed edge, lifting it up and pulled out a folded piece of white paper.

Meet me tonight at Langhorne Bridge. Midnight. I have urgent information regarding your daughter's death. It wasn't an accident. Julia is in danger.

The note was stamped with an insignia. A capital 'C' sitting atop a scroll.

'The Chroniclers.' Molly gasped. A feeling of nausea settled in the pit of her stomach. Molly rushed to the doorway again, this time running to the fence line and glancing back and forth along the worn road and damaged curb of their street. Apart from a stray dog sticking its nose into a neighbouring bin, there was no one to be seen.

Molly read the note again, then pressed it to her chest. She ran back to the house, to check on Julia, who was still playing happily with Caleb.

'Come inside!' Molly called, opening the back door.

Julia frowned. 'But why? We're still playing!' she whined.

'Julia Marie, I said inside, now!'

Julia and Caleb trudged inside and Molly closed the door behind them.

'It's not fair, we were having fun!' Julia said, flopping on the couch.

'Well, now you can have fun in here instead.' Molly replied.

'Can I show Caleb my magic in here?' Julia asked, sparking up at the prospect.

'No, dear. I'm sorry. No more magic today. Why don't we bake cookies instead?'

Caleb jumped up. 'Yeah, cookies! My mum never makes cookies.'

'That's because she's busy looking after your siblings. Now come on into the kitchen and we can get baking.'

When the children were busy mixing and rolling cookie

dough, Molly slipped outside to Caleb's house and asked his mother, Lauren, if she could have Julia for the night.

'Of course, Molly. But what's the problem? You don't have a date, do you?'

'Don't be ridiculous.' Molly replied. She felt hesitant to tell anyone about the letter. 'I just have some business I need to sort out.'

'You're not sick, are you? Is it the radiation? You know I'll have Julia here anytime you need, forever if need be.' Lauren asked, her face furrowed in concern.

'No, no. Nothing like that. There's no need to worry, I just don't know what time I'll be back.' Molly knew what Lauren would say if she told her about the meeting. She would warn her off going.

The Chroniclers were a secret organisation responsible for recording events for future generations. Nobody knew who they were or where they met, or worked, or lived. They were meant to be neutral, separate to society and the Fortress, and even to the Imperator himself. Governed by their own rules, they were to be impartial and unbiased, never to meddle in events. For one to reach out in person meant one of two things; either something was really wrong, or they couldn't be trusted. Or both.

'Are you happy to feed those two dinner, and send them over afterwards? They can help me put the twins to bed and stay here tonight.' Lauren said, motioning to Julia and Caleb next-door.

'No problem, thanks Lauren.'

WHEN DINNER WAS DONE AND THE CHILDREN HAD MADE THEIR way to Calebs, Molly set about keeping herself busy with her work until it was time to leave. She couldn't ignore the request to meet. It mentioned Julia being in danger, so she had to go. It also mentioned information about Sara's death. If Molly was honest with herself, something had always grated on her about her daughter's untimely death. But she had put it down to the grief of losing her only daughter, and focused on caring for Julia. Sara had worked within the Fortress walls, as a researcher and scientist. Gifted with the power of fire, attention to detail and a curious mind, Sara was a respected member, working in a team directly under Imperator Vaarem to help him discover a cure to the radiation. Sara had been killed during an experiment, because she had failed to seal her safety gear appropriately. Extreme radiation had seeped in, killing her almost instantly.

At least that's what Molly had been told. But Molly knew Sara was extra careful, she always talked about not getting paid enough for the dangers she faced with her research. It never sat right with Molly. But Molly also knew better than to question the Imperator. He had a reputation for being volatile. Molly had witnessed his temper first hand many years ago.

Molly remembered the day as if it had only happened recently. A few years his senior, Molly used to babysit the Imperator, back when he was just Ivan Vaarem, the oldest of four boys.

'Ivan, you'll hurt your brother if you keep being so rough. Please stop.' Molly had asked while the boys wrestled in the backyard, fighting over a football.

'I don't have to listen to you, your not my mother!' Ivan had called back, before shoving his little brother, Seth. Seth fell but got straight back up.

'It's my ball, Ivan. You can't have it.' Seth tried to grab the ball back, but Ivan held him at arms-length.

'Ivan, please give Seth the ball. Or I'll have to tell your father how you've been behaving.' Molly threatened. Ivan's father was the only one Ivan seemed to respond to. A large man, who worked long hours and drank too much. He didn't say a lot to anyone, but his boys all respected him.

'Whatever. There you go, baby!' Ivan tossed the ball up high, and shoved Seth again while he was looking at the ball. Seth fell to the ground awkwardly and immediately cried out in pain.

'My shoulder! Ow!'

Molly had rushed to the younger boys' side; he couldn't lift his arm and cradled it with the other.

'Show me where it hurts.'

Seth pointed to his collar bone, and Molly winced when she saw a lump had already formed. 'I think you may have broken it. I'll call my mum and get her to come get you.'

Molly watched Ivan storm inside, slamming the door behind him. He showed no remorse until his father came home, and Molly told him what had happened. It was only then that Molly thought she saw Ivan falter in his arrogance, quiver even. Molly was sent home immediately. She'd seen Ivan sporting a black eye in the days following, but was never asked to mind the Vaarem brothers again.

· · ·

It was a twenty-minute walk to Langhorne Bridge, and at 11.30pm, Molly could wait no longer. Wearing her black coat with the hood pulled up, she was about to leave, before deciding to grab the small knife she used to pry open the back of watches. Just in case. She clasped the knife in her pocket, running her finger over its smooth handle. It helped to settle her nerves while she walked. By this time of night, it was quiet, and Molly didn't pass anyone on her way to the bridge.

Langhorne Bridge was built over what used to be the Langhorne River, before the radiation flare. It was now nothing more that a dry crater filled with rubbish, rusted cars, rocks and dead tree branches. Molly was lucky to be one of the few who could remember what it used to be like. Although the water had always been murky in colour, it used to flow freely, flanked on either side by banks of green grass and wildflowers. Her father used to fish a bit further downstream, while Molly and her little brother would swing from an old tyre hung over a low branch, and jump into the water. The memory made her smile momentarily before the bridge came into view.

Molly kept to the shadows, crouched behind a crumbled piece of concrete wall, waiting to see who would show up. A single car passed her, and a few rats, while she waited. At 11.59pm exactly, a dark figure on a bicycle rode up. They paused in the middle of the bridge, but stayed on the bike - one foot on the ground, the other resting on the pedal. The figure removed their helmet, shaking out shoulder length black hair, and glanced around them. Molly squinted then realised she recognised the figure as Pete, a colleague of Sara's. Sara and Pete had been friends for a couple of years before her death, and Pete had been very considerate after she passed, dropping in to check on Molly and Julia, and bringing Julia toys on occasion. Molly wondered for a time if Pete was Julia's father, but Sara had always been insistent that he wasn't, and that she didn't know who exactly was the father, after a drunken dalliance at her work Christmas party.

Molly stepped out from her hiding place. Pete grasped his handle bars, but relaxed when he realised it was Molly.

'You received my note?' He called to her, as she closed the distance between them.

'Why all the secrecy Pete, why didn't you just come to the house?'

'I'm being watched, Molly. We all are. You and Julia too.'

Molly frowned. 'But why? What's going on? And are you really part of the Chroniclers now?'

Pete held up a hand. 'One thing at a time. But we have to be quick.' He glanced around to make sure no other people could be seen. 'I've always been a Chronicler, Molly. My assignment was to work inside the Fortress, under-cover. My friendship with Sara was organic though. I promise you that.' Pete brushed his hair behind his ear.

'How can you be a Chronicler, and work inside the Fortress? Isn't that a conflict of interest?'

Pete smiled and Molly noticed the wrinkles around his eyes, he looked tired. 'Not all Chroniclers are the same, or tasked with the same sort of jobs. I'm more of a research and report agent. Anyway, that's not important.'

Molly frowned again, confused. 'Why are we in danger, Pete? What do you know about Sara's death?'

Pete sighed. 'I'm so sorry, Molly. I promise you I never knew any of this at the time. If I had, I would've protected her. I loved Sara, you know that, right?'

'I guessed as much, but why didn't you ever ask her out, marry her for Christ's sake? Are you Julia's father?'

Pete shook his head. 'I can't be married. Or have a girl-friend. It's against the oath I took. And I'm definitely not Julia's father.' Pete closed his eyes for a moment. 'But I know who is.'

'How? Who?'

'Sara knew too. And you're not going to like it. It's Vaarem.'

Molly gasped. Then laughed awkwardly. 'Don't be ridiculous. That's impossible.' But a nauseous feeling began sweeping through her belly. Vaarem was old enough to be *Sara's* father, let alone Julia's.

'Were they in a relationship?' Molly asked, bile rising in her throat.

'No. Vaarem was her boss. But that's not the worst of it, Molly.' Pete reached into a satchel bag strung over his shoulder. He pulled out a small device that looked like a tiny radio or walkie-talkie. 'This belonged to Sara.' He handed the device to Molly. 'I found this taped to the top of the drawer inside her desk. This explains everything.'

Molly took it from him. 'A voice recorder?'

Pete nodded. 'She used it to record her notes and find-ings on her research while she was working, and then used it to go back and make her detailed notes and reports.'

'So, what do I want with it?' Molly asked.

'There's more. In the months before her death, she

began recording other things. Secrets and truths about what was going on inside our division.' Pete explained.

'What kind of secrets?' Molly asked, cautiously.

A car back-fired in the distance, and Pete jumped, looking around to ensure they were still alone. 'Let's move down here.' Pete motioned for Molly to follow him off the bridge, down towards the junk-filled river bed.

'What secrets, Pete?' Molly asked again when they were hidden from street view.

'Sara wasn't the only woman Vaarem got pregnant. Apparently, he's got a penchant for getting girls drunk and having his way with them. Some of them he's even drugged.'

'What!' Molly whisper-screamed.

'I know, its revolting.' Pete said, shaking his head.

Molly felt her blood boil as her heart began to pound. She wanted to race up the hill to the Fortress and strangle Vaarem. She wanted to punch him in his face and kick him in his groin before stabbing him in the chest.

'How can he get away with this?' Hot tears filled Molly's eyes.

Pete raised his eyebrows at her. 'He's the Imperator.' As if that explained it and made it acceptable.

'Why didn't she tell me any of this?' Molly cried.

'Probably because she feared for her life. And yours. He threatened her. Do you know what Vaarem is working on? Why he runs the trials to find the strongest in each field of magic?'

Molly shook her head, trying to clear her thoughts and shrugged. 'He needs the strongest to reverse the effects of the radiation, and restore Symador to how it was before the flare.'

Pete nodded. 'But that's not the only reason. He wants to harness the power for himself. He's found a way to strip the power from the wielder, and imbue it into himself. All five types. At once!'

Molly threw her hands up in the air. 'And then what? He already holds power over the whole damn city!'

'Then he plans to conquer the world. There're other cities like ours, hundreds of miles away. Unreachable because of how strong the radiation is past our borders. He'll be invincible with the combination of power inside him. Unstoppable.'

Molly breathed heavily. 'It doesn't explain why he's raping and impregnating innocent women.'

Pete pulled a large envelope from his bag. 'He's discovered a serum which elevates intelligence and magical ability in the growing foetus. If the mother consumes the serum, the baby absorbs it.'

Molly felt a cold sweat break out over her body. 'He gave the serum to Sara, didn't he?'

Pete nodded.

Molly squeezed her eyes shut as new tears threatened to spill. 'Julia. My Julia.'

'I'm so sorry, Molly.' Pete reached out and rubbed her back.

Molly's shoulders dropped. 'Is that why they're watching us? For signs that Julia is one of his weapons?'

'Yes. And it's why he killed Sara.'

It was too much for Molly to bear. Her legs buckled and she fell to the ground, hard. Sharp rocks dug into her knees and skinned the palms of her hand. Pete knelt to help her into a sitting position.

'Why?' She choked.

'Sara found out what he'd been doing, and what his plan was. She was a liability. He made her death look like an accident, but he'd unstitched a seam in her suit. There was video footage, but it's since been destroyed. And the security guard who discovered it is also dead.' Pete searched through his bag and pulled out some bandages and antiseptic wipes. He gently cleaned and bandaged Molly's hands.

'What else have you got in that bag?' Molly asked.

'In my line of work, you just never know what condition you'll find people in. But I do have something else for you.'

Molly sighed, unsure she could handle any more surprises.

'Here.' Pete handed her an item wrapped in white cloth. Molly carefully unwrapped the item, fumbling slightly with her bandaged hands. Inside was a chunk of rock.

'What's this?' Molly asked, confused.

'It's a piece of the meteor that caused the radiation flare. A piece of the core.'

Molly turned the rock over in her hands. It was dark grey in colour, but flecks of light silver caught the moonlight and glimmered.

'Sara discovered that the core of the meteor acts like a shield to the radiation. And to magic. If someone with magic is holding a piece of the rock, their powers are suppressed. She was keeping it for Julia, to protect her from Vaarem discovering her power, if the serum had worked.'

Molly wrapped the rock back up. 'Julia is already showing strong signs of Energy. She can produce sparks of electricity at will.'

'That's a clear indicator she will be exactly what Vaarem wants when she comes of age.' Pete said.

'What am I going to do? She is so strong-willed. She already talks about competing in the magic trials. It's against the law to stop children being tested.' Molly rested her head in her hands.

'You make jewellery, right?' Pete asked. 'Make her something, say it was a gift from her mother, and that she needs to wear it at all times. That it means Sara is with her, watching over her and protecting her. It wouldn't be a lie.'

Molly nodded. Feeling steadier, she ungracefully wobbled to her feet with the aid of Pete.

'I just wish Sara had told me about all of this sooner. I might have been able to help her, protect her.'

Pete looked at the ground. 'I know, I feel the same way. I'm so sorry to dump this all on you now. But I needed to warn you. Even though I could be killed for sharing the information, I had to do it, for Julia.'

Molly grasped Pete's hand. 'Thank you, Pete. I'm glad you told me.' She gazed up to the night sky. 'I will keep our girl safe, my darling. I promise.'

Observations of the Head Chronicler

Liv Evans

"The true meaning of life is to plant trees under whose shade you do not expect to sit."
- Nelson Henderson

Every story that has ever been told is one of sacrifice. They differ in type and magnitude, of course, but there is always an element of sacrifice in there. Whether it is a grand gesture of someone who gives their life for a greater cause, or it is as simple as someone offering the last bite of their favourite food to another. History is built on the back of humans making concessions. For better or for worse.

The thing that is given up is not always obvious or even tangible. This is why people don't always realise what they are reading about, even as their eyes skim the page. Not all sacrifices are altruistic or moral, either. Sometimes a person is just waiting for the right excuse to relinquish their moral compass for ill-begotten gains.

But this observation is not about morally questionable

actions. It is not about the twisted, anarchic grabs for power and control. It is to highlight the pinpricks of light. The morning stars that shine brightest in the dawn after the dark. It is about the quenching touch of rain on a parched landscape. The warmth of a loving embrace at the end of a cold day.

The Chroniclers are no strangers to sacrifice. As folks who weave our way quietly through society, we give up much in our quest to record our observations. Whether it is our ambitions, time with loved ones, or our own subjectivity... it takes immeasurable willpower to stand back and watch, to not intervene, whilst we let others exercise freedom of choice.

Although not all Chroniclers stay the course, the tenets of the organisation state that impartiality is the goal. Those in the know understand this is impossible. As humans, we Chroniclers are just as susceptible to bias as your next-door neighbour. The difference, however, is in the intent. It is the amount of effort that goes into maintaining some semblance of objectivity when no one else need bother.

Then, there are those of us who cannot remain in our roles. For one reason or another, the burden of the history we carry on our shoulders becomes too heavy to bear. Even though we would never advertise it, there are many of us who have left our ranks to join rebels and outcasts, to try and use the knowledge they have gained to improve the world for the people they developed such a fondness for through their observations. This is not something we encourage. It is not what we see as our role. Yet we do not punish those who leave. We would not claim to free them from the captivity of social veneer only to trap them behind philosophical bars. So, whilst we strongly discourage deviance, we will never stop someone from leaving.

As the Head Chronicler, people would assume I frown upon these leavers the most. This couldn't be further from the truth. Despite all logic, I have a tender spot for the people who have enough fire and passion to sacrifice their vows and try to make the world a better place for others. Their patience is lacking, of course. They are already working on the goals they profess to be deserting for, but they just get swept up in the stories and forget the long-term plan.

I can't blame them for their short-sightedness. After all, what is the power of a good story if not luring people away from the trappings of their own mind?

But I digress.

If we return to the notion of patience, I can think of only one group of people whose general levels of the trait outweigh our own as Chroniclers.

Carers.

The people who choose to care for another, more vulnerable, human being. They sacrifice everything, from sleep to food, money, clothes, morals, and even their own dreams. They have the patience to take a child from a mewling, needy creature and nurture them until they become an independent person all in and of themselves.

The parents and carers who aim to raise whole, moral humans play the long game. They are constantly sowing seeds of love, ethics, and learning into their wards. They weather all sorts of challenges, heartbreaks, and triumphs in hopes that, decades later, they venture independently into the world and thrive.

Part of raising a child this way means carrying some burdens for them so they need not shoulder them themselves. These are the family secrets an adult holds closely to their chest so their child does not feel the taint of their knowledge. It does not always work, of course, but the intentions are usually sound.

In some cases, these secrets are held across generations. For some, the original knowledge fades out until the power in them fizzles.

Others?

Well, some of those secrets are like a rolling snowball that gathers up every bit of powder in its path until it becomes unstoppable. These are the kinds of secrets that smash through the veneer of history and have the power to change the world.

And the person who first shaped that snowball? The one who set it on the ground and gave it a gentle tap to see it on its way?

Those are the people who sacrifice the most.

Those are the people who give up the most important thing a human can have.

Hope for themselves.

They let go of their own aspirations, setting them in a neat little package that they pass down through generations on the chance that maybe, just maybe, their descendants will get a chance at something they could never have.

They are the true beacons of humanity. Of selflessness and sacrifice. The true harbingers of change.

THE SECOND LIFE OF WREN

GR THOMAS

THE SECOND LIFE OF WREN

GR THOMAS

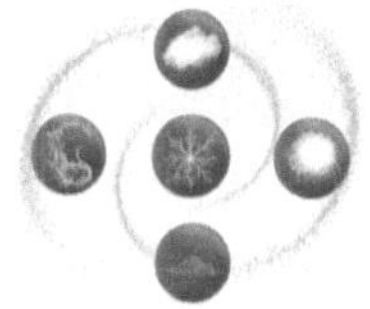

"How much you gonna get for those, Wren?" Busta asked, his hollowed cheeks puffed out as he ogled my stash.

"As much as I can, here, you take this and don't tell a soul or I'll flatten you, okay?" I passed two slightly rusty lithium disks into his hand. Busta's fingers snapped around them instantly, and he hugged them against his chest, his eyes darting left and right.

"Thanks, Wren, thanks." His stomach growled; he hadn't eaten in a while. I looked up at the sky, a foul brown smudge; was it a wish I was looking for, a dream of something better for little Busta? I didn't really know as I drew a deep breath, trying not to wretch on its distinctive metallic smell.

"Find yourself some lard, anything fatty. I'll try to bring you back something better after I've seen Ash. I'll put some meat on those bones." I squeezed his cheek playfully. He shied away, a flash of colour blushed his ashen cheeks. He giggled; the sound was rare around here.

"I'm expecting a good haul on my next fence, so I'll be

able to get to Ash, and bring her back here with us if she needs protection." I wanted to smile at the possibility, but my face remained flat as I thought on the shit life I'd been dealt... that most of us had been gifted by war and death, by a world in utter chaos; and that society left kids like Busta and I only one choice to survive with any semblance of dignity... fencing.

Stealing is a way of living... for us Regs...that's Regulars, those who have no magic, or very little. We're the ones of no value to the Western Districts ... or anywhere, so they say. If we were born elsewhere in Symador, perhaps we might've had a chance, but the West desired the most powerful, the least *defective* citizens. Rumours of other districts being more tolerant were rife, but they were impossible to get to without magic or something incredibly enticing to bribe your way in. I had just enough to survive, and for now, it had to do.

Busta looked up at me with wide, hungry eyes. Tears unexpectedly hung onto his lashes.

"I'm scared you won't come back, Wren," he said, blinking those tears free, leaving muddied steaks in their wake.

I turned his shoulders around, faced him towards home. Calling anything around here home was nothing short of a truth stretch.

"Get outta here, I'll be fine, ya little rat." I nudged him gently.

"Promise you'll be back?" Busta peered over his shoulder; eyes watery again.

I swallowed hard; promises were the least reliable of things in our world.

"Sure kid, now get!"

Busta dashed ahead, along the rim of the wall that protected Symador from... well, apparently everything. On our left, was the wastelands, a black smudge of the last known forests in the West. In the far distance, the blueish, vertical outline of the capital city. It was huge, I'd only ever been there once. Once was enough seeing the power and tech it sucked from its indentured, magic-laden workforce, power not shared with the majority of Symadorians. It's why I was now running along the perimeter of the wall as a nobody, an outcast.

A wild ocean crashed to our right, the air salty and sharp, but a whole lot fresher than the thick sludge that coated the air within the walls. I sucked it in as though it was life itself. The churn and bump of the last two wave-powered generators ground rhythmically as we ran. The only traditional source of power left, and if we were seen anywhere near the generators, we'd be mincemeat.

The only true power Symadorians do have, is freedom to live under the protection of the system, if we're lucky enough to escape relegation to the sewers or the world outside the wall after the coming of age trials. I'm actually not sure what's worse though, living the way I do, or what exists beyond the great wall that surrounds Symador, the barrier between survival and the unknown world. All I do know, what we've all been taught since birth... inside is life, outside is certain death. Yet, the life I live in the cesspits of Symador could be questioned as another form of death.

My mind snapped back to the present as I felt the air move above us.

"Busta! Eagles… run!" We dashed, Busta harder than me, his life, in that moment in greater danger. New to the life of a Reg on the run, he would still be hunted for extermination. Taller and faster, I dashed past him, pulled his hand and almost threw him at the ladder that led back down to the shadows and hidden nooks we lived in.

Busta slid down it at an alarming rate, arms and legs curled around its edges just as the bird crossed overhead. It didn't notice me, they never did anymore. The scar on my wrist was a testament to what Regs will go through to survive. It hurt as I watched Busta hit the ground hard, roll into a screaming ball, before dragging himself off into the undergrowth towards the sewers. I rubbed the phantom pain of my scar and recalled my first months, running, terrified just like young Busta.

I was destined for the sewers too, as Busta was, sifting excrement for my entire life after failing the West's magic tests. Mum was horrified, embarrassed by me, not so much as a hug goodbye when I was sent to work in the treatment plant. A purest, Mum desired the social improvement that magic offspring offer.

It was no surprise to me when I hit sixteen that my future was quite literally shit. It was either that or banishment outside the wall for refusal… neither suited what I wanted, so after an agonising appointment with a rusty knife, my wrist and a tracking chip, I just disappeared. Two full years of hiding in the shadows, I nearly starved to death until they stopped looking for me. This is why I took Busta under my wing. I'd been just like him, and hopefully, when he's brave enough, we'll cut that chip from him too.

I became a memory, my existence erased. Symador

would never admit they failed. I knew I'd been culled the day I stumbled across a Sentry Eagle... deadly weaponised guardians of the realm. No one survived being on the wrong side of one.

I'd been searching for drinkable water. My regular source, in a usually un-patrolled area, had dried up. Symguards had been spotted there recently. I swear they knew it was a safe haven for Regs. I'm convinced Vaarem, that effed-up dictator, sent his lackies to seal off any natural water supply to kill off those like me. It wasn't just Busta and I out there on the hop, there were many to be hunted down. I'd found the odd corpse or two, starved to death by the system. In truth, I'd found hundreds, there's no point in not saying it how it is.

On that day, thirst and a healthy fear of death had forced me deeper into the grasslands, away from the relatively safe, hidden nooks of the outer wall. Pampas grass surrounded the outskirts of the Western cities, their razored leaves rimmed the only land that grew anything edible. It was a clever ploy by Vaarem, few dared venture through Pampas that could have you bleeding out before you realised the danger you were in... from a plant.

I'd had no choice back then; just a seventeen year old kid. Ostracised by my community, I was scared, starving and desperate, and hadn't learned the skills of thievery I now taught to others. So, that day, desperation had me crawling on my belly, scraping myself to shreds on the bite of those bushes until I reached a dense clutch of trees.

My clothes, whilst never really clean, glued to my skin with blood, the smell of it made me gag and reminded me of my own failed blood trials. Air filled with the metallic tang of death, of screams for mercy... me calling for Mum, and Mum turning her back on me. I'd shaken my thoughts clear, curled my hand into a fist and tapped on trunks one by one, waiting to hear that delightful reverberation that gave away a secret supply of fresh water.

Dad had snuck me a spile not long after my trials. Families were allowed a last visit with failures like me, those whose genetic makeup didn't express a power to contribute to the betterment of the Western District, and Symador at large.

That was the last time I'd seen Dad, or my sister, Ash. Mum had refused to see me after my failure. I could still feel the tremble of Dad's hand as he slipped the spile up my sleeve. Dad knew I'd run. The spile was his way of telling me there was a way to survive. That small point of metal was my most valuable possession, it was my only possession, and had saved my life more times than I can remember. On that day, barely a year ago, I'd just tapped it into a particularly lush looking tree when I'd heard the wings of the eagle. My body froze, but I'd ducked down too late, it had seen me.

I'd fallen flat on my back, the ground bit into my ribs, agony held me there as my throat dried up. The desire to scream for help was pointless, there was no one to hear, or care, and besides that, my chest had constricted so tight I literally pissed myself as the eagle's attention locked onto me.

Its mechanised eyes scanned me, clicking diagnostically, whirring left and right. My pants filled with piss again, until it looked away, flapped its immense wings and flew upwards, attention lost. That meant no life detected;

my chip had been deactivated from the system, the chip they were trained to identify. I was essentially dead to the history books of Symador. The West would have written me off, no record of birth or death, the capital ignorant I'd ever existed at all. Being *dead* was the best thing that ever happened. I could actually start living. Yet, no one advertised for the dead, the forgotten, no one welcomed those who had bucked the rules, so I forged my way through life in the only way I could... I became the best damned thief and fencer of the wasteland's lands. Busta was my protégé.

He'd long disappeared now. I slipped from the ladder and checked for a trail.

"Good boy, no footprints," I mumbled. "Ahh, Busta!" I'd groaned almost immediately after as I pulled a piece of fabric from the thorns of a bur bush. I shook my head. "Sloppy." I screwed up the fabric and slipped it in my pocket.

Fencing was punishable by death, of course, as was practically every crime in Symador. There were no second chances, no do overs. In the ancient past, people were kept in prisons apparently. In my world, there weren't resources for that, just death.

"Your place is privileged in a delicate and recovering world. Those who live beyond the bounds of societal expectations choose a life that is void." Ms Robchen of junior school drummed this in. So lovely to hear as a ten year old.

I couldn't tolerate the thought of that happening to little Busta. I'd have to force him to be *dead* to the system sometime soon. It was liberating, it was life-saving.

Once I knew I was *dead*, I took myself off to the old lands, to the tips and dumps, the gutters and disease-ridden holes to find whatever I could to fund the dark economy which was all things power. And there I stayed.

Energy sources of the old world that were both banned and supposedly long lost, in my time, were a valuable commodity. Lost they weren't; cause for capital punishment they were. If found in possession of any, rich or poor, seller or buyer, magic or not, your freedom was at an end. The fact was, people simply didn't have enough elemental power to survive, but Vaarem would not, could not acknowledge this. Propaganda was the loudest voice in my world, a world that showed no sign of redemption, at least not from what I could see and smell.

I waited the day out after Busta scarpered. When the moon was high, I'd set out on the hunt. Working the night hours, I scavenged the old cities for flint, batteries, liquid fuel, the odd dry matchstick, even a light bulb. Anything that could generate power. It's a competitive business that often involves a bloodied nose or the odd slit throat.

I'd kept my manners clean so far, I was a runner, not a fighter. My long legs, and apparently appealing appearance were in my favour, so if I needed to, I'd smooch up to anyone to keep my heart beating and my belly full. Busta, being small, I'd taught to scatter like a mouse if confronted, he'd never survive a fight.

The night was busy with the soft rustling of Regs, secreted amongst the dump. I had a favourite spot. A stinking area where the capital's scraps were dumped quite conveniently on the roof of what used to be some kind of giant supply store. I was one of a few who fought through the gut churning smell, the rats and rabid dogs to find a prize.

It was a lucky night. A particularly frighteningly large dog with five legs and one eye was dragging a bag out of the tunnel yours truly had dug out six months prior. One quick well-aimed rock, and it howled away into the shadows. The bag, whilst slimy with shit-smelling slobber, beheld a dead rat, a smattering of roaches, the head of something I didn't recognise... and large D-size batteries.

"Mother fu..." I hushed my joy as something rattled nearby. I slipped the batteries into my pockets and backtracked out.

This will be enough for a fare. I had to get home to my sister.

I haven't been home in 2 years. It's dangerous walking around the boroughs. Symguard and eagles patrol practically every square inch of land and sky. If I was caught, it wouldn't matter that I have no recordable history, that I'm no one. I'd be shoved out the Symador gates in a heartbeat.

I had to go home though. Ash turned sixteen in two days. I *had* to be there, to make sure she's okay. If she was powerless like me, I had to save her from the shit hole I was sent to.

But first, I needed a customer.

"Wren, you're late! We've been out for weeks!," Solana du Mark snapped.

I chuckled, and curled the batteries back into my hand.

"Ma'am, it's dangerous work, I need recompense for the danger I put myself in for your betterment. Supply is lower every month; competition is high. Westerners are desperate for a little moonshine power. You want a few weeks using a flint and a stick? Dare to use your own elementals without appropriate permission? Bask in darkness? Makes no difference to me." I waved my hand dismissively and backed away. "Or, do you want to pay a fair price?"

She crossed her arms, her eyes were daggers.

"Fine by me. I hear Miriam is paying 5 pounds of potatoes and a whole chicken for these," I smirked, waving my battery-laden hand at her. I turned, pretending to leave, hoping she'd fall for the lie. Solana hated Miriam who lived in the upper West, her social standing and elemental power just that bit better.

"Stop!" Solana snapped. I spun around, but not too enthusiastically.

Solana's lips thinned, then pursed, her eyes flicked nervously at my hands, worry shaded the strange violet that tinged her eyes, a peculiarity of the more powerful magic populace.

"Greedy OGM, you are. Wait there!" The door slammed; her profanities breached the door. I looked around her courtyard while I waited. A sconce burned away the evening insects just outside a portico, it stunk like roast meat, the pig fat soaked wick especially rancid. A rat scuttled by, probably lured by the smell.

"How rude... OGM!" I muttered to the indifferent vermin. OGM was an insult for sure, but a death sentence if heard in the wrong company. Reg is the nicest thing people like me are called, a peculiarity of the Western districts, the most hateful of Symador. Outdated Genetic Material, or OGM, was the nastiest of slurs. My blood is as

OGM as it could be, as though I'd been born in the 21st century.

The door banged open; Solana's face florid. "Here, you greedy runt!" She threw a bag at my feet. "I'll not have Miriam with more than me. She already has two of her kids well-appointed in the capitol." Solana blew at the sconce, the flame flickered brighter; orange ember magic floated on her breath, giving the light more substance.

I wrenched the sack open. It contained two headless chooks, a dozen muddy potatoes and a sprinkling of nuts. My mouth watered. I handed her one battery; she slammed the door in my face.

The bag was heavy enough to lift my hopes. It was just what I needed to hail a night cart back home, enough to bribe a Carter to keep their mouth shut.

"A whole chicken?" I'd drive you outside the wall for that!" The Carter said. His horse stamped impatiently. I patted its neck. I liked horses, they didn't ask for much, a mouth of grass, a scratch behind their ears. And they were invaluable. Next to elemental power, they were the most valued commodity across Symador. Passed down through families, often fought over in wills and seemingly unaffected by radiation. Horses were the main transport option throughout outer Symador, and because of the expense, few could travel, and when a population couldn't move, they were easily controlled. The system seemed to feed itself well.

"A whole chicken for your silence," I said as my hand

slipped from the horse's mane. "Your complete and eternal silence."

"For what? You killed someone?" He adjusted a leathered filter mask across his face. He didn't have to smell the fetid air.

Lucky bastard.

I held up my wrist. Flashed the silver of the scar in the moonlight.

The Carter snickered, "You'll wanna give me more than a dead chook, you stinkin' OGM, if you don't want me to call on the Symguard." His eyes squinted; a blush of power set his eyes to sparkle.

I could've lost it, made a scene of how much of an arse he was, but that's the exact opposite of what I wanted. I needed silence, to be as inconspicuous as possible, and I was only going to get home that way if I was dropped off expediently by a Carter. They needed payment with a Symbar, a nano implant tattooed into our wrists. Every Symadorian received one the day they were born. Each time they're scanned, credits are taken, our daily activities are managed by the government, and of course, they track us. Those credits are earned by sharing our elemental power to run the city... well, I couldn't do that now, could I?

The pain of gouging mine out was too easily remembered, and I know he saw that pain in my eyes. Hence the power kick he got when my scar flashed in the moonlight. I was erased, nothing, and he knew it.

My hands fell into my pockets as he pulled his scarf down, revealing a leering grin. He suddenly seemed to notice my breasts. *So* not going there with this creep.

"Here, these will last you 6 months." I stepped

forwards, dropped 10 SR43 coin batteries at his feet. It nearly killed me to hand them over. These were like diamonds, six months' worth of food. His eyes bulged. He scooped them up quick as a whip.

Greedy bastard.

I knew he'd sell them on the Undermarket, just like I do. Horse owners didn't need the extra, they were among the wealthiest Symadorians, but this one was an extra greedy pig. Actually no, that was an insult to pigs, he was a slug.

"Get in! Where to?" The gloating of his voice made my fists clench. I'd love to have sunk my knuckles into his thin lips and split them against his teeth.

"The 4th borough, south end of the old highway," I said, climbing into the rear of the carriage. It wasn't exactly where my family lived, a few blocks back, but I wasn't dumb enough to take him straight to my front door, he'd still snitch for sure. The reward for an AWOL OGM would be too enticing.

THE TRIP WAS ROUGH, THE NIGHT AIR COLD AND FOUL. I PULLED my hole-ridden scarf over my mouth, it really made no difference, the smell still burned my throat, the taste of it never got better. Dust blew in on a midnight wind like a stinking, airborne scythe. The grit of it stung my eyes. I couldn't imagine living beyond the wall in the wastelands. I'm sure nothing actually did live there and that's why I had to be there for Ash... just in case she was like me, just in case she somehow found herself banished.

The 4th borough was a good hour away. Nerves bit my skin with each passing moment. I watched the back of the Carter, the peak of his collar, the way his head tilted. The flea-bitten green mountain hat they all wore sat lopsided on his balding head, and it irritated me.

As we approached a checkpoint, my heart thundered hard. In the grand scheme of things, I was a veteran, but checkpoints still made my bowels turn to water. I thought I might shit myself right there in the cart.

I drew a deep breath, but my limbs still trembled. I looked up as the breeze blew a little harder, revealing an unusually clear night. The moon had arced a quarter way down, it must be about 3am. Hopefully the Symguards were dozy.

I peered anxiously towards the checkpoint. The blueish torchlight on their post was low, no Symguards in sight. I bit my lip, my hopes a little higher.

"You'll wanna keep your eyes down and your mouth shut Missy," the Carter said. "Let's hope they're full of Raptor; usually they are this far out," he chuckled.

Raptor was something I refused to deal with. Whilst people starved, and they kicked Regs like me to the gutters, the powers that be certainly found the time to *not* police illicit drugs. Raptor was not the worst, but it did send enough off the rails to the point that they did dumb things, like climbing the wall and jumping off, thinking they could fly. Idiots, deserved it really. Sorry, my empathy has waned over the years.

The horse's hooves slowed, their clip clop increased pitch as we moved from dirt to paved road. We came to a stop at a boom gate, the blue lights seemed too bright now, and the annoying buzz of mosquitoes added an extra edge to my nerves.

The Carter slapped a mozzie from his face. "Oi! I need thoroughfare. You fools on the job?"

I slunk lower, disbelieving of his tone towards Symguards. A door slammed, the bright red of a Symguard uniform emerged from the darkness.

"Reverse your horse! Get your ID out," the Symguard slurred. The Carter clicked his tongue, pulled on the reins and the horse complied.

"Lay down, cough, look sick, and say nothing," the Carter whispered through the side of his mouth. I did as he said, I had no other option.

"Late cartage. Why?" The Symguard asked.

"This one's had too much Hype, she shoulda stuck to Raptor. Taking her to Remsin Infirmary."

"Remsin? Shit, must be hard up! Wouldn't send a dog there!" The Symguard's words bled together.

"How'd she pay, Carter?" The Symguard snickered.

"How do ya think?" The Carter laughed. Bile lapped in my throat; it wasn't a stretch to imagine the other ways I could be paying my way through life... I'd done many things close to that, not that I judge those who do, whatever helps you see the next sunrise is fine by me, but so far, I'd kept that kind of payment under control. This night, well, it felt all levels of out of control.

The cart lurched as the Symguard slapped the horse. "Get on then, you might find a bonus payment before you arrive," the Symguard laughed again whilst I vomited in my mouth. I imagined pushing him off the wall into the radioactive dust of the wastelands.

THE ROAD WAS ROUGH THE CLOSER WE CAME TO MY HOME district. Houses sagged under time, poverty and apathy; paths narrowed from smooth pavement to pot-holed gravel. Even the air was different, holding a more pronounced tang of rot and excrement. Those with little magic, just enough to stay this side of the wall or sewers, scrounged a meagre existence on the outer boroughs.

Professor Tamwin of 6th grade emphasized that those who descended from regions furthest from the radioactive fallout evolved differently from the survivors of the epicenter. My fingers curled, I peeled my gloves back, let the night air taste my skin. My skin looked no different from those of the inner boroughs, those whose DNA kicked them in the right direction. Yet, what dwelled deep within my tissues, far away within the fabric of myself, was not enough, it would never be enough.

When the bomb hit long ago, the future was predestined for thousands before they even knew it. My ancestors didn't hit the DNA jackpot, living in sustained generational poverty. Only a scant few relatives scraped by with enough elemental power to be recognised as something rather than nothing.

Mum works the pump station of the local power plant; well, she did last time I saw her. Her kind of power fuels its pumps, controlling the water flow through the sewers towards the filtrators that recycle it for consumption. Yeah it sounds gross, but rain doesn't fall enough and whatever they do to the water, it seems to make it tolerable to consume. It's yet to taste like literal shit and piss, so I can't complain when I do get the chance to drink from a tap. To be honest though, I'd prefer my spile and a tree any day.

DAWN WAS AN ORANGE SMUDGE ON THE HORIZON WHEN MY borough came into view.

"Get out, you can walk from here," the Carter snapped, and I was grateful. I hauled myself out quick as a whip and disappeared down an alley where the houses leaned as though they were depressed. I couldn't blame them.

The odd unsanctioned rooster crowed as I dashed through the shadows, head low, gasping as I kept my speed as steady as I could. The further I ran, the sparser the homes became, and the more decrepit.

I reached the block I grew up on and stood under the waning light of the night lamp. These were few in the outer districts, powered by the weakest, and it showed. I may as well have followed the moonlight, and I did all the way to the rotting front door of my childhood home. The smell of garlic and onion soup made my mouth water. It was humble, a fairly tasteless meal, but it stirred something deep inside me.

Candlelight flickered inside as dawn drew the sun higher in the sky. I wasn't going to make my presence known; it would only put Ash in danger. All I could do was be nearby, listen in, follow her into the town square, when the Symguard came for Ash to take her to her blood trial.

The problem was... how was I going to follow, how would I get into the testing arena? My nails clicked, I bit my lip, and broke a decent sweat thinking about it.

The answer came to me as the sweet sound of the rhythmic clip-clop of horse hooves. That same Carter just happened to pass by the top of my street, hoping for a day time fare. My hands sunk into my pockets. Did I have enough to bribe him further?

I backed away from home, away from soft sobbing eking from a part opened window... Ash. Mum's hazy silhouette hugged Ash behind thin curtains. I couldn't stand to see it, and struggled to suppress memories of my own trial. I couldn't stand to see Ash disowned just like I was. Dad's silhouette wasn't there.

Where are you?

The Carter rang his bell, touting for business. What an idiot, no one here could afford a Carter; but perhaps...

I hunched down, running quickly to the top of the street. Keeping hidden in the last gasps of the night, I dashed through the overgrowth of spindly weeds on the side of the road, my feet wet from the stinking run off from house waste. I shivered from the cold wicking up my pants. The Carter pulled over at the end of the street, the horse's snorting sent plumes of white over his head. I dropped down and watched as he pulled a flagon from under his seat.

"Yes..." I hissed quietly as his belch launched birds from a nearby tree. A plan was in the making. Watch, listen, smell the intoxication build, then pounce.

The sun was a thin wedge of glaring yellow when the Carter's body began to slump, but it took for his horse to lurch forwards, startled by a fox after an errant chook, for me to be assured the lurid Carter was easy pickings. He fell forwards, limp in his seat.

"Easy," I mumbled as I slipped into the cart; hand tight around one large DD battery.

"Hey, want this?" I elbowed him. He snorted, farted and opened bloodshot eyes. His fat fingers reached for the battery. My face crinkled, he stank like the sewers.

"You get this if you take me into town for the trials," I said as I leaned away.

He squinted at the battery, and lurched again.

"No, I already gave you a sack of food." I eyed the bag in the back. "Cartage to the city, then you get the battery."

"You'll pay up first... little lady."

I gasped. He wasn't as drunk as I thought. His hand clamped around mine, my fingers flushed red, then blanched white.

"Let go!" I hissed.

"Or what? You'll scream? Alert a Symguard?" Spittle fluffed in the corners of his smile. He leaned in, sniffed my hair, his hat fell at my feet as he reached for me.

"Fuck off!" I leaned back and kicked hard at his chest. He yelped, rocked backwards and fell from the cart. There was a thump and a groan. Breath held; I edged forwards and looked down. The battery rolled from the Carter's hand; blood pooled under his head. His eyes were dilated and dull.

"Oh shit!"

SKIN PALED TO A PASTY YELLOW, HIS LIPS A SICKLY BLUE, THE Carter was deader than half the batteries I fenced. It seemed an eternity before I could draw a breath, before the shake of my body eased. A bird squawked, jolting me from shock. My eyes darted about; relief released my chest as I realised I was alone. No one had seen... I hoped. I dragged him towards a ditch on the roadside. Sunlight streamed close, its fingers nearly reaching my crime scene. Sweat ran down my back, my heart thundered as I heaved the body along the gravel, ever aware of the blood trail left behind. He was heavy, fat with riches and food he didn't deserve. It took all my strength to yank him to the precipice of the ditch; I pushed. His body made a strange sound as it flipped over and over, finally splashing into a puddle of fetid water.

I was sliding down the embankment before a plan had really formed in my mind. He was heavy, his dead weight entrenched in mud as I wrenched his coat off. I slipped back and he rolled on top of me, his last breath groaned from his dead lungs. Vomit filled my mouth, my body slipped awkwardly, also gripped by sludge. Gasping, twisting, eyes stinging; I slipped free of his corpse. Hands on thighs, I struggled to draw breath, my face burned, I vomited again. Such as waste, I needed that nourishment on the inside.

The first strike of sun hit my back, a thin finger of it probed near the body, urgency poked like a jab in the ribcage. The Carter's signature mountain cap in hand, I scrambled back to the road, slipping into his stinking coat.

Coughing for breath as I climbed back into the cart, my vision warbled, my body numb. The horse chewing roadside thistles, seemingly unaffected by my crime, twisted its head back.

"You... gonna give me... trouble?" I stuttered

The horse snorted and yanked another thistle.

"What to do, what to do?" I panicked. Sweat slicked my skin as I grappled multiple lengths of leather, trying to figure out the reins and what the hell I was doing.

THE MORNING SKY SNAPPED WITH ELECTRICITY, BLUE AND WHITE wisps of elemental power buzzed overhead as the locals stirred. It broke the quiet of dawn, and magic-driven field generators spun to life. I slapped the reins hard, the horse lurched forwards. The cart jolted; I fell backwards. Luckily, the horse stopped, and I scrambled back into the seat.

"How do I drive this?" The horse looked jittery, so I clicked my tongue gently, as I'd seen the Carter do... the dead one. I cringed at the memory of his gasping mouth. The horse pulled away more gently. Turning, now that was a problem, and a new sweat ran down my face. The poor beast complained, flicking its head in annoyance, snorting and stomping as I grappled with the leathers. The sun warmed, the air thicker with the pollution blanket of a new day before I managed a full U-turn back to my street.

Two years ago, the Symguard picked me up for my blood trial mid-morning. I had time, and a plan was coming together in my mind. I'd get to Ash first, take her to the outer Western districts, remove her chip and set her free with me. The plan evaporated as the horse turned the next corner.

"Woah!" I pulled hard on the reins and we shuddered to a stop.

"No, no, no!" Dread iced my insides.

The Symguard was early, parked right outside my house. Ash hushed Mum with a hug as a Symguard impatiently urged her into his carriage. The Symguard took off, Ash in their possession as I stupidly froze in place

"GET IN!"

"Wren?" Mum was ashen seeing me, the one she thought long dead, the one she wished dead.

"Get Dad, I'll get us all to safety."

She stared, glassy-eyed at me, as though I was a ghost. I *was* a ghost.

"Get Dad and get in!" I snapped. Mum backed away.

"It can't be you..." Her mouth gaped.

"I'm gonna save Ash!"

"You killed your father, running away... you..." Her eyes narrowed; her hands clenched. "He was hung for protesting your blood trial."

My body went to ice.

"Mum... I... what?" I couldn't feel my body.

"You'll get her killed too!" Mum's eyes glimmered, flickers of energy sparked from her fingers.

"Just go Wren, go back to wherever you've been. Ash has a chance... unlike your father."

Tears nearly blinded me. My heart hurt.

"She doesn't and you know it! Dad..." My breath hitched. I could mourn him later, I *had* to be strong. I drew a deep breath, imagining what Dad would want of me. "Dad was weaker than you, Mum. If I had no power, Ash won't either, and she won't know how to survive. Get in Mum..."

She turned away, head shaking, her body aglow.

"Mum...please? We can start over!" The words were a lie and I knew it.

The front door slammed shut. For a stunned moment I sat there, the carriage jiggling underneath as the horse fancied itself to bolt. Tears burned down my face.

I let the horse have its way, and followed the Symguards wheel tracks.

THE SKY SPARKED WITH ELECTRICITY AS THE CITY OF THE 13TH borough of the Western district came into view. The closer to the centre, the grander the skyline became. Those who could pay for the likes of Mum to stand for eight hours a day powering their generators lived here, with more than they deserved, all because radiation changed their DNA just that little bit better.

It clenched my gut with rage. Gravel roads turned smooth again, fringed with neat paths. People spotted the towns, increasing in numbers where the roadside power poles were draped in red flags announcing the yearly blood trials as though it was some kind of celebration. I'd lost the Symguard a while back, but I was on the main road into the city now, I just had to follow the throng of people heading into the city square. It was all very public, the joy and the shame of baring your unmagical soul.

More carriages appeared, clogging the road, slowing my progress and whipping my anxiety into a frenzy. Once we hit walking pace, at least one decision was made. It was dumb, it was stupid, and it would probably kill me, but what choice did I have?

I pulled the cart off the main road, stopping in a quiet alley near a blacksmith. That would seem perfectly normal. Blacksmithing was the only respected trade not requiring magic. But, like Carters, those skills were familial, if you weren't born into it, you couldn't do it.

The bang of iron against an anvil fanned a brewing headache as I unlatched the horse from the cart. The buckles were endless. The horse stamped impatiently as I pulled him away, leaving just the bridle in place.

"Mother of fuck, what am I doing?" I whispered, smoothing the horse's already sweaty back. "Please don't kill me?"

I bounced on my feet and jumped; one leg hooked over the horse's back.

It skittered about, I held onto the reins, fingers twirled through the mane, knees dug into its ribs. "Woah, woah...'

After a few circles the horse settled, I didn't. My stomach was in knots.

"Good boy, good boy."

After a shaky, deep breath in, I tapped my ankles against his flank. He took off at a gallop, I barely stayed on, my arse stung as it banged against the spine.

A thickening crowd split, some screamed as the horse bolted through, I may have knocked one or two down.

It wasn't normal to see a single rider, only the elite had such luxury, and I think that's what held them back from reaching for me. They couldn't be quite sure the wild-eyed rider wasn't way above their station.

I didn't know how I was still on the horse to be honest, but I'd seen the Symguard that took Ash only a block ahead, and it was all I needed to keep my arse in place.

The city square was only two blocks away. It was now or never.

"Get on, go!" I squeezed the horse's belly as people dove out of the way.

"Ash? Ash?" I screamed as I approached the slowed Symguard. The startled crowd and my yelling caught the Symguard's attention. Eyes wide, they looked confused as I bared down. Ash turned; brows furrowed. Those eyes, I could tell from this far away, they were plain, they held no sparkle of magic. This was her only chance.

"Ash…" I screamed, leaning one arm out, waving towards myself, hoping she'd understand. One of the Symguard stood, drew a weapon from his back and fired. I ducked the arrow, felt the breath of it, nearly slipped off. The horse's back was white and foamy, slicking my legs this way and that.

"Ash… Ash…"

She stood; a guard pushed her down. She struggled; he smacked her across the face.

"No!" I yelled; I was maybe a hundred feet away.

"Wren?" Ash finally called my name. She struggled as the guard hit her again. Their cart stopped moving, I gained ground. Their cart started rocking, I was closer, and closer…

The crowd surged and pulled the Symguards from the cart. My horse slid to a stop as the crowd stomped the guards, a strange, frenzied look across their faces. Their power snapped overhead.

"Well get her, hurry up!" A violet-eyed man shouted, "We can't hold off any others when they arrive."

Speechless, I nodded, he nodded back. "Get her to safety," he said as he lifted Ash from the cart and up onto the horse.

Ash hugged into me, sobbing. The crowd parted behind us, the horse swung around and someone slapped its rump as the cries of more Symguard sounded. As we thundered away, I dared look back, through the stream of Ash's auburn hair. The crowd closed over the road, blocking the Symguard, giving us a chance.

THE HORSE HAD TO STOP; IT WAS EXHAUSTED AS WE HIT THE outskirts of the Western districts. The skyscrapers of the city faded, far enough away that we slipped from the horse, knees wobbly. I took the bridle off.

"Good boy, thank you."

It snorted, lay down and rolled the sweat away.

Turning around, I held Ash's face in my hands.

"You ok?"

Face red and tear-streaked, she nodded. "We thought you were dead."

I chuckled, "I thought that for a while too, but I found a way."

"Mum..." she began.

"Mum will survive, but we won't if we don't keep moving.

Like the cruel hand of fate heard my words, there was a sting across the top of my head. Ash gasped, as my hand came away bloody. Another whoosh sounded past my ear.

"Symguard!" Ash screamed.

We were running, dashing around the trash of the garbage dumps, through the thick smell of the open sewers. Arrows zoomed with increasing frequency as we dodged around the filth, through sludge and shit towards the wall.

"Where are we…" Ash's words cut off as I pulled her to the ground, a finger pressed to my lips. "Shh," I pointed to the wall.

"Where?" She mouthed.

"Out," I replied pointing up.

Her eyes bulged. I clasped her hand tight. The Symguard were in numbers, their voices closer by the moment.

If I head to my cesspit home, I'll expose everyone. They'll all be killed.

Eagles buzzed overhead, their whirring eyes scanning. They'd be looking for Ash, they'd have her ID on high alert.

"But, Wren, it's death out there," Ash whimpered.

"It's certain death here, out there… maybe we have a chance, at least for a while," I whispered, now wondering what the hell I'd done. What if she did have a chance at the trials? What if there'd been even one nanoparticle of magic in her?

My blood ran cold. *I've killed my sister*

The eagles circled closer, arrows thumped overhead, one twanged in a dead tree stump above our heads.

"Let's have one amazing adventure," I smiled weakly.

Ash's fingers laced into mine. She didn't smile.

"One, two..." On three, we dashed for the wall, the high-pitched squawk of an eagle sensing Ash knocked the wind from me. The wall felt so far away.

"Over there!" I pulled Ash until she stumbled, arrows and shouts filled the air. I felt the eyes of Regs, other OGMs, peering from the shadows. No one would help, I wouldn't help if I was them.

The wall was closer, the mildew ridden stink of it invaded every breath, then something punched me. I fell, Ash screamed, and pain seared through my chest.

"You're hit!" She cried.

I felt the tip of an arrowhead poking just below my collarbone, blood bloomed through my sweat-soaked top.

Gritting my teeth, I pulled myself up. "Go!" I stuttered, and we ran the last fifty feet to the vine-clad service stairs I used every other day to stare out at the ocean, to wonder what lay beyond it.

It was now Ash pulling me up each step, my breaths laboured.

"All the way up?" She asked.

I nodded, it was all I could do, grateful the eagle and the Symguard couldn't see us behind the overgrowth.

Their shouts became fainter, the air thinner, I struggled the last few levels, falling at Ash's feet at the top. She stood there, silent, gasping, eyes wide at the view, taking in the ocean turbines, the salty smell, the taste of something other than this life.

"Wren?" Ash turned; she paled as an eagle hovered overhead. Ash rubbed the small swelling in her wrist, knowing the presence of her ID chip meant she couldn't evade detection. Ash looked over the wall, down at me, back at the crisp outline of Symador... the city that took and gave nothing back.

"Come on," Ash pulled me to the edge, the eagle locked onto her, the sound of its mechanised eyes whirred. Its call to the Symguard was a death warrant.

"An adventure, sis?" Ash nodded.

"Adventure," I whispered.

As the eagle's razored claws descended for us, Ash pulled me over the edge. Light dark, light dark; we tumbled forever until the cold grip of the ocean engulfed us.

"FINALLY," ASH'S VOICE WAS DISTANT AS MY EYES PULLED AT THE glue that held them shut.

"Wren? Wake up," she urged.

My chest felt tight, I sucked in a breath, it hurt, but not as bad as when the arrow had struck. Glare hit me when I finally opened my eyes, the ground was moving. Nausea hit and I threw up.

Someone laughed, "Ah, you'll get your sea legs soon."

I sat bolt upright, tried to stand, but slipped back down when the ground lurched and I was face to face with a bearded stranger.

"You two are lucky we did a second sweep last night, you'd be shark bait otherwise," the man said, his foggy eyes smiling along with his mouth.

I sat up, shook my head, Ash urged me to my feet.

"You won't believe it, Wren, you really won't," she said.

I struggled to get my balance, and the bearded man

helped Ash hold me steady as they guided me to the side... of a boat.

"What?" My entire body trembled. "What's... what's happening?" I mumbled as I looked across a still and mirrored ocean, the enormous wall of Symador a blur on the horizon.

"You're numbers 649 and 650. That's how many we've saved from that hell-hole," the bearded man said. I noticed then that he had only three fingers on each hand.

Ash held my hand tighter and pointed in the opposite direction of Symador.

"Is that...?" I mumbled.

"A safe place, yes. Whilst the world and its people aren't as perfect they once were, it isn't what you've been told it is," he said.

I blinked hard, tears flowed hot, gasps of anger and relief wracked me.

"There are other places out there, Wren, slowly healing from the war, places that don't demand you be magic," Ash said.

As the nausea abated, and shock settled into a strange tingling feeling in my fingers and toes, I hugged into Ash as a new land closed in. Land with trees, lots of trees. Land with a shoreline and other boats bobbing in the water.

Land with hope, land with a future.

OBSERVATIONS OF THE HEAD CHRONICLER

LIV EVANS

"The totality is not, as it were, a mere heap,
but the whole is something besides the parts..."
- Aristotle

THERE ARE MANY LAYERS OF CIVILISATION IN EVERY CITY, AND SO few of them are ever recognised for their contributions. As humans, our attention is always drawn to the powerful; to the shiny, untouchable idols that hover loftily at the pinnacle of our society. They are the levels we aspire to, even though we know so little about them. But it isn't the person that really matters, it is the facade, their image. To truly know them would be to remove their power.

The illusion of grandeur works well to protect the ruling class. It keeps everyone and everything working just as intended. From the very top rung of the ladder right down to the feet buried in sludge and waste. Every person in that hierarchy has a role.

It can be hard to see how all the parts of a society come

together when you are enmeshed in it. It is, as they say, difficult to see the forest for the trees. However, when one is able to take a step back and watch the machinations of the world, it soon becomes clear that one part cannot function without another.

Even though those in power like to pretend society would fall apart without their indisputable valuable guidance, the world would be equally disrupted by the loss of someone else in a completely different position. Every change causes a ripple. Some are small, some are large, but there is *always* an impact.

Every person matters.

UNTIL THE END

KRISTEN DOVNIK

UNTIL THE END

KRISTEN DOVNIK

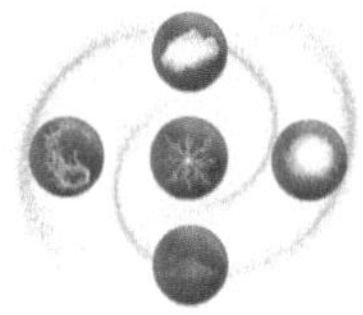

"WAIT UP, CALEB!" I CALL OUT TO MY LIFELONG FRIEND WHO runs through the crowd ahead of me. His brown curly head bobbing in and out of the throngs of people is all I see as I chase after him. This sector, which is usually empty around this time of day, is absolutely buzzing with patrons waiting to see who will pass the tests. Everyone is milling around Hollow Fountain, an old sandstone structure that's deteriorated over time. A sea of shouts erupts the moment water explodes from within the three-tier structure. Liquid brown as dirt gushes over the sides, forcing those around to jump back. We all know it comes from deep within the Earth and how dangerous it can be. My mother told me it's like acid, it burns through the skin before you even know what's happening.

"WATER!" The people begin to chant. I can't help but feel a sense of happiness with them. Around twenty years ago the Imperator announced that we would conduct tests for the magic wielders in the hopes to find the strongest in each element. He believes that if we combined the powers of all five wielders, it might just cause enough of an imbalance to reshape the Earth. Bringing back the peace we so long for.

Many eons before I was born my grandmother mentioned a great destruction that took place all over the globe. Radiation began to seep up through the cracks in the ground making ninety percent of the world inhabitable. My family were lucky to find Symador as it was a place the radiation hadn't touched. Many of those who survived hid behind its great walls hoping that it would protect them from what lies beyond.

It didn't take them long to realise that even though they were safe from the devastation beyond the wall, they faced an even bigger threat inside. Food turned poisonous and the water was contaminated. They built machines to purify the water, and all was well until those within the fortress came and took them away, only supplying the people with just enough to survive. The people fort back and many died trying to gain control over the fortress, it was a time of great sorrow.

Around the time my mother was born, those who had children found that when their offspring became teenagers, they had unbelievable powers. No one knows how they came to be except for the fact that every person who birthed a child was exposed to the radiation in one way or another. Thankfully for my family they were close to Symador when it happened and weren't really exposed to it.

Many of those who live down by the wall don't survive long enough to see a change, but I'm one of the lucky ones. Since the time of the radiation, my family has had a good position in the middle. We make clothes for the upper class and send the scraps down to those who cannot pay. My grandmother told me to always look out for the less fortunate. 'You never know who may need our help, Julia.' I miss her sometimes, especially now that I am alone. Thankfully, I have the anklet she gave me when I was a small child, a token I hold so dear to my heart.

"Hurry up slowpoke, the next one is about to start," Caleb calls out.

He's standing on the far side of the fountain. I squeeze my way through the crowds just in time to see a long blonde-haired girl step up to the microphone.

"Name and date of birth?" A woman in her late forties with jet black hair asks beside her. Her suit is absolutely perfect, with not a single crinkle to be seen. She definitely comes from within the fortress. There is not a soul around who is as clean as her.

The blonde's lip trembles. She licks the dry surface of her lips and nods.

"Racheal Adams, and the 12th of June 2205."

"Ability?"

"Fire."

"Begin." The woman says abruptly as she jots things down on her clipboard before lowering it to watch the girl cast her magic. Racheal's clothes are in tatters, proving that she is not from around these parts. I wonder why she came all the way up here to do the tests and not down in her district. Maybe it is because of the rumours going around about the anticipated uprising. I heard just the other day that the fortress is going to be cutting back their rations once again. They only get them two times a week, the poor people will starve if they cut them back anymore.

Racheal raises her arms and points them towards an artificial plant brought in just for the tests. I can see her concentrating but nothing seems to be happening. She lets out a huff of frustration before trying again. Her eyes are glazed over and focused on the plant but still, nothing happens.

"Has your magic come in yet?" The woman asks impatiently while tapping her finger against the edge of her clipboard.

"Yes, it has. Please believe me. I can do this." Racheal looks nervously at the crowd as she fiddles with the sleeve of her coat. It's not a crime to take the tests and have little to no powers. Loads of people do it and the fortress folk hate it. The longer they are down here the more likely they are to get radiation poisoning. They just don't understand how badly people want to get out of their homes near the wall. The fortress isn't a better place, not by far but it's further away from the radiation leaking through the cracks in the stone structure protecting us.

The woman points towards the plant whilst staring at Racheal. "Try again." She says through gritted teeth. The girl closes her eyes and takes a deep breath. For a moment she does nothing, just stands there and the black-headed woman looks like she's about to explode. Racheal opens her eyes and focuses solely on the leaves that blow ever so slightly in the afternoon breeze. Her eyes seem to grow wider with every passing second and still nothing happens.

"Enough! I don't believe you possess any powers and if

you did, they most certainly wouldn't be strong enough to survive the trials. Next?"

Racheal's facial features turn from frustration to embarrassment as she steps away from the microphone. I feel sorry for the poor girl. She was definitely trying.

"Hey, it looks like there is no one else lined up. You should go now, go show them what you can do before you miss your shot," Caleb mutters as he looks down over his shoulder at me. We both know I can manipulate the elements. I've been able to for a few months now. Even way before my eighteenth birthday, I knew I had a connection. Now it was my turn to show them.

I hold up my hand flashing my crossed fingers. "Okay, wish me luck."

A sly smile plays on Caleb's lips as I step away and head over to the black-haired woman. "I would, but you don't need it," he calls out bringing a similar smile to my face. Butterflies swarm in the pit of my stomach the closer I get to the woman. The buildings that contain our tiny homes, stand weathered and aged along the edge of the vast space around us. I step up to the microphone and it feels like all of Symador is watching me.

"Name and date of birth?" The woman lifts her clipboard. It's only now, being this close, I see a list of written names. I thought she was only taking notes, but it looks like she is marking off everyone who participates in the tests and is writing a number next to each name. I wonder what the numbers are for.

"Julia Gardner. Born the 9th of June 2205." People are smiling as they eagerly await to see what I can do. They push and shove each other trying to get closer to the props put out for the tests. If I were them, I wouldn't want to be anywhere near the instruments just in case a tester lost control of their abilities. It's happened before. Many years ago an electric lost control and fried an innocent bystander. I think the people may have forgotten that, but I haven't. I still remember blood hitting my face after they exploded. My stomach rolls at the memory of the metallic smell of blood coating my face.

"Ability?"

"Electric," I declare with confidence as I watch everyone's eyes light up with glee. There are not many of us out there, and I'm proud to be one of them.

"Begin." The woman says, and I turn towards the beat-up car sitting off to the right.

A few people back away from the hunk of metal and yet, Caleb walks over. He is such an idiot, he's always trying to get in on the action. I know he would be able to move the Earth, blocking my powers from ever touching him, but would he be fast enough? He is strong but nowhere near the top of his class.

"Energise," I whisper, holding my arm out and the old station wagon comes to life. Sparks of electricity fly out of every nook and cranny, narrowly missing a man standing just a little bit too close. I feel my power coursing through me. It flows from my feet all the way up my body and out my fingertips.

"ENERGY!" The crowd roars, and I can't help but smile as my heart bursts with pride. I look over at Caleb and he too is smiling from ear to ear. He knew I could do it.

"You have twenty minutes to pack your belongings and say goodbye to your friends and family. You better hurry, I hate waiting." The black-haired woman glances at me and grimaces. She eyes me from head to toe, giving me a look of disapproval before turning her back on me. With haste, she walks over to the shiny SUV waiting on the path leading out of the middle sector.

"You did it, Jules. I always knew you would." Caleb puts his arm around my shoulders as we head down the hill towards my house. Our feet kicks up the red dust that lingers along the surface of the stone pathway. It must have come in with the last dust storm.

"Yes, and I'm over the moon. I just hate the fact that I must leave." It suddenly hit me what this actually meant. Up until now, I had only focused on doing my trial. Now reality slammed into me, causing my stomach to clench in fear. "What if I never see you again? What if I never return to this sector but I am forced to stay in the fortress for the rest of my life?" My mind wanders to the nightmare I had of entering the fortress and never coming out. Thankfully it was just a dream.

"Come on Jules, you're overthinking this." Caleb roughly rubs the back of my head forcing me to push him away. He chuckles beside me, and I quicken my pace knowing he's coming after me.

That's one thing I've always loved about Caleb, he tries to find ways to cheer me up even if the situation isn't in our favour. "Hey, they will take you up the mountain and you will do what needs to be done and be home by lunchtime. Easy peasy." People smile at me as we walk past them on the street, some even reach out their hands wanting to give me their blessings. I accept them all although I'm not really sure what I'll need them for.

"If only it were that simple. I just hope I'm strong enough to face what's to come."

"You're a Gardner, you can face anything." We walk up my front steps, and I unlock the door. I held it open just long enough for him to follow me in. The smell of old fabrics hits my senses and I breathe it in. I'm really going to miss it here, but if I have a chance to help heal the world, I'm going for it.

"I hope you're right."

"Hurry up and say goodbye, I need to get away from this place." The black-haired woman frowns at those still milling around the Hollow fountain as she opens the car door and hops into the driver's seat.

"I guess this is it, Jules, you're going to the top." Caleb stands less than a foot away with his hands in his pockets. For a moment all we do is stare at each other before he swings his gaze to the fortress on top of the hill. All our lives we have longed to see what is up there, and now, I'll finally get the chance.

"I'll see you soon, yeah?" I almost whisper. My heart breaks knowing I may never see him again. My eyes are rimmed with unshed tears. Why does it have to be so hard?

"Come on Jules, don't cry." As if on cue, my tears begin to stream down my face. Caleb reaches out and grabs my shoulders, pulling me into his arms. "You're gonna kill it up there. You're going to fix our world and be back before you know it. I'll be waiting right here when you get back."

"You promise?" I whisper while tightening my grip around his waist. I know I have to let him go but I don't want to. He smells like home.

"Always," he whispers against my hair.

I jump in fright as the fortress woman honks the horn reminding me to be quick. "You better go," he says, placing a sweet gentle kiss on my forehead before dropping his arms.

"Yeah, I better," I nod as I step back and wipe my tears away with the back of my hand. "I'll see you soon, Caleb." I cross the short distance over to the car and open the door. I take one last look, branding his image into my memory as I climb in.

His smile is sad and yet also proud. He knows that my going to the fortress could potentially be our ticket out of here. If myself and the other four magic wielders are able to restore the balance and contain the radiation that is poisoning our planet, only then may we finally leave Symador. The walled city we have all lived in our entire lives. Don't get me wrong, I don't mind living here but grandmother always spoke about trees that would blow in the wind. Streams of clean fresh water that would travel down from the mountains. About the beautiful oceans as far as the eye could see, and the amazing animals that used to live in amongst the forests. I long for those things to come back, to be able to witness such amazing wonders with my own eyes. To not see greyish clouds all day long or to have air so thick in areas you almost choke.

"You are to keep your mouth shut and only speak when spoken to, do you understand?" The woman beside me snapped me out of my daydream. I'm jolt around in my seat as the woman races up the narrow walkways towards the top of the mountain.

"Yes ma'am," I whisper.

"You are heading to the fortress for one reason and one

reason only. If someone asks you to do something, you do it. Got it?"

"Yes."

"Good, we're almost there." My heart skips a beat as my driver slows the car down until we are just slightly rolling on the road. People crash into the car windows trying to get a glimpse of the next magic wielder entering the old medieval structure. Smiling faces lined with eagerness greet me as the car rolls up to the entrance.

"Energy wielder." The woman says bluntly to the guard manning the gate before he waves us through.

There is an old metal fountain in the middle of the courtyard. It's covered in so much rust that I doubt it even worked before the world was plagued by radiation. We come to a stop at the base of some stairs leading up to huge metal doors. For a split second, I regret ever stepping foot into the tests. What if the trials are not what they seem? A guard walks past my door, and I quickly shake off the sickening feeling that washes over me. Get a grip, Julia, you're just overthinking things as always. I can feel energy pooling beneath the car and know I have the power to do this.

"Get out." The woman says opening her door.

I step out and am momentarily stunned by what lies before me. Over the city and past the walls are vast open spaces as far as the eye can see. Whirlwinds of dust linger near the lower sectors along the edge of Symador, and I see now why they always wear face coverings. Who knows what sinister things those winds bring with them? Thankfully I never had to endure hardship like that living in the middle sector.

"Come here girl," the woman spits angrily from her place at the base of the steps.

"Oh, sorry," I mutter, dashing over to her side.

A bald-headed man speaks as he descends the three steps in front of us. "Avery, you finally returned, and who is this?" He is wearing brown armoured pants with a matching jacket. An outfit that wreaks authority. He eyes me from head to toe like a prized lamb ready for slaughter.

"Miles, it's always so good to see you. This is Julia Gardner from the raised sector. A powerful energy wielder. Definitely a ten, she's the strongest I've ever seen."

"Strong you say? Interesting." Miles contemplates her words for a moment before turning his head to talk to the guard standing next to him. "Take her to the court, the others are already waiting there. Let's see what this little lady can do." He smiles at me, and I can't help but nervously smile back. I wonder just how strong the others will be.

Another guard descends the steps and grabs my arm. He pulls me towards the open doors and into the stone structure. The bricks are old and worn with age. The ceilings are as tall as two story buildings and there are statues of armoured men lining the walls. I don't see much as we hastily walk through the hallways and out the other side. The floor is soft beneath my boots as we step out onto artificial grass. The entire courtyard is surrounded by even more greenery and for a second I think it's real. Trees line the walls which blocks all view of the outside world. With water and earth wielders at their beck and call why not get them to liven up the place? However, when I pass by one of the trees, the shiny texture of the leaves is a dead giveaway that it's fake.

Standing in a circle, with a vacant spot for me, are four young people about my age. A guard dressed in all black stands behind each teen watching their every move. With a clipboard in hand, I can only begin to wonder what they are monitoring.

"Energy wielder." The guard behind me pushes me forward, forcing me to stand with the others.

"Hi," I mutter nervously but the others look at me wide-eyed in alarm and shake their heads. But their warning comes too late.

"No talking!" A blonde-headed woman, who stands behind a tall lanky boy, scolds me with a vicious look on her face. "Raise your arms and hold onto the person standing next to you."

Is she talking to me? I wonder as I watch those around me grip each other's wrists. Not wanting to anger the woman more, I do the same. The teenagers look tired, like they've been at this for hours, maybe even days. Their shoulders are slumped forward and their heads look too heavy for their bodies.

"Harness your gift deep within you and focus on the stone in the middle of the circle. Channel all your powers into the rock. You need to create a vortex of power strong enough to cover the entire globe." I look down between us and see a tiny stone maybe an inch in diameter lying flat on the fake grass.

"Focus newbie," My eyes shoot over to the dark-skinned man circling around behind us before they return to the rock.

Breathe Julia, you've got this. I close my eyes and pull up the energy that burns deep within. It zaps through my veins and uncontrollably down my arms into the wielders standing next to me. Oh no! Their painful groans echo beside me and it's my instinct to pull away. I don't want to hurt them, but they hold strong. Fire burns its way up my arm as water freezes the veins in my other, this time it's my screams that fill the courtyard. Pain as I've never felt before rushes through my entire body. My eyes spring open and above the small rock on the ground, an orb has formed and spins around with our combined power. I can feel our magic entwining with each other's. The glowing ball moves this way and that, forever revolving, preventing our powers from escaping. Fire, water, air, and electricity are evidently present with only a hint of earth. Dirt swooshes around inside the orb before crumbling to dust and disappearing. I look over at the wielder and see the moment she blacks out, collapsing to the floor.

"Fail." The guards say in unison behind us and the wielders next to me drop their arms.

Two men dressed in white enter the courtyard heading straight for the girl with black curly hair. She mumbles something as they lift her up by her arms and drag her off towards the entrance on the far side. There is a small commotion behind me, and I can't help but strain to listen in.

"Earth wielders are so hard to come by, where will you find another?" The blonde woman asks, and I'm guessing she is the one in charge around here.

"I've seen one, a level eight."

"Go retrieve them. I want to continue as soon as possible." The blonde-haired lady commands and the dark-skinned man leaves the courtyard.

"Take them back to their cells. Give them their rations. We don't want anyone else passing out today." The sound of a gunshot reverberates through the air making us all jump. My nightmare resurfaces the moment I heard the pop and my initial feelings about coming here come flooding back in. Grandmother warned me about the fortress, she told me to be cautious, but I thought she was only saying that because she never liked the Imperator. My gosh, I've made a huge mistake coming here.

We walk in a quiet line back through the fortress. Not a single soul dares to make a sound. My body trembles in fear as they lead us around a few corners and down a flight of stairs before we are forced into a cold dark room. The guards close the door and lock us inside. I look over at the others ready to speak and yet the eyes of a red-headed girl say not to. I'm about to say what the hell when a wooden panel midway down the door opens up and the wielders rush forward to grab their rations. Not wanting to miss out, I do the same. I'm handed a small bottle of green liquid and a medium-sized paper bag. Within the blink of an eye, the panel is slammed shut and the sound of heavy footsteps move away from the door.

"What's your name, newbie?" A lanky boy asks. He is crouched in the corner biting into an apple. Even in this dimly lit room, there is no way I would miss the dark circles that lie under his eyes. Under all their eyes for that matter.

"Julia, what's yours?" I reply and lean my back up against the brick wall.

"Finnick. Going by your clothes I'm guessing you don't live too far away."

"Not really, I just design clothes for the upper class. I'm from the middle sector."

"You had me fooled." The girl beside Finnick chimes in. "I'm Stacey and this is Eris. We are from the lower sector." Both of them are super skinny and have the whitest hair I've ever seen. I wonder if they were born that way or if it was caused by the radiation.

"Nice to meet you. What happened back there? To the Earth wielder?"

"Isla wasn't strong enough to handle our powers. The Imperator only wants the strongest of each element. Those who fail his trails... well they don't ever leave this place if you get my drift," Finnick says before taking another bite of his apple. The memory of the gunshot enters my mind sending a shiver down my spine.

"Why not just let us leave? Why do they kill us?" My voice is shaky as panic rises within me.

"Because some of them never make it through the trials. They don't want the word to spread and it causes a rebellion," Stacey says before she turns away and takes a sip of her green fluid.

"What is this by the way?" I ask, holding up the bottle.

"It's vitamins. It's everything you need if you want to survive this place."

"Fair enough." I unscrew the lid and take a whiff. Bile rises in the back of my throat and I quickly move the bottle away from my face, forcing myself not to throw up. "It smells like vomit." I pinch my nose, never wanting to smell the vile green liquid again.

"And it tastes even worse," Stacey says, raising her bottle to me before swallowing every last drop.

"Great." Holding my nose with one hand, I place the plastic to my lips and down the liquid in a huge gulp. If I were to ever mix dirt with battery acid, I bet this is what it tastes like. It hits my stomach and for a second, I think it's about to come back up, but I won't allow it. I pinch my nose and force myself to count to ten, thankfully it stays put.

"You better eat too, they will have the next wielder here before you know it," Finnick mutters from his spot in the corner.

I didn't ask him where he was from, but going by his clothes, he was most certainly from the upper sector. His brown suit doesn't seem to have any tears and from this far away I can tell that the stitching is impeccable. A suture that is only reserved for those in the upper sector. I wonder if he was a part of the elite group of people rumoured to have trained kids to withstand the trials.

"Don't we get a break?" I ask, feeling my excessive magic use weighing heavily on my body. I take a seat on the floor, pull my knees up to my chest and run my hand along my anklet. Grandmother was always wary of the fortress, I completely understand why now. This is not a place of happiness, but one of sadness.

"This is our break. Once the Earth user is found, they will bring them back here and we will conduct the trails again. We rest when we can, eat when rations are given otherwise we will not have the energy to move forward. They want to finish this and they don't care what we have to go through to achieve it." Finnick says as he rests his head back against the wall.

I nod slightly in understanding not wanting to say anymore. I will do as he says and eat. If he is right and we will be put through that again soon, I'll need my strength.

WE PASS THROUGH THE LAST DOORWAY AND OUT INTO THE courtyard. The sky is dark with clouds hovering as far as the eye can see. The flicker of fiery lanterns lines the walls illuminating the vast space. The newcomer has their back to us, but I could never mistake those brown locks for as long as I live. Can it really be?

The guards move away allowing us to take our places and I rush over to Caleb's side. Knowing I'll be reprimanded for speaking, I grab his hand and squeeze it tight. He glances down at me, and his shoulders soften the moment our eyes connect. He opens his mouth, and I quickly shake my head. Silently telling him no. He eyes me warily before mouthing the words 'are you ok?' I shake my head. If we pass their trails tonight, we might be able to stay alive but if we fail, one of us will die. This whole day has been one whirlwind of a ride and yet I'm so glad to have Caleb back by my side.

"Raise your arms and hold onto the person standing next to you." The blonde guard says behind me.

I let go of Caleb's hand to grab ahold of his arm while Finnick grabs my other. Anxiety flows through my veins remembering just how much this is going to hurt. I focus on the rock in the centre of our circle and try to calm my raging nerves. Breathe Julia, let's end this. I close my eyes and pull the energy up through my feet and into my core. It zaps and fizzes through me like lightning as I force it forward down into the rock. The guys groan beside me as my energy works its way through me and into them. Air hits me like a hurricane from the left as my veins fill with dirt on the right. My body becomes stiff the longer I hold onto Caleb's arm but we can't stop. I open my eyes and stare at the revolving ball in front of us. Pain worse than ever before takes over my body, and I clench my jaw not wanting to give them the satisfaction of hearing me scream.

"More!" The blonde woman shouts. I force my powers forward and down into the orb, watching it grow larger by the second. "MORE!!" She screams again and we do as she says.

A wind turbine forms in the centre of our circle; it's almost strong enough to knock us off our feet. I feel untouched energy beneath my boots and reach for it. However, just before I can touch it, a wall goes up, cutting me off and my powers begin to diminish. No! What is happening? I try again and again but it's all the same. My body feels heavy as my powers fade and before I know it I crash to the ground.

"NO! We were so close; I could feel it!" The blonde woman screams as my eyes blink away the fogginess lining my vision. Caleb drops down beside me and brushes the hair away from my face. He hovers over me, asking me questions I cannot hear. His lips pinch in a thin line as he has no idea what just happened. A guard walks over and pushes Caleb out of the way before rolling me onto my back. He flashes a light into my eyes before looking up at the blonde woman shaking his head. The woman lets out an enraged growl as she stomps over to where I lay on the ground. She glances at me for only a second before lifting her clipboard and crosses off my name.

"Get rid of her and bring me the spare."

Get rid of me? What? No! Two guards from the side of the courtyard step forward and pick me up. My legs drag along the ground as they begin to whisk me away. My heart hammers in my chest as I try to think of something, anything that will stop what is about to happen.

"Where are you taking her?" Caleb yells. I can hear the panic rising in his voice and know I have to get away. I can't let them kill me.

"Be quiet!" The blonde woman shouts.

Stacey sniffle's and I know she's crying. They will kill me just like the others, and I begin to wonder just how much death they have had to witness because of these trials. You need to fight Jules, give it everything you've got or you will die today. Something stirs deep inside, an innate sensation to not give up.

My body kick-starts into overdrive as adrenaline fills my veins. I dig my heels into the fake grass knowing I only have minutes before they put a bullet into my skull.

"Please stop," I say, trying to pull my arms out of their grasp. The guards don't even look down as my boots slip off my feet. I feel energy just below the surface of the ground and try pulling it into my core. I might be able to gather just enough to zap them so they let go.

"Hurry up, we have a job to do," Blondie barks at the guards as we near the edge of the courtyard. My body flails between them as I frantically try to get away. I look around and catch a quick glimpse of Caleb. Finnick holds him back knowing that if he were to chase after me, they would probably execute him too.

We pass over the threshold, and I kick my leg out trying to hook my toes on the door. Instead, my anklet gets caught, halting our movements. One of the guards grunts in annoyance. The other pulls out his gun. For a moment my heart stops.

"Could this one be any more annoying?" The guard places the barrel next to my temple, and the sound of the bullet moving into the chamber. I won't allow my body to succumb to my fear. Ripping my leg away from the door, my anklet breaks. I kick the one holding the gun in the ribs. He drops the revolver, his hand quickly moving to his side.

"Maeve will punish us for this, hurry up and stop messing around." Energy like never before awakens all around me, and I pull it in. I'm winding up like a coil that's about to explode. Anger burns through me, making me feel stronger than ever before. These men were willing to hurt me because of my failure. I'll show them just how wrong they were.

"She kicked me or did you not see that? Hey, what's she doing?" No longer holding me, my body floats off the ground. Small lightning bolts emit from within me, crashing into the lights that are lit up along the hallway.

"You better run," I declare, raising my body so I'm hovering less than a foot off the ground.

"Oh shit!" The guards say in unison. They dash back into the courtyard with me following behind them.

"Julia?" Caleb asks in shock as everyone turns to see

what the commotion is about. The blonde guard known as Maeve, glares at me in utter annoyance.

"I'm glad to see you've recovered. Now stop messing around and get back in line." She orders, but I do no such thing. She wanted to kill me and it's only fair I repay the favour.

"How many of us have you killed?" I ask never taking my eyes off of her. Her stance is one of authority, and I can see the guards around us are starting to realise I mean business. I will make them pay for what they have done.

"That is none of your con..."

"ANSWER THE QUESTION!" I shout.

"One hundred and ninety four." A woman to the left of Maeve blurts out and my jaw drops in shock. Maeve flicks her eyes to the black haired woman, and I see death for what she just said lingering in her blue pupil's. Sadness and fury over those who have died rises within me, and I can no longer contain the power within my core. The hairs on my body stand on edge as my energy lifts me even higher off the ground. Electricity flickers from her core making the fiery lanterns around the courtyard spark brightly.

"You will pay for the lives you have taken," I seethe through gritted teeth while raising my arm towards her.

"Julia don't!" Caleb warns, but it's too late. A bolt of lightning leaves my fingertips, hitting Maeve in the centre of her chest. Her eyes bulge as she claws at the hole as wide as her head before she collapses to the ground.

Without another thought, every guard or observant within the facility faces the same fate. They try to flee away from me, but I am faster. I release more bolts of electricity hitting two guards on the right and three on the left. I know there are more hidden within the building and I send a shockwave of my powers through the fortress, slicing through every guard that stands in its way. In a blink of an eye my powers are diminished and it's only us wielders who remain.

"What did you do?" Stacey asks as her eyes dart from one body to the next.

"I don't know, but I know it had to be done. They wouldn't have let us live after we restored the balance." I let go of the rest of my powers and allow my feet to settle back in the ground.

"How did you do that?" Caleb asks coming to stand by my side. He looks at me like I'm an alien. Like he doesn't want to get too close in case he catches something.

"I honestly don't know. A guard put a gun to my head and it was like all of a sudden a wall came down and I could access everything." My grandmother's anklet comes to mind, and I walk over to the door to retrieve it.

I lean over and pick up the thin chain from the ground. The second my skin touches the metal I get this odd feeling. It's like something is blocking my mind from access my full potential.

"How strange," I whisper.

"What is it?" Caleb asks, standing not too far away. I don't say anything as I walk over and hand him the anklet. A look of confusion crosses his face but so does something else. He glances down at the anklet in the palm of his hand as dirt swirls around in the centre of his other.

"It's blocking your powers isn't it?"

"Yeah but how? It's just a piece of metal?"

"I'm not too sure, but it would be why my powers deflated earlier. I could feel the electricity beneath my feet, but I couldn't access it. I originally thought it may have had something to do with the power usage as I've never used that much before, but now I see it was this." Grandmother always told me the anklet would keep me safe and protect me from the Imperator, but she never explained why. I glance over at the others and see they look lost. They stare at the deceased on the guard unsure whether to stay or run. Without the guards around, they don't know what to do.

"We should leave. The other guards will be making their rounds soon." Finnick mutters as he glances over at the door leading into the courtyard.

"Actually, I think we should stay. We should finish what we started. With my powers no longer blocked I really believe we can do this."

"But what about the guards? They will come for us." Stacey holds onto Eris for dear life. They know what the consequences are for killing the others, but I say let them come. They will suffer the same fate.

"Let them. With our powers combined we will be indestructible. They will not defeat us."

"You really think we can do this?" Finnick asks a little too sceptically.

"Absolutely. We were close before, but we can do it again."

"Are you sure Jules? They look pretty tired." Caleb rests his hand on my shoulder while he glances at those around us. I feel it, the toll my powers have on my body but if we don't do it now, when?

"We have to try. If we stop now, who knows when we will be able to try again."

"I agree with you. Although if the guards come, we are as good as dead," Stacey says as she looks at Eris. Going by the look on his face, he doesn't want to stop. He knows the risks and still wants to end this, just as much as I. "Stuff it, let's do this," Stacey declares as she walks back over to her place in the circle. Finnick joins in and so do Caleb and me. I glance around at the four other magic wielders and mentally give them my thanks. Thanking them for believing that we can do this and pray that no one else has to die today.

"Are you ready?" I ask not only them but myself too. They nod, and I take a deep breath. Raising my arms, I link them with Finnick's and Caleb's before closing my eyes. "Let's begin," I whisper. The air turns cold around us flicking up specks of dirt and water in my face. The vortex opens and spins around in front of us. The energy from within the planet's core rises up through my body, and I force it forward.

I grit my teeth. It's no longer just Caleb's and Finnick's powers seeping into my veins but also Stacey's and Eris's too. Our powers channel through us like a never-ending wave moving round and round.

I open my eyes and watch the orb grow bigger and bigger until we are standing inside it. Fire, electricity, water and earth twirl together like ribbons on a breeze. Shouts and screams come from somewhere beyond our powers but we don't stop. My powers are strong, and yet, I know I can still give more.

I turn my head to look at Caleb beside me, needing to

see him one more time before I allow my powers to completely overthrow me. His smooth features and his loving face stare back at me. The man I could always count on whenever I needed him. I just wish it didn't take me this long to realise what he meant to me. There are small rocks piling up inside of his beautiful blue eyes and I know he's already too far gone.

"Caleb," I whisper as a small tear slides down my face before getting caught in the wind. Not wanting to see anymore, I close my eyes and let my powers take over. I burn stronger than any energy current known to man.

I feel the last wave of my control leave my body as a supersonic boom erupts from the middle of our circle. The force of our powers throws us back to the outer walls of the courtyard. A force like never before rushes through my body, crushing me against the cold stone walls. My screams fill the air as the onslaught never seems to end.

My body deems it can't handle anymore, and I fall to the ground. My mind going blank.

I INHALE AND NOTICE THERE IS A SHIFT IN THE AIR. IT'S CLEAN! I breathe in deeply, loving the feel of the fresh air in my lungs. My body fills with excitement as my eyes flutter open and the sky is no longer grey but a beautiful shade of blue. Did we do it? I sit up and look around. A massive hole lies in the centre of the courtyard; a crater large enough to fit a small field.

The wall behind me no longer stands as it was crushed by a wave of power. The towers which once stood at each corner are gone, and I can now see past Symador's outer walls without being outside the fortress. It looks almost the same as it did when I arrived yesterday but somehow different. The fields beyond the walls look brighter than ever and the hills seem to sing in the new light.

"Thank my lucky stars," Caleb whispers, his big strong arms circling around me to hold me close. He rests his head in the crook of my neck while I raise my arms and hug him tight.

"Did we do it?" I ask not wanting to let him go. I could have lost him today, and I never wanted to feel as heart-broken as I did when I saw his powers take over.

"I think so but how will we know?"

"I'm not sure but right now, I don't care. I just want to stay right here."

"Me too... Are you all right?" He asks, trying to pull away, but I don't let him.

"I don't think so, but I will be." My voice is muffled as I speak against his chest. Tears of joy slide down my face because moments ago I believed I would never be able to hold him again.

There is a rustling of footsteps not too far away and my heart stops at the thought of the guards. Caleb stills only for a moment before his body relaxes back to normal. A few muffled voices fade away, and I'm guessing whomever it was wanted to leave before anyone saw them.

"Hey, are you guys ok?" Finnick calls from where he stands on the other side of the courtyard.

"We are, but what about them?" Caleb removes one of his arms from around my shoulders and points at something in the distance.

"Yeah, we are ok," Stacey calls out, and there is a grunt from Eris. Without another word, they all make their way over to where we stand. Even though I don't want to, I lift my head away from Caleb's chest and wipe away my tears.

Caleb feels me move away and lifts my chin so we are eye to eye. For a moment he just stares at me before he leans forward and places a sweet gentle kiss on my lips.

"You don't know how long I've been dying to do that."

"So, why didn't you?"

"I never realised before how much you loved me too." A smile creeps onto my face as I lift my hands and pull his face down to meet mine. A kiss as sweet as the air we now breathe rests on my lips, and I savour every moment.

We may not know what our future holds but as long as we are together we can conquer anything.

OBSERVATIONS OF THE HEAD CHRONICLER

LIV EVANS

"But isn't everything here green?" asked
Dorothy.
"No more than in any other city," replied Oz;
"but when you wear green spectacles, why of
course everything you see looks green to you..."
- L. Frank Baum

Stories are rarely ever make-believe, even the ones in books labelled fiction.

Fairytales and fables have been used throughout recorded history to help people make sense of the world, to warn children of dangers in their environment, and to impart wisdom and morals. Later, as humans evolved, they became a way to reflect society. To hold a mirror up to humanity.

There was a story once, a very long time ago. A tale about a girl who was lost in a coma dream and travelled to a world with yellow brick roads, silver slippers, and cities made of emerald. Only, the city wasn't really made of emeralds. The leader decreed that everyone within its glimmering walls had to wear glasses with green lenses to make the buildings appear as though they were made of the precious gems the city was named after.

Symador is a lot like the city from that story.

Whenever the Trials are on, the people witness the fallacies of the Imperator through green-tinted lenses.

There is talk of people with elemental powers being tested to see if they can save our dying world.

There is prestige in being selected as a strong wielder because you will be part of solving an impossible problem.

There is a sense that all the violence, the sickness, and the danger... maybe it is all worth it to find the right person.

After all, there is no way to survive outside the bounds of this city, right?

These are the things Vaarem wants everyone to believe. This emerald-hued facade is the only option he allows. This life, the way he demands it is lived, is the only one on offer.

For the most part, people believe it. After all, it is far more comfortable to view the world in limited hues of green than it is to tear off the lenses and see the true complexity and depth of the colours all around.

Humans are odd creatures; they are willing to put up with all sorts of atrocities to avoid seeing just how messy reality is.

It is far easier to be uncomfortable than it is to be enlightened.

Enlightenment brings its own special burden. There is

an inevitable sense of responsibility that comes with it all, where one must stand on the precipice of everything they have ever known and see how they have been complicit in their own deception.

Then, comes the question: Am I brave enough to face this?

The need for survival often dictates that the answer to this is no. So, people slip back into their old lives. Into the comfort of the stories woven by those in power to keep things running just right.

Others, the daring few, eschew the glasses. They will never see the world quite the same way again. Like the girl in the story about the yellow brick road and silver slippers, they will return to their home irrevocably changed and never quite sure if they imagined it all.

ABOUT THE AUTHORS...

Kate Schumacher

Find out more!

Kate Schumacher is the author of the epic fantasy series The Fires of Aileryan (Shadow of Fire and Heart of Flame). Her latest romantic fantasy novel, The Call of the Sea, is the first book in The Grail Cycle, a reimagining of Arthurian legend.

When she isn't writing, Kate is reading her way through an ever growing TBR pile and trying to get enough sleep. She finds time to write in the in-between moments of life, and is inspired by landscape, poetry, music and politics.

Kate completed a Bachelor of Arts in Creative Writing and Journalism, and an Honours degree in Screenwriting, followed by a Graduate Diploma in Education.

She lives in Northern NSW, Australia, with her partner, two children and three very spoiled cats.

Liv Evans

Find out more!

Liv Evans is the pseudonym for an Australian-born author who delights in crafting stories just as much as she enjoys devouring them.

Always one to question authority, Liv prefers to write stories with fully fleshed out characters and immersive worlds. Her favourite aspect of writing is weaving a tale that makes the characters and readers question what they think they know about themselves and the world.

Central themes in Liv's work include never blindly accepting authority, finding the strength to stand up for what is right, and the power of the human spirit.

JUDY LIU

Find out more!

Inspired by her love of Marvel, sci-fi, old Taiwanese dramas, and ridiculous anime, Judy scribbles mini-stories wherever she can (and subsequently forgets them!).

She graduated from Rice University in Houston, Texas, studying history, Asian studies, and education. Judy is not unfamiliar with extensive writing, having published multiple pieces. She spent some time living in rural Japan before working in the legal and compliance sphere.

With her debut novel The Vending Portal, Liu hopes to meaningfully add to Asian American literature to further enrich the YA genre.

Outside of work and writing, Judy enjoys dancing with her teammates and friends, exploring unknown spots or cities, caring for her plants, and making nonsense sounds to her sister.

J.P. MCDONALD

Find out more!

JP lives in Western Sydney with his family and an army of puppies.

Before publishing Sci-fi adventure novels, JP focused on writing songs for the melancholy masses and in complete contrast, also developed vibrant and catchy children's songs.

JP has published a space opera duology and a standalone scifi adventure.

You can find him posting bookish parody videos on social media, planting native bush foods in his backyard and chasing the sun through rivers and national park trails.

EA Robins

EA Robins is just having fun. She has crippling attractions to well-dressed villains, research cleverly disguised as fiction, and jokes that require some base form of general geekery or nerdification.

Ursula K. LeGuin, Carl Sagan, Malcolm Gladwell, and Natsuo Kirino are her current literary heroes.

EA travels the world, tries all the snacks, and makes all the mistakes. Sometimes twice. But, she's learning.

Katie Civitelli

Find out more!

Katie grew up in Meriden, Connecticut. Reading, writing, and music have been her lifelines since she was a child and she had always been told she had a gift for telling stories.

She graduated from Middlesex Community College in 2015 with an Associate's Degree in General Studies, focusing on English Literature and History, and she is a big fan of Fantasy and Historical Fiction novels.

Katie currently lives in Wethersfield, Connecticut, USA with her Bernedoodle, Floki. The Fallen Light series is her first published series, with the final novel released in February 2023.

Emmie Hamilton

Find out more!

Emmie Hamilton is forever inspired by the "in-between" moments. You know the ones - the empty spaces between the chaos of life. The conversations that are never said, the days filled with waiting, the silence after the emotion calms down; those are what Emmie's stories are built off of.

In her free time, Emmie likes to fulfill her passion for "life" whether that's writing emotional connections, reading addictive novels, traveling the world or trying new food.

Emmie received her MFA in Creative Writing in 2019 and has since had poems and essays published with Scary Mommy and Pure Slush Press. Her debut novel, Chosen to Fall, was released in May 2021. Its sequel, Fated to Burn, was released November that same year.

Victoria Jade Moss

Find out more!

Victoria is an Australian writer living on the idyllic Gold Coast. Though she has explored all styles of writing, she is most drawn to understanding life through poetry and escaping through fantasy.

When not creating or tackling her interminable TBR pile, she enjoys long walks on the beach with her obstinate Border Collie, Skyrim, spending time with family and friends. She is also forever planning her next adventure.

Victoria has two poetry collections releasing in 2024.

Danielle Hughes

Find out more!

Danielle is a fantasy author from Melbourne who writes enchanting stories full of magic and adventure for pre-teen and YA readers.

Her debut Mystica Trilogy draws on childhood loves of Peter Pan, Alice in Wonderland and The Neverending Story.

While her new fairytale novella The Princess and the Fawn, is inspired by an original Grimm's Brothers story.

G.R. Thomas

Find out more!

Grace is an Australian author of paranormal urban fantasy, dark fantasy and gothic horror.

Her stories are inspired by a vivid dreamscape, the places she visits and the people she meets. An avid, lifetime reader who began with the fantastical world of Enid Blyton.

These days, she reads widely with a love of most genres. When not drafting a new story, she is a wife, a mum, a nurse, and lives on a farm with many fur babies. Can be found in the wild stalking bookstores.

Kristen Dovnik

Find out more!

Kristen loves to write just as much as she loves to read. For years, she's imagined wonderful characters and exciting storylines, just waiting, waiting to be brought to life.

Now that her children are a little older, she has the time to enjoy her passion for writing and is putting pen to paper, giving life to her characters and stories.

Kristen resides in Sydney, Australia with her husband Robby, and three very energetic, young children. She loves nothing more than spending time with her family or sitting down with a slice of vegemite toast, a good cup of coffee and writing the next exciting chapter for her characters.